OUROBOROS

LOPHII
PRESS

OTHER TITLES BY KEVIN KAUFFMANN

⚘ THE ICARUS TRILOGY ⚘

Murder of Crows
(Book 1)

Phoenix Rising
(Book 2)

Swan Song
(Book 3)

⚘ THE FORSAKEN COMEDY TRILOGY ⚘

From Hell with Love
(Book 1)

Ghosts of Earth
(Book 2)

In Defiance of Heaven
(Book 3)

⚘ STANDALONE ⚘

Ashes for Ashes

Rumplestiltskin the Third
(Releasing 2021)

Daytrippers
(Releasing 2021)

Check out other books we love at

25andY.com

OUROBOROS

KEVIN
KAUFFMANN

Published by Lophii Press
an imprint of 25 & Y Publishing
25andY.com

Cover Design by Peter J. Wacks

ISBN: 978-1-953134-14-1 (Paperback)
ISBN: 978-1-953134-15-8 (Ebook)

Printed in the United States of America
11 10 9 8 7 6 5 4 3 2

CHAPTER 1

DOWN THE RABBIT HOLE

I.t was such a small, little thing, but Jeremy's dealer had promised this square piece of paper held another universe. Turning it over in his hand, he noticed a green infinity symbol printed on the other side. The internet forums told stories of acid and mescaline covered in anarchy and freemason symbols—even the star from Super Mario—so the infinity symbol seemed like a lazy signature. However, if this truly was Escape, it could have a diseased penis on it and Jeremy wouldn't have cared.

So, skeptical and scared out of his mind, Jeremy placed the paper on his tongue and stood in his kitchen.

This was the first time Jeremy had done anything so serious; he had tried mushrooms once and almost threw them up, but Escape was supposed to be the ultimate hallucinogen. *Supposedly,* a dose of Escape allowed the user to imagine and live in the world they wanted. Jeremy was skipping a few tiers of drugs and going straight for the hard stuff—DMT was the only thing that was even close—but he thought it was worth it. The way the community talked about it, there was no going back to real life after the first dose, and it would not be much longer before law enforcement would crack down on it.

But as he stood there in the kitchen, rapping his knuckles against the fancy countertop of the kitchen island, Jeremy was getting impatient. He had read it took twenty minutes or so to kick in, but he had already waited so long just for the package to arrive. Taking a much bigger risk than he had wanted to, Jeremy had purchased a full sheet of Escape from someone on an online forum and it had arrived a week later, smuggled in the belly of a hand puppet.

The puppet was still sitting there on the kitchen island, a green, somehow adorable version of Cthulhu of Lovecraft fame, and it made Jeremy smile. He hadn't had a chance to read any Lovecraft yet—he was only sixteen and preferred to play video games—but he liked the idea of the Old Ones. Jeremy loved the idea of gods dwelling just outside the realm of sanity, just beyond his ability to perceive them.

However, as much as Jeremy liked the puppet, that was not what he had bought; that was not why he had taken such a big risk. Right now, he was supposed to be looking at an altered version of this world, but Jeremy still saw the same, shiny, barely-used kitchen. Sixty percent of the time he lived off of frozen fare, the other forty percent was fast food, and the kitchen looked like it belonged in a model home because of it. If she was ever around, his mother would only bother to scatter bottles and glasses of wine that would eventually be cleaned up by their housekeeper.

Most of the time it just looked like the rest of the house; sterile and abandoned.

His mother was gone again, of course; she was always gone during the week. Another important something or other must have come up, because she hadn't even called Jeremy to say that he should make his own dinner. At this point he was used to it—he had already made a pile of chicken tenders and washed them down with the unhealthiest soda possible—but that certainly did not make their relationship any better. Part of him felt awful for it, but Jeremy had given up on his mother years ago.

Starting to get angry, Jeremy stomped away from the kitchen to find something to distract him, but he turned around once he remembered his drugs were still lying out in plain sight. After shoving the sheet back into the hand puppet and throwing it into the cardboard box, Jeremy walked through his empty house with the box under his arm—past a living room large enough to hold thirty people—and climbed the main stairway two steps at a time. Even if it winded him slightly, Jeremy was too impatient to go any slower. Once he got to his room and threw the box on his bed, he immediately turned around and went into his bathroom.

"C'mon, you bastard, just work already," he muttered, setting his hands against the counter and gripping the porcelain. What he saw in the mirror was disappointing for a number of reasons—his weight, his acne, the way his ears stuck out too far—but he had learned to ignore most of his imperfections over the years.

The only reason he was staring at the mirror was to see if anything had changed in his perception. Jeremy remembered one of the coolest parts of taking mushrooms was seeing his own face shift and distort in the mirror, growing and shrinking and becoming someone else's face while he watched. Of course there was more to the experience—he remembered feeling a surge of pleasant emotions and getting the giggles at more than a few points—but he thought that a drug like Escape would perhaps manifest first as a shift in perspective.

But ten minutes after setting the infinity symbol on his tongue, Jeremy was left seeing his pathetic reflection as always. He was still the same, pudgy, pasty white kid other teenagers mocked every day. He was still the same rich kid who didn't have any friends, resorting to using drugs to escape his world.

"Goddamnit," Jeremy said before sticking out his tongue and seeing the wet paper clinging there. This was how he supposed to do it, or at least that was what he had read. After closing his mouth, Jeremy glared hard at his own face and shook his head. The stranger on the forum had promised the real experience, but Jeremy was starting to doubt his integrity.

With a grunt, Jeremy turned from his reflection and left the bathroom, trudging to the stairs with his head down. The open space around the staircase had always made him feel small; the architect had apparently loved the idea of the house wasting as much money and space as possible. Jeremy couldn't walk through the house without feeling like he didn't belong there—that he was on display—and it was just another reason he resented his mother. Not only did she push away his father, but she had to go and buy a gigantic house with the settlement and make Jeremy feel even smaller.

"This is bullshit," he grumbled, turning at the end of the staircase and walking back to the massive living room. After falling onto the leather couch they had brought with them from the last house—the only one Jeremy liked—he picked up the remote and turned on the giant television hanging on the wall. After the display warmed up, the sound system erupted into the chaos of people talking over each other on cable news. His mother was an addict of the twenty-four-hour news cycle, and she must have been watching before leaving for work.

"I just can't understand how this is even a question," a dignified woman with short, blonde hair said on the left side of the screen. Displayed underneath her picture was her name, Lynn Stafford, but Jeremy already knew that.

It was hard to ignore anyone trying to be the next Nancy Reagan.

"It's *not*, that's the thing," her opponent replied from the other side of the screen, an overweight man wearing an oversized suit. This one was an unfamiliar face, but Benjamin Childress was displayed underneath his part of the screen. "It's an individual right, Ms. Stafford. An individual right to treat our bodies the way they want, and I certainly don't want the government to infringe on my rights."

"This has nothing to do with rights, Ben," Stafford replied, shaking her head and offering a condescending smile. "It is an abusive substance. A substance that leads to addiction, leads to self-destructive tendencies, to *violence*, to criminal behavior! It's a well-known gateway drug and it is becoming more and more difficult to keep it away from our *children*."

Fucking hypocrite, Jeremy thought as he watched Childress trying to hold back his own reaction. As nice and dignified as she seemed, Jeremy knew Lynn Stafford was no angel; it was practically public record that she had a number of prescriptions she abused on a regular basis.

Still, they were legal, so the woman got to keep her soap box.

"Couldn't you say the exact same thing about alcohol?" Childress asked, hoping to argue logically with the congresswoman. "Every link you've established there—even if there *isn't* one—could be said of alcohol. What we're proposing is to introduce marijuana into the system legally and tax it, which would lead to more revenue which we could use, Ms. Stafford, to improve the state of our nation. As a member of Congress, I would *think* that would be one of your priorities."

Damn straight, Jeremy though with a smile.

"What would you say to that, Ms. Stafford?" the host of the program asked, trying to sneak in a word between the two opponents. Rolling her eyes, the woman threw up her hands before leaning forward.

"What I would say to that, Chris, is that it is not only an absurd argument, but it is morally irresponsible to consider the idea—"

"Absurd, what's so absurd about—" Childress tried to interrupt, but the congresswoman put up her hand and talked over him.

"It is *morally irresponsible* to consider the legalization of marijuana and perpetuation of a drug culture. The citizens of this country are hurt every day from the advent of this drug and the absolute *last* thing I would want is for our children to grow up thinking that drug use is acceptable." Stafford teared up on cue and stared straight into the camera. "If my child turned to drugs—if he threw away his life like that—I would be *devastated.*"

"Do you *drink,* Ms. Stafford?" Childress asked, ignoring her emotional plea entirely. Leaning back in her chair, the congresswoman tried to dismiss the question with a slight shake of her head.

"That has little to do with it—"

"Do you drink, Ms. Stafford?" he repeated, and Jeremy was pleased to see her eyes flash with anger.

"I have the occasional drink, Ben, but that is beside the point," Stafford said, at which the overweight man wagged his finger.

"It *is* the point, actually. There is no real difference between your occasional drink and the occasional smoking session of a recreational user of marijuana. There are certainly people who abuse it, but there is more than enough evidence to show that alcohol abuse is—"

"It's illegal, Ben, that's what it is, and for good reason," she interrupted, causing Jeremy to growl and pick up the remote from his chest.

"Will you let me speak?" Childress asked, drawing a scoff from Stafford.

"I'm just not a fan of listening to nonsense. There are studies that show the harmful effects of marijuana, and no matter how many states legalize this drug, I would never allow such criminal activity to invade my state and my home," she said triumphantly, the host of the program enamored as he listened to Stafford's every word.

Although Jeremy could see her opponent bristle with anger, he also knew that Childress would not be able to get another word in, so he changed the channel until cartoons were on the screen. Even though he was not particularly interested, it was better than watching that televised circus. After a few minutes, he remembered why he was watching television, why he needed a distraction.

"It's fake, it has to be," Jeremy said as he looked at the ceiling, admitting his failure. Whoever *KilgoreMKUltra* was, he had obviously stolen Jeremy's money. Seeing that laughable name on the forum, Jeremy should have been more skeptical, but he had been desperate. He had wanted something more than this life; he had wanted more than this loneliness. A few hundred dollars seemed like an even trade for true escapism.

Closing his eyes, Jeremy thought of Allison and felt a tickle crawl up his spine.

She would never be with him, no matter how much he liked her. She was pretty, with blonde hair that fell past her shoulders, and she had a perfect smile. Not only that, but she had always been nice to Jeremy in class and in the halls. They didn't have anything in common—Jeremy had almost nothing in common with anybody at school—but she gave him a smile every once in a while.

It was more than anybody else would give him.

Opening his eyes with a sigh, Jeremy turned to look at the cartoons blaring from the television. It was a dumb show about a talking fruit, and Jeremy could only watch for a few seconds before wanting to hurl something at the screen. Picking himself up so he could sit on the couch, Jeremy turned off the TV and threw the remote to the side. He had already lost all that money; he didn't need to punish himself by watching visual poison.

Burying his face in his hands, Jeremy thought about what he was going to do next. Escaping to another world had been his plan for the night—even if he had school the next day—and there was nothing exciting happening in his gaming communities. Even the games he *hadn't* played held no appeal; Jeremy had bought dozens of them and hadn't even started half, but he knew it would give him no satisfaction. What he wanted was to *be* in another world, not just another night of pretend.

Frustrated, Jeremy lowered his hands so he could turn the TV back on, but then he saw something that changed his entire night. Leaning forward, he tried to understand just how it had happened. Sitting there on the coffee table was a crystal vase with a single rose inside, which wouldn't have been so remarkable anywhere else in the house.

Except that it had not been there before he closed his eyes.

Reaching out with a trembling hand, Jeremy tried to touch the rose and was surprised to see it shift before his eyes. The rose crystallized and sparkled as light from a nonexistent source shined through a hundred different facets. Jeremy could only gape in wonder, pushing himself off the couch so he could look at the mysterious object from a different angle.

"Oh, that's fucking cool..." A giant grin was on his face as he reached forward again, fear abandoned completely. However, as soon as Jeremy touched the rose, the entire room changed and made him fall back to the couch in shock. Spreading from the vase holding the rose, every surface in the room was soon covered in brilliant crystal, and Jeremy laughed as he looked at his new house.

"Incredible..." Jeremy stood up and was drawn into the brilliant purples, violets and light blues of his walls, seeing the different crystal formations covering the walls and floor. Crouching down, Jeremy ran his hand along the carpet, which was covered in a million tiny crystal projections, and for a moment he forgot he was under the effect of a powerful hallucinogen.

For that moment, as he ran his hand along the ground and felt the cool touch of crystal, Jeremy thought he was in another world.

"Shit! Shit, keep it together," he said as he jumped back up and looked at his living room. It was amazing and he would have been content with this on any other drug, but this was *Escape*. This was supposed to be the world he wanted; the world in his imagination.

Closing his eyes, Jeremy tried to imagine the world he wanted to experience. On the forums, he had read that the only limitation was that his hallucinations were layered over reality, so he couldn't imagine that he could run around forever unless he wanted to run into a wall.

Keeping his house in mind, Jeremy tried to will another world into existence.

When he opened his eyes, Jeremy was so shocked that he had to cover his mouth. Fantastic, otherworldly plant life had exploded into reality in that instant; neon blue vines hung from fuchsia tree limbs, brilliant red ivy wrapped around the gigantic emerald tree trunk that had sprouted out of his carpet. Walking forward, Jeremy ran his finger along one of the leaves and felt the velvet texture and laughed as he experienced another world.

"Oh my god," he said—could not stop himself from saying— and he was shocked once a small insect landed on his outstretched finger. When Jeremy brought it up to his face to look closer, he found that its wings were made out of diamonds; that it stared at him with great, big black eyes.

"Oh my god," the insect repeated, lifting up its torso to reveal a face that looked remarkably like Jeremy's own. "My god. Our god."

"What? What the hell?" Jeremy whipped back his hand and made the insect take flight, flapping its crystalline wings so fast that it hovered like a hummingbird.

"No Hell. Hell is gone," it said before it flitted away, leaving Jeremy to marvel at the world surrounding him. Before his eyes, a magnificent jellyfish lowered from the sky, pulsing with soft, yellow light, and Jeremy's jaw went slack as he saw it hit one of the outstretched branches of the tree and then split into a dozen smaller, identical versions.

"Hell is gone," Jeremy repeated under his breath as the jellyfish scattered around his living room, bathing his vibrant surroundings with pleasant light and heat. It felt like the entire world was wrapping him in a warm embrace, and Jeremy looked down to find small animals munching happily on blue roots beneath him.

Crouching down, Jeremy put out his hand to one of the animals—a bundle of purple fur—and it looked up at him once it felt his touch. It seemed like some distant, blue cousin of a ferret, and it instantly started to purr once his fingers were buried in its soft hair. Before he knew it, the animal climbed up his hand before wrapping lightly around his upper arm, settling its head on Jeremy's shoulder never once stopping that thrum of a purr. Using his other hand to pet its forehead, Jeremy saw the creature smile and close its eyes, almost falling asleep on his shoulder.

"There, there," he said, remembering the old days when he had pets. He missed the affection and the warmth, even if he didn't miss the responsibility. Smiling, Jeremy was about to pry the creature off his arm when it seemed to take a mental cue, climbing up his arm until it could perch on his shoulder. Leaning down to nuzzle against his ear for a moment, the animal then leapt and grabbed at one of the neon vines hanging from the nearby tree.

Jeremy watched it go with a hint of sadness, but eventually he was distracted by a large beast coming from what should have been the hallway to the stairs. A giant wolf stepped over the archway of tree limbs Jeremy had left to signify the hallway, but once it turned to look at him, Jeremy saw it open its mouth and roll out a green tongue before approaching him like a loyal dog.

Lowering its head in reverence, the wolf set its forehead against Jeremy's body and radiated with affection. It was all Jeremy could do to wrap his arms around its massive head, and he stayed there burying himself in its coarse hair before realizing that he did not want to spend his entire trip cuddling with animals in a neon rainforest. Closing his eyes, Jeremy said goodbye to the creature before imagining another layer to his reality.

He tasted salt air before he even opened his eyes, but Jeremy was still excited once he was able to see the chain of airborne islands connected by suspended rope bridges, and he jumped in excitement as he climbed onto a nearby boulder, what he realized was probably his couch once his feet sank a few inches. From his vantage point, Jeremy was able to see cascading waterfalls coming from the source of a distant mountain, and that water flowed through the landscape until it poured off cracks between the islands of his new home.

Jeremy had put those cracks there to signify the walls of his reality, but he had already started to forget there *was* a reality. This new world had been part of one of his favorite games growing up; he would hack and slash his way through bushes for money—days at a time—and Jeremy instantly felt like a little kid again. Making his way to the rope bridges to his left, Jeremy ran through his house at top speed before climbing up the steps etched into the rock formation that led up and over his current island.

He only vaguely remembered that these were actually the steps of his house.

Taking the steps three at a time and not bothered by the exertion of it all, the world shifted around him like an MC Escher painting and Jeremy was unable to think rationally. To him, this was the new normal; this world could not be questioned. When he made his way to the top of the stairs, Jeremy turned left and right—forgetting momentarily where he had been going—but then he remembered he was searching for his room.

Not bothering to close his eyes this time, Jeremy watched the world change around him, the island adventures from his youth replaced splinter by splinter with a sleazy, apartment building mashed together from dozens of dystopian science-fiction stories. Jeremy knew he was not prepared to face any of the anti-heroes from his favorites, but he grinned wide as he considered what it might be like to run into a replicant, fight aliens on a spaceship or even imagine that he was on the surface of Mars. Instantly his world phased into a red wasteland, but Jeremy put a stop to that by lifting his hand.

Laughing at the sight of his own arm as the world reverted to the dystopian building, Jeremy could not help but shake his head at the gnarled, alien fingers in front of him. Somehow, he had become someone else entirely, and Jeremy looked at his legs to find that his new knees were bent backward. Setting that discovery into the back of his mind, Jeremy let his own self-image become dominant and turned back into a teenager, but he knew it would not be long before he experimented again.

"This is so awesome," Jeremy said as he pushed into the dingy apartment, seeing trash and body parts scattered around what was supposed to be his room. He was momentarily shocked—he did not expect his imagination to get away from him like that—but he was here for a purpose. Hopping over to a chair attached to a futuristic interface, complete with five monitors and several peripherals he did not recognize, Jeremy tried to focus on reality for the moment.

Suddenly, the computer monitor in the middle reverted back to what he knew, and Jeremy saw a window into his old world. Displayed on his computer monitor was the Escapism forum, and Jeremy eagerly clicked through the menus so he could return to his personal thread.

Guys, this is amazing, he typed. *I only does half an hour ago and I'm already seeing incredible stuff. Seriously, I had no idea it could be like this. Big fucking thank you to the community, because I've already been to three different worlds. It's SO FUCKING AWESOME.*

Clicking on the button to submit the post, Jeremy leaned back in his chair and let his fantasies wash over him. Forgetting about the dystopian apartment covered in blood, Jeremy allowed himself to think he was on the bridge of a starship that was open to the vacuum of space, watching a nebula undulate before a star went supernova in front of his eyes.

If it was real life, he knew that it would spell trouble for his ridiculous spaceship—that it was probably not possible in the first place—but this was just a show he had created. Jeremy let the heat and stardust wash over his open cockpit and felt joined to the universe, only remembering that he was talking to people online after a few moments of ecstasy. After he turned his attention back to reality, he leaned forward just as the window into his real world opened back up, clicking the refresh icon on his browser once he got his bearings. There was already another post, but Jeremy found the other user had said what he already realized on his own.

Fantastic, man, but don't waste your time on her when you're about to peak. Just enjoy it.

With a smile, Jeremy nodded and tried to follow the stranger's advice, leaping out of his chair and running through his doorway. When he got into the massive room holding the staircase, Jeremy let the stars fall away and replaced them with rolling fields and wisps of clouds flowing through the air. More importantly, he let a person solidify at the bottom of the stairs, more beautiful than he remembered.

"It's about time, Jeremy," Allison said, her light hair falling past her shoulders in loose waves. A warm breeze flowed against her in that moment, causing her hair to drift behind her, just like the red dress that covered that perfect, ideal version of her body. Unable to speak—to even breathe—Jeremy just watched as Allison brought up a hand to keep the hair out of her eyes and looked up at him with a knowing smile.

"You didn't have to do that. Come down here," she lilted, beckoning him with her other hand. Looking down, Jeremy found his stairwell was made entirely out of golden light and, more surprisingly, that he was not himself. At least, he was not the pudgy, pasty white boy he had been just a few minutes ago.

What he saw was an idealized version of his own body; tall, thin but muscular, and covered in magnificent plate mail. Without his knowledge, Jeremy had transformed into the knight in shining armor he had always imagined for himself. As happy as a teenager could be, Jeremy had to stop himself from running down the steps to meet the girl of his dreams.

"I'm coming, Allison, I'm coming." Jeremy mustered his fabricated confidence as he made his brilliant entrance from the sky. "You're pretty impatient, you know that?"

"Only because I see what I want," Allison replied as Jeremy came down to join her. "Though I think I'm going to have to wait a little longer."

"Oh, and why is that?" Jeremy gave a crooked smile in his best Han Solo impression, unaware that he was supplying both sides of the conversation. "I'm right here. There's no reason to wait."

"But I'm a lady, *Sir* Jeremy, and you're a knight, even if you don't act like one," Allison teased as she walked forward, setting her fingers on something attached to Jeremy's neck. When he looked down, Jeremy realized it was an amulet of a snake eating its own tail, but that thought was pushed away when he caught her scent.

"It's pretty difficult to act like a knight when you're around," he said, bringing up his hand to caress the back of her neck.

"I'm sure it is, but you know that a knight only gets his lady after he slays a dragon," Allison locked eyes with him, and seemingly on cue they were interrupted by a loud roar. Turning with her still in his embrace, Jeremy saw a gigantic lizard breathing out fire just past a steep valley and waiting for him to meet it.

"Well, I guess I have to be a knight after all." Jeremy turned back to face Allison, who was looking up at him with big doe eyes. "Tell me, though, is there any way I can get a kiss before you send me off?"

"Hmm, it's against the rules, you know," she said, tilting her head slightly, "but since you're about to save my life and all, I don't see why not."

"Perfect," Jeremy said, leaning down and pressing his lips to hers. It was just like he imagined it, love and warmth flowing between them, and it was hard for him to stop. Upon hearing the dragon roar again, however, Jeremy withdrew from her embrace so he could draw his sword. "Now I have the courage to fight."

"Off you go, my good knight. Kill 'em for me," Allison requested with a wink, and Jeremy found all the courage he needed.

Turning around, Jeremy ran through the steep valley, his

blade shining brilliantly in his grip. By the time he met the dragon, Jeremy was yelling—completely lost in his battle—and he could not stop himself from feeling like this was where he was supposed to be. Even though he was fighting a hallucination in his living room, this was more of a home than he had ever known.

With the aid of just a small piece of paper, Jeremy had found his way to Escape.

CHAPTER 2

FOR THE CHILDREN

T.ell me, Sharon, why exactly did I stoop to arguing with a pothead on national television last night?" Lynn asked after walking into her office, finding her secretary at her desk.

"Maybe it's because you've backed yourself into a corner?" she replied, earning a sneer from the congresswoman. Sharon was sitting back in her chair now and looking pleased with herself, and Lynn walked up to the desk before placing her knuckles against the surface.

"Backed myself into a corner? Is that you how you talk to your boss?" That earned a shrug from her secretary as she turned back to the computer screen.

"It is when we've known each other for a decade. You have a call with Senator Price in ten minutes, just so you know," Sharon said as she moved her mouse around. "Oh, and you have a meeting with your gun control committee in an hour."

"I know that, why do you think I came into the office so early?" Lynn said before she stood up and set her hands on her hips. Although she was buried in her thoughts for a moment, Lynn watched Sharon out of the corner of her eye and noticed something suspicious. Leaning forward, she rotated her secretary's monitor and found a screen full of cartoonish farms.

"Hey, stop that," Sharon said as she reached out and turned the screen around, causing Lynn to back away and cross her arms.

"*Really?* Taxpayer money is funding your virtual farm?" she asked, but Sharon only shrugged while clicking at the screen.

"Call it a subsidy," she muttered, waving off her boss with her free hand. "When it gets in the way of my job, you can complain then."

"I—fine, you win. But as soon as it does, don't expect me to treat you like another constituent," Lynn said as she walked to her office, but her secretary scoffed at the threat.

"What, you'll use my pain to better your public image? Hey, you remember when you used to make a difference?" Sharon teased after her, but she didn't expect an answer. Lynn just shook her head and laughed before stepping into her office and closing the door behind her, hoping to get some time to herself before the senator called.

Yawning, Lynn stepped around her desk—made out of rich, dark wood that cost more than she was comfortable admitting—and sank into her chair. It was only the start of her day and she was already exhausted. Last night's debate, and subsequently dealing with its consequences, had kept her up past her bed time and gave her no chance to recover. Sighing, Lynn sat up so she could turn on her computer, and it was not long before a login screen was staring at her.

"...why do I do this?" Lynn asked herself as she typed in her password, a version of her son's name substituting half the letters with numbers and punctuation. After just a few keystrokes, a cluttered desktop was sitting there waiting for her attention, dozens of abbreviations and groups in the filenames. It was already causing her stress, but Lynn had other concerns for the moment. Clicking on her web browser, Lynn typed in her own name and the news program last night with the hopes of positive feedback.

"Shit," she muttered, lifting her hand to massage her temple. The response to her appearance on Chris Harmon's show was less than positive; most of the internet criticized her for being too aggressive and having nothing important to say, and Lynn secretly agreed with them.

Lynn Stafford didn't care about marijuana at all—she had a *great* time in college because of it—but this was all about appearances. Siding with the government in the War on Drugs gave her a lot of allies and campaign funds; support she desperately needed as a junior congresswoman. It had always been an uphill battle to keep her station, and it was only made worse once her husband had left.

He claimed it had been the stress she had brought into the relationship—and the fact that she was never home—but Lynn knew better. He wanted a newer, better model, one without stretch marks and fading looks, and Lynn had discovered this when she walked in on the new model stretched across their marital bed. At that point Lynn was not sad to see him go—it meant half the family fortune was hers—but it did make her suffer in the polls. Constituents tended to view single women as weaker, or at least that was what Lynn and everyone else assumed.

So she had joined the War on Drugs, but the world was changing on her. The youth culture had shifted dramatically— accepting and enjoying drugs as a way to escape the everyday tedium and the miserable world her generation had created— and it was becoming obvious that the war would soon be over. Whenever she appeared on one of these programs, the internet would be up in arms at her behavior, but they were not her target demographic.

Her constituent base was the paranoid, delusional audience that would flock around any threat to their children or their way of life, and so she had to play the part.

When the phone rang, Lynn remembered she had been waiting for this call and hastily paused the video of her speaking mid-word. Although she lifted the phone from the stand, her eyes fell on the still footage and she hesitated, remembering just who she had been. In the past, Lynn had tried to defend the righteous, tried to be a person who could change the world. Back in college, she had wanted to make a difference.

After a few years in office, she had become just another politician scrambling for votes.

"This is Lynn Stafford," she said in an authoritative voice, shoving back her memories and focusing on the present.

"Lynn, it's Bill Price. You know why I'm calling, right?" a gruff voice answered her, and she dropped the act immediately.

"I'm guessing it's because of the Chris Harmon show. I hit all the high points, Bill," she argued, knowing the senator likely intended to chew her out for some perceived weakness.

"*High* points, Lynn? Nice choice of words to use for a debate against a pothead. Tell me why you let him talk at all."

"I can't just interrupt everyone; I have to give some semblance of rational—"

"You know what? It doesn't matter," Price interrupted, causing Lynn to swallow her words. Looking back at her face mid-speech, she had to agree with him. "We have something more important to talk about."

"And what is *that*, Bill? Am I to rage against weed in some other public forum? How much more do you want me to do for this pet project of yours?" Her voice was weary, but the senator surprised her by laughing on the other end.

"No, I think we can safely say that it's time to stop beating the horse. It's dead as a doornail now that more and more states are making it legal," he said, groaning as Lynn scoffed. "No, we have a new target, something that will be incredibly persuasive to voters."

"A new target? What are you talking about?"

"There's a new drug. It's called Escape. Already illegal in certain contexts—something about it being a mix of different restricted substances—but it's brand-spanking new-and it's starting to catch on with the kids. Some bullshit about how you get to live out your perfect fantasies." After that explanation, Lynn had to massage her temple again.

"A hallucinogen, Bill? And it's already illegal? Why the hell would we care?" she asked, and her fellow representative let out a bark of laughter.

"*Because it just killed its first kid.* Lynn, the bastard was only twelve and now his parents are raising hell. Best part about it is that it's in your home district!"

"Oh my god," Lynn uttered out of pure reaction—the words meaning little—but Price seized on the moment.

"Oh my god is *right!* Lynn, you get yourself a group of mothers and use this dead kid as your mascot, and you can ride that train all the way into the inner circle. Hell, you can probably get a subcommittee going and really make a name for yourself," Price explained, sounding entirely too pleased with himself. Lynn was horrified at first—she had never considered anything so monstrous—but then she looked at the woman still frozen on her screen.

It might have been reprehensible to use a dead child, but that woman had started on this path a long time ago.

"Jesus," she said, gulping down her personal disgust and breathing out slowly. "This is… it's—"

"*Great*, I know. You're fucking welcome, by the way," Price said, his chair creaking loud enough for her to hear it over the phone. "I almost gave it to Werner, but I thought I would throw you a bone. That broadcast last night was pathetic."

"Yeah, well," she said, closing out the browser on her display, "we do what we have to do. Thanks, Bill, I'll get something together later today."

"Today? You need to move on this *now*, before anybody else gets hold of it. The press is about to break it, and you definitely don't want Janice or Gretchen to jump on it first. What else do you have to do?"

"I have my gun control meeting in half an hour—"

"Cancel it; you have more important things to do. I've emailed you the number to the parents and a few other influential groups. Get an aide to start working on a plan and get a move on. Hell, it probably wouldn't be a bad idea for you to visit the parents sometime this week and really sell it. Then we can get the media circus going."

"Bill—"

"Lynn, I'm trying to *help* you. Without this boost, I'm not sure we can keep you around after the midterm elections," he said, his tone darker than before. "This isn't *doubt* I'm hearing, is it?"

"No, not at all. It's just... sudden." She hoped it would convince the senator. Truth be told, Lynn did not feel entirely comfortable, but she had stopped telling the truth back during her first campaign.

"Well, I can get Janice to support you, I guess. Something this big, we can share the credit among a few members of Congress. She's been dealing with MADD for a while now, too, so she has some experience with this kind of thing," Price suggested before breathing in deep. "So can we trust you with this?"

"I..." Lynn said as she stood up and turned to an old picture of her son smiling up at her. It had been taken years ago and he didn't look like that boy anymore, but she still felt the same. Even if this Escape drug wasn't necessarily harmful, she still didn't want it to end up in his hands. Something like that would be dangerous for a boy his age.

"Yeah. You can trust me, Bill. I'll call the parents after this."

"Good girl. This will be good for you, Lynn, I promise you that. Anyway, I gotta go. Have a pro-life benefit to get to, and the hands of my campaign investors won't shake themselves. I'll tell Janice to swing by your office," he rushed through the statement, the last words barely audible as he set the phone back in its cradle.

"Do that," Lynn muttered to no one, holding her phone to her chest. She stood there for a moment—trying to think up an excuse to give her gun control committee—but then she realized that was what Sharon was for. After sitting back down in her chair, Lynn pressed the intercom button on her phone and cleared her throat.

"Sharon, I'm going to need you to move the committee meeting to sometime next week," she said, hearing her secretary sigh through the door.

"You can't move it, Lynn. You're not in charge of this one. I can tell them that you can't make it?" she suggested, and Lynn realized she would have to take the hit.

"I guess that's how it has to be. Something big just fell in my lap," Lynn said, sighing heavily as she opened her email client on her computer.

"Got it, shattered pelvis," Sharon quipped, and Lynn's eyes widened at the remark.

"Something I can explain *away*, please," she asked, hearing Sharon laugh through the door.

"Don't worry, I'll tell them your son got sick and needed to see the doctor. No one questions kids," she said, and Lynn immediately felt awful. Turning to look at her son's picture again, her heart broke just a little.

"No, they don't," Lynn agreed before releasing the intercom button, touching the frame of the picture and pursing her lip. She told herself again that she was doing it *for* him—that she was trying to leave a better world for him and his generation—but years of politics had left her jaded.

Turning from the picture, Lynn looked at her computer screen and found Senator Price's email, reading the blurb about the dead child and his parents. It was a terrible story—even if the boy was being admittedly foolish—and it was perfect press fodder. Convinced that she knew enough details, Lynn found their number and picked up her phone, using her other hand to enter the number. It rang four times and Lynn was about to hang up, but a deep, male voice eventually answered her.

"Hello?"

"Hello, is this Mr. Crenshaw? My name is Congresswoman Lynn Stafford, and I wanted to offer my condolences in these tragic times."

Only two hours after Price had hung up, another woman burst into the office and caught Lynn in the middle of a call to an anti-drug group based in her home district.

"What is this *bullshit*, Stafford?" she demanded, but fortunately Lynn had already covered the speaker to her phone.

"Hey, Jerry, something just came up. I'm going to have to call you back," Lynn said before she set the phone back in the cradle and stood up to meet the rude visitor. She was a middle-aged woman with dark red hair, a little overweight, and she was dressed in a frumpy, grey pantsuit, but her looks were entirely secondary.

Her name was Janice Pearson, and Lynn knew exactly why she was upset.

"It's nice to see you, too," Lynn said, her tone more than just condescending. "Can I get you something to drink?"

"Oh, yeah, offer a supporter of Mothers Against Drunk Driving a drink in the middle of the day." Janice crossed her arms, and Lynn sighed as she leaned over her desk.

"It didn't have to be alcoholic, Janice," she said, gesturing to the seat across from her. "Sit. We'll talk this out like adults."

"We're going to talk about this like adults, huh? Is that what it's called when Bill goes behind my back, gives you such a fantastic lead and then tells me to *support* you?" she asked, cocking her head slightly. "I'll think I'll just stand."

"I didn't ask for it," Lynn said as she sat down in her chair and crossed her legs, "but it makes more sense this way."

"Makes sense? How does it *make sense?* I've been handling press for angry mothers for years now, and it's not that far from my district in the first place! It's a *goddamn* insult for me to be running second on this," Janice explained, but Lynn just gestured calmly to the seat again.

"Just sit. If we're going to work together on this, we can't be hostile," she said. Though she did not let it show, Lynn was surprised when Janice surrendered and plopped down on the seat, the leather cushion creaking under her weight. "It makes sense because I'm already in the anti-drug camp."

"So *what?*"

"So I already have the association with drugs, even if all I have to show are clips on YouTube showing how bullheaded and irrational I am. I'm already in the position to jump on this and really force the point home that the drugs that are illegal need to *stay* illegal. Honestly, your position is a little too harsh," Lynn explained, and she could see indignation spread across Janice's face.

"Too *harsh?*" she said, pressing her fingers to her chest. "I'm too harsh for a *drug-demonizing* campaign?"

"Just a little bit, Janice. While no one is going to *support* drunk driving—whether or not they realize it—people view MADD and organizations like it as a modern temperance movement. With you at the helm, we would only gain the exact same supporters you already have. We would be seen as old grandparents trying to stop the kids from having a good time," she explained, leaning over her desk and lifting a glass of amber liquid to her mouth.

"Are you seriously *drinking* in front of me?" Janice glared at Lynn as she smiled and sipped at her drink. After swallowing down the sweet liquid, Lynn laughed softly as she looked at the plain glass.

"Just a little brandy, calms the nerves," she said, making eye contact with the furious congresswoman. "I don't hide that I drink—I never have—and so I seem like a more moderate and acceptable spokesman against a new wave of dangerous drugs. A modern congresswoman with modern tastes. Hell, if I acted normally, I *almost* think I would have more support."

"Too late for that now," Janice replied, forcing a nod from Lynn.

"*Definitely* too late for that. Both of us are way too far down this path to change now, but if we work together, we can both benefit from the advent of Escape. Have you read anything about it?" she asked, reaching forward and hitting a button on the screen. After a moment, the printer on a nearby shelf whirred to life and Lynn turned her attention back to a confused Janice.

"I haven't had a chance yet. Bill only told me half an hour ago what you were up to."

"It actually sounds like a really good time. It affects your perception so you see what you *want* to see," Lynn explained as she walked over to the printer and picked up the pages, collecting them into a neat stack. As Janice watched her, Lynn walked back over to her desk and picked up the stapler near her monitor. "If I was right out of college and there wasn't a drug test for it, I would probably jump at the chance."

"That's because you're a hedonist at heart, Stafford. That's why you're no good for this." That only caused Lynn to smirk as she stapled the pages in her hand.

"On the contrary, it makes me the *perfect* choice. I understand the appeal," she replied before tossing the paper at Janice, forcing the woman to uncross her arms to catch it. "Read that over, it'll tell you what you need to know about the drug and what happened to that little boy."

"I can't just know that it killed him?" Janice asked while waving around the printout, but Lynn shook her head as she walked back around her desk and sat down.

"*Technically*, he killed himself—jumped into oncoming traffic—which is why you need to know what it affects. Escape really only establishes a change in perception, the world around them stays the same, and the biggest danger to someone who takes the drug is themselves."

"So the drug *didn't* kill him?" she asked, causing Lynn to tilt her head and scrunch her face.

"No, not really, but we can certainly *blame* it on Escape. When they interviewed the boy's friend, he said they dosed on the drug and that the kid thought he was a superhero attacking a meteor. Without the drug—"

"He would have known it was a car," Janice interrupted her, but Lynn forgave it with a nod.

"Right, though it was a bus. As long as the user knows what they're getting into, Escape is harmless, but a dead child draws all kinds of sympathy."

"A bus? School or city?"

"City, and the parents' attorney were going to sue the hell out of them, but once the police investigated and found the drug on his tongue, it got messy. That's half the reason we found out so fast, before the press really got wind of it. The city is trying to cover their ass," Lynn said before leaning back in her chair. "And *we* are going to be the ones who do it."

"How is that?" Janice raised an eyebrow, and Lynn almost forgot that the congresswoman had burst into her office all fire and brimstone.

"I'm going to go meet the parents, rub elbows, and I'm going to convince them that it was not the bus driver's fault, that it was all because of Escape. Once we do that, we can go public, turn Escape into the pariah we need it to be, and you and I will get all the national attention we desire," Lynn concluded, but her statement was met with skepticism.

"So you fully intend to bring me in on this, as your *second?*"

"Think of it more as a *partnership*. We'll both be making appearances, though I'll obviously be making more of the public statements and doing more of the grunt work. Honestly, your best contribution will be the support we can get from MADD and your other projects, and we can turn this movement into a powerhouse. Bill didn't explain all this?" Lynn asked, but Janice responded with a roll of her eyes.

"That cocky bastard just told me to 'give Stafford whatever she needs.' Made it seem like I was taking a hit for the group," Janice said, letting out a loud sigh as she shook her head. "Still seems that way, but I can see the appeal of working together on this one, especially since you've already gone and made arrangements with the parents. Wouldn't be smart to step on each other's toes now."

"I wouldn't be surprised if Bill planned it that way. And trust me, I didn't want this solo, anyway. It's a whole lot of work and I don't have the best reputation right now. However, with the two of us together, we can grab some others, make a full-fledged subcommittee out of this thing and ride it all the way."

"See, *now* you're talking. Alright, well," Janice said as she shoved herself out of the chair and stood up, "I'm still not happy about it, but I probably would have done the same thing if I was in your shoes."

"I'm glad you understand." Lynn stood up and walked around the desk, offering her hand.

"Oh, I do," Janice said before taking Lynn's invitation and shaking her hand. "But let's be *clear*, Stafford. You screw this up and we're going to have problems."

"You're such a dear friend, Janice," Lynn said with a fake smile, causing the congresswoman to release her hand and sigh in disgust as she left Lynn's office.

"It was good to see you, Ms. Pearson," Sharon said as Janice stomped through the room and out into the hallway, disappearing from sight within just a moment. Lynn watched as Sharon turned to her and whispered. "What a magnificent bitch."

"Hey, you wait to say that kind of thing until they're out of earshot," Lynn cautioned her secretary, pointing at her like a schoolteacher, but Sharon smiled as she turned back to her computer.

"Wasn't talking about *her*. Tell me," she said, peering over the edge of her monitor. "How did it feel to drink booze in front of her?"

"Probably would have felt fantastic," Lynn said as she leaned against the doorframe, "but it was just my iced tea from lunch. The ice melted."

"What a magnificent bitch," Sharon repeated as she looked down at her screen again, leaving Lynn to her own devices. The congresswoman walked over to her computer and looked at the information Price had gathered for her. Only after a few minutes of memorizing details about the boy's family did Lynn remember what she had been doing before Janice had barged in.

"Oh, Sharon, can you get Jerry back on the line for me? I'm going to try to make an appearance after I meet with the family, get this whole thing rolling."

"So you're going to make a weekend out of it?" Sharon asked, but Lynn shook her head even though her secretary couldn't see it.

"No, probably the same day. There might be some sort of service later that night, but I think I only need a couple hours with the family," Lynn said as she started skimming the profiles again.

"Well, aren't *you* confident," Sharon commented under breath while looking through her own resources for the telephone number, and Lynn scoffed in dismay before muttering to herself.

"Yeah, well, I need to be."

"Oh, thank you, Susan," Lynn said as she accepted a saucer with a steaming cup of tea, smiling at the woman barely able to hold back tears. It had only been four days since the boy's death—two since Lynn had heard about it—but here she was, sitting in the victim's living room. Taking in every detail of the cozy home out of her periphery, Lynn maintained eye contact with Susan

Crenshaw until she joined her husband on the couch across from Lynn. They were normal, white Middle-Americans—making them all the more appropriate for Lynn's agenda—but she tried to hide her satisfaction.

"Thank you for coming to see us, Ms. Stafford," the father said, making stubborn eye contact with her even though he was clearly affected by grief. "It means a lot that you would come from D.C. just to visit."

"Daniel, please," Lynn said, tilting her head slightly and giving him a compassionate look, "it's the very *least* I could do. When I heard about what happened—in my own district—I didn't have a choice. I couldn't ignore such a tragic accident."

"It wasn't an accident," Susan squeaked, holding her husband's arm tightly. "That woman ran over my poor boy."

"Sue, he jumped out in front of her," Daniel said, looking to his wife and interlacing his fingers with hers. "You can't blame that woman forever."

"She could have *stopped*. Buses aren't *supposed* to go that fast," Susan replied, shaking her head stubbornly. "If she had been going the right speed…"

"Sue, stop it," he whispered, turning back to Lynn before continuing. "I'm sorry, we're still raw, we… it's hard for us to talk about it."

"I understand, Daniel, Susan, I really do." Lynn set her saucer on the coffee table and sat back up. "If I lost my son, I'm not ever sure I could ever recover."

"But Susan, I hope you know that Ms. Fields—the bus driver that day—she feels just *awful*," Lynn said, drawing the gaze of the poor woman. To these good people, it might have even sounded like the truth. "I've spoken with her and she couldn't make it three sentences before breaking into tears. She had *no* intention of hurting Tommy, she just couldn't react fast enough."

"She could have stopped, she could have swerved," Susan said, tears starting to fall from red-rimmed eyes, and Lynn realized this might be a harder sell than she had thought.

"She could have, that's true, but we make mistakes, Susan. Maybe she was thinking about something else, maybe someone on the bus was distracting her. Maybe, well, maybe Tommy didn't see the bus. There's so much we don't know, *can't* know," Lynn said, hoping the last statement would hook one of them. It was hard for her not to feel satisfied when Daniel breathed out deep and shook his head.

"We *do* know, Ms. Stafford," he started, and Lynn interrupted him by shaking her head and touching the table in front of her.

"Please, Daniel, *Lynn*. There's no need for formality now," she said, drawing a nod from the grieving father.

"Al—alright. Well, we do know. I'm not sure if they told you, but Tommy… Tommy wasn't in his right mind when the accident happened."

"No, Dan, no—"

"*Stop it,* Sue," he said, just a little too strong, and it forced his wife to cower back. Lynn could see Daniel regretted speaking up like that, but he turned away from his wife and continued his explanation. "It's not Ms. Fields' fault, Lynn, Tommy was… he was high when he jumped in front of the bus."

"Oh my god…" Lynn breathed in, covering her mouth with her fingers and pretending to be shocked. When she lowered her hand, Lynn let herself tear up. "Tommy smoked *marijuana?*"

"No, that's not… no," Daniel said firmly, believing in his son's memory even if he did not know for certain. "Tommy didn't do that kind of thing. One of the neighborhood kids, Derrick… he gave Tommy this drug. The police found more of it at the boy's house, and it's called Escape. It's like acid."

"Dan…" Susan pleaded, but he shook his head and patted her hand.

"We have to be *honest*, Sue. We loved him and he may not have known what he was getting into, but Tommy wasn't… *Tommy*… when it happened," Daniel said before looking back to Lynn, who was pretending to look at them with concern. "Derrick… Derrick said that Tommy thought he was some kind of superhero and… and he thought he was saving the world."

"Saving the world?" Lynn asked, but Susan cried out and threw away her husband's hand.

"I told you! I *told* you that we should never have let Tommy hang out with that boy!" she shouted, rising to her feet and pacing around the room. Daniel stood up quickly to try to pacify her, but she slapped him away before backing up against the wall. "We should… we should have never let him…"

"Sue," Daniel pleaded, his wife holding him at a distance. "Sue, please, they were just being kids. They were just experimenting—"

"Just experimenting…" Susan said, burying her face and sobbing before throwing them away and screaming at her husband. "He was *twelve*, Dan! That was not *experimenting!* They weren't in *college*. That little *bastard* gave our son hard drugs!"

"Sue…"

"Someone has to *pay*, Dan! If it's not his parents, if it's not the city, *who's* going to pay! *Someone* is responsible!" Sue shouted, sinking down against the wall until she was sitting against it, covering her face in her hands.

And though her heart broke for them, Lynn knew this was her opportunity.

"Susan," she said, walking over to the woman before kneeling down beside her. After placing her hand on Susan's wrist, Lynn pulled her hand away with tenderness and looked her in the eye. She even let tears stream down her cheeks. "Susan, I'm so sorry."

"*Why?*" she asked, and Lynn thought at first that the woman was asking her why she cared, but her fear was misplaced. "Why did it have to be *Tommy?*"

"Sometimes… sometimes no matter what we do, it's just not good enough," Lynn said as she placed her hand against Susan's cheek, breaking eye contact at just the right moment. "We all make mistakes, Susan, and sometimes our loved ones get hurt."

"But that's why," she said, lifting her face and staring straight into Susan's eyes. "That's why it's up to *us* to try to stop it from ever happening again. And it's *not* because of Ms. Fields; it's *not* because of the boy down the street. Tommy... Tommy isn't here because... because he got his hands on something that *shouldn't* exist."

"What are you..."

"Tommy is gone because someone out there thought it would be a good idea to push this... what was it called," she started before turning to Daniel, who was standing behind them. "Escape, was it?"

"That's right," he said with a nod, and Lynn turned back to the mother she was trying to manipulate.

"Someone gave this powerful drug to *children*, to this Derrick, to your *child*," Lynn said before looking down. "And I can't imagine what I would do if someone gave this terrible drug to my son. I can't even think about the possibility. I can't—I just can't..."

"I'm sorry," Lynn said, turning away from them and breathing out shakily, letting the Crenshaws watch as she recovered from her thoughts. Lynn let the moment go on too long, she knew it, but she had unintentionally started to think about the possibility of her son getting hold of the drug. It was painful—with all of his issues her son would not cope well with a drug like Escape—but Lynn tried to remind herself that she was on stage. Sniffing back her tears, Lynn turned back to Susan and pursed her lips.

"I'm sorry, I got... caught up," she said, lifting her head and placing her hand on Susan's shoulder. "I know you probably think I'm being overdramatic—my son is alive and healthy—it's just..."

"No," Susan said, placing her hand against Lynn's face, and Lynn knew she had already won. "No, don't you apologize. You understand, I know you do."

"I do, or... I think I do," Lynn said, smiling briefly before making eye contact with Susan again. "We can't let this happen again, Susan."

"Wh—what should we do?" she asked, and Lynn took Susan's hand off her face and held it between both of her hands.

"We need to let people know, Susan. We need to let people know the dangers of this terrible drug. We need to warn them, to show the world how we won't let these drug dealers hurt our children anymore."

"How—how would we do that?" she asked, and Lynn knew she had her mascot.

"Don't you worry, Susan, Daniel," she said, turning briefly to nod at the father standing by.

"Just leave that up to me. We'll find the criminals responsible, and we'll make them pay."

CHAPTER 3

BABY COME BACK

M．arc sat in the corner of his living room and pulled his legs in closer, unable to stop the pain seizing his chest. It never stopped hurting; no matter what he did, no matter where he went. Everywhere he tried to forget her, old memories would surface. Every time he breathed, her scent hung in the air. Whenever he found strands of hair on the ground, he couldn't bear to sweep them up or throw them away.

He couldn't forget Kara, but he also didn't *want* to.

Although he thought he was hearing things at first, Marc eventually realized that a song was playing, and it took him a few more seconds to realize that someone was calling him. When he had first gotten his smart phone, Marc had created a ringtone out of "She Blinded Me with Science" and had never bothered to change it. In this moment, the noise completely contrasted his mood.

Looking down at his phone, Marc watched it vibrate along the ground, cheesy 80's music playing all the while. The photo on the screen was his friend Lewis spitting out fire—a relic from their college days—and it was almost enough to make him laugh. However, it wasn't long before Marc realized why Lewis was calling, and he contemplated answering. After ten seconds he realized he wasn't brave enough to talk to his friend, so Marc swiped the screen and sent the call straight to voicemail before dropping the phone back to the ground, not caring if it would break or scratch.

Marc buried his face into his knees and trembled, feeling tears escaping his eyes against his will, but it wasn't long before the same, stale song started playing again. After lifting his head, Marc saw the phone still vibrating, but it had landed face down.

Although it would certainly gain some new scratches as it made its way across the hardwood floor, Marc couldn't bring himself to pick it up. As good a friend as Lewis was, Marc did not know if he could even speak to him. He had tried talking to himself earlier, but each syllable was so painful in his throat that Marc could not bear to think about it.

Eventually, the phone stopped ringing and Marc let his head fall back against the wall of his apartment. This was what he wanted right now; he wanted to be alone in his misery and grief. A couple weeks ago there had been another person living in this apartment. A couple weeks ago he would have seen her smiling face, touched her warm skin, heard her soft laugh.

But this was not a couple weeks ago; this was now, and Kara didn't live here anymore.

A harsh grinding that sounded like a trash compactor resonated through the apartment, and Marc realized that Lewis had left a voicemail for him. He didn't know why that sound was so much louder on his phone, but he assumed it was because he had downloaded the noise from a Transformers fan site. However, since the sound did not bother him much, Marc had given up trying to fix it and left it as his message notification, even if it practically shook his apartment.

Picking up the phone, Marc turned it over and saw the screen did not have more scratches than before, but he did not particularly care. What he could not ignore was the reminder on the screen that a message was waiting for him, and it did not take a genius intellect to figure out who had left it. Setting his thumb against the screen, Marc wondered if he could handle hearing Lewis' voice, but an accidental twitch started the process and he brought the phone up to his ear in a hurry.

"You have… one message," the feminine, artificial voice said before Lewis coughed into the phone, causing Marc's heart to drop out of his chest.

"Marcus, call me back, man. No one's been able to talk to you for a week, and we know you're hurting. I came by earlier and pounded on the door a bit, so I'm sorry if I scared you, but we're just worried. I know you have your phone on you, otherwise I wouldn't have been sent to voicemail early with the last call," he said before sighing.

"Dude, just call me back. Don't do anything stupid. Don't... don't do you-know-what. I know it used to be all fun and games, but that kind of thing can mess with your head and you aren't in the place for that. Call me back and we can get stupid drunk or something. Just—"

"Press five to delete this message or," the artificial voice broke back in—apparently Lewis had run out of time—and Marc lowered his phone and pressed the touchpad to delete the voicemail. He didn't need to keep Lewis' message. It was everything he already knew, it was everything he had already been told. They were all worried about him; that's what they said. And those who knew about their little secret business had already told him to stay away from his own merchandise, but the warning had come too late.

There was a square of paper with a green infinity symbol stuck to Marc's tongue at that very moment.

It would not be much longer before the Escape kicked in—he knew from experience—but he did not know what to expect in his current state. He had never heard of anyone taking the drug under this kind of stress, with these kinds of thoughts. Although *that* was not much of a surprise; Marcus Wright led a sheltered life with only a few friends. Half of those friends were currently drug dealers, but he didn't judge them for that.

Especially since he was the one who created their supply.

Laughing at the absurdity, Marc tossed his phone to the side—where it miraculously landed on a couch cushion on the floor—and set his head back against the wall. If his parents could see him now, taking a hallucinogen he had created just because of a girl, they would probably disown him. They had paid for his chemistry degree and he had turned around to create one of the new, hip designer drugs flooding the streets.

Adding that guilt to the mountain already crushing him, Marc pushed himself to his feet, using the wall to balance himself once he was standing. It would only be minutes before his brainchild would take effect, and Marc stumbled through his living room—using the counter that doubled as his kitchen wall and his breakfast bar— and tried to make his way to the bathroom. He didn't know why he always needed to pee right before he started to peak, but it was ritual at this point.

Entering the bathroom, Marc was distracted by his own reflection. Somehow, even with his dark skin, he looked pale. Turning to face himself head-on, Marc turned his face and ran his fingers along the black stubble covering his cheek, realizing how much he had let himself go in the last week. He couldn't even remember the last time he had eaten, but that was of no consequence, so Marc turned on the faucet so he could get a drink of water.

After making a cup out of his hands and lowering his face to the stream, Marc realized he did not want to dilute the effects of the Escape, no matter how thirsty he was. Letting go of the water in his hands, Marc lifted himself up and turned off the faucet before undoing his belt. Setting his pants around his ankles, he sat down and waited for his pre-peak urination to start.

It took about a minute before his bladder finally surrendered, and he guessed it was because he felt self-conscious. Not because he was sitting down—he had always preferred the lazy approach— but he guessed it was because it would mean the start of his trip. He was nervous, he had never done this kind of thing before and Lewis had been right; taking Escape in his current condition was dangerous and could give him a whole host of issues. The mind does curious things when exposed to traumatic events, and Marc was playing with fire.

Breathing in deep and realizing he was out of urine, Marc

stood and picked up his jeans in the same motion, settling them on his hips and zipping them up before clasping his belt. Walking over to the sink, he turned on the faucet and let the water run over his fingers, but he did not bother to use soap. Because of the way the water flowed over his skin and the way he could barely feel it, Marc was more than just distracted. The Escape was finally taking effect and his world would change in front of him.

Forcing himself to maintain his current world, Marc closed his eyes and prepared himself for what he might see. He could keep this bathroom the same—this was within his power—but whatever was beyond the door could very well break his mind. That thought caused Marc to laugh, and he opened his eyes with renewed confidence.

His heart was already broken; he may as well break his mind to match it.

Pushing open the door, Marc stepped through and found himself standing in the exact same apartment, which was what he wanted. Almost every detail was the same; movie posters were still scattered around the room, his TV was still in the corner, his bookcase was still filled with books he had read years ago and others he would probably never get around to reading.

Everything was the same except for the girl with short, black hair sitting on the couch. When Marc breathed out in shock, the girl turned to him with a smile.

"What took you so long? You fall in?" she asked with a smirk, and Marc fell in love all over again.

As he walked around his cheap furniture, Marc took in her every detail. She had a black miniskirt on, revealing the blue legwarmers with stylized skulls printed all over them, and she wore a torn, white shirt with holes showing her dark bra and pale skin. Dark eyeliner and the rings in her eyebrow made her blue eyes pop; he could only stare as she played with the snakebite piercing in her lip. This was how Marc best remembered her—the first time he had seen her again after high school—and he remembered how it felt to see his crush out of nowhere years later.

It was not so different than what he felt while she sat on that couch.

"You lost your tongue or something?" she asked, uncrossing her legs and leaning forward. "Dude, what the fuck is going on?"

"Kara," Marc muttered as he sat down next to her, causing the girl to look at him like he was a homeless person.

"*Yeah*, that's my name, hosscat. You hit your head?" Kara raised an eyebrow, but then she tilted her head and scowled. "You just smoked a big ol' bowl without me, didn't you?"

"No, it's not that," Marc said, reaching out to touch her leg and marveling at the heat flowing from her skin. Most of him knew Kara wasn't real, but his brain was doing a lot of work to convince him otherwise. When he saw her pale hand cover his dark finger, Marc's rationality abandoned him and he looked up to find her squinting at him.

"You made a new drug and tried it out *yourself...*" she muttered, but she could tell from his reaction that she was wrong. "Okay, what the fuck, dude? This is starting to weird me out."

"No, it's just... I'm fine, Kara. I just haven't seen you in a long time," he said, causing the girl to snort and fall away from him to the other end of the couch.

"You must be *super* fucking high, man. We've been living together for a year and a half and I sure as *shit* haven't left the house in days," Kara said before sitting back up and placing her hand on his shoulder. "If you hadn't noticed, we've ordered delivery for three days straight. I'm starting to get a little gut from all the pizza I've been eating."

"I... I must have forgot," Marc excused himself, looking at his girlfriend with a smile and seeing his reflection in her eyes. "And you're fine. I don't see a gut on you."

"Well, good! I need to stay sexy for now. Since you're not gonna put a ring on my finger, I have to make sure I still look good when you break up with me." She used her foot to poke at Marc's ribs, but he grabbed her leg and brought it across his lap, using his fingers to massage the bottom of her foot once she was settled.

"I'd never do that, Kara. Besides, you're not *exactly* the poster child for tying the knot," Marc joked with his hallucination, and Kara was kind enough to oblige him, making a face filled with mock surprise.

"Says Mister Anti-Commitment! That's why we fucking *work*, dude," she said before kicking him with her other foot, Marc only half-heartedly knocking away her play strikes. "*Neither* of us want that shit and you know it. We don't need rings, we don't need to abide by the traditional family unit."

"You and me?" Kara said before leaning forward and throwing her arms around Marc's shoulders, looking up at him with a sly smile.

"You and me just need a good bed where we can screw each other's brains out, a couch where we can cuddle and jobs that don't eat our souls. And *guess what*, handsome? We got *all* three," she said before pulling him down into a deep kiss, eventually letting him go with a laugh.

"Don't need rings," Marc muttered, smiling at his girlfriend before waving his hand around his face. "Says the girl with rings just all over her face."

"Hah, if I wore a wedding ring on my face, that'd be one hell of a piercing," she said before drawing away. "Besides, you like the metal in my face. Least, you *said* you do."

"I like *you*, Kara, rings or otherwise," Marc said, lifting his finger to tap the ring in her lip. "Might even say I love you."

"Only if you might want me to throw up." Kara rolled her eyes, but she did not get to do much more before Marc leaned down and kissed her, rubbing his hands along her back and down the side of her torso. When he finally let Kara go, she was looking up at him and having a difficult time breathing normally.

"*Fine*, you asshole, I love you, too."

"That's all I wanted to hear," Marc said before throwing an arm underneath her legs and the other underneath her armpit, standing up with her without much effort. She squeaked as he tossed her lightly, settling her in his arms, but then she put her hand up to his cheek and scrunched her face at him.

"You're too strong for a nerd, you know that?"

"Eh, it's probably because I'm black. All those Africa genes give me super strength," he joked, earning a smile from the girl in his arms.

"Yeah, *super strength*. Lifting a hundred and twenty pounds means you're the fucking Hulk," Kara said, but she was not prepared for Marc to look down at her in alarm.

"Hundred and twenty? *Damn, girl,* you *did* get fat," he said as he walked to their bedroom, and he got slapped for it.

"Hundred and twenty looks good on me, you jackass. You don't see me pointing out that new paunch of yours…" she said, looking away as Marc came to a stop above their bed.

"Paunch?" Marc used a mock angry tone as he tossed her on the bed and watched her bounce before catching herself. She turned over and looked flustered, but Marc had already taken off his shirt to show his muscular physique. "How's *this* for *paunch?*"

"You are so fucking fat, dude, it's disgusting," Kara teased, and she was rewarded with Marc jumping on her and holding her close as they rolled around the bed.

They kissed for a few moments, groping each other as clothes flew off their bodies, but eventually they came to a stop with Marc on top of her and staring down at her in adoration.

"Super strength," he stated with confidence, earning a laugh from his girlfriend.

"Okay, Hulk, fine. You're *super* strong."

"Hey!" he said, lifting a finger and nodding. "*Fucking* Hulk."

"Oh yeah, sure," she said, shaking her head before lifting an eyebrow. "We'll see about that."

"Hulk smash," Marc said before lowering his head and giving her a deep kiss, completely losing himself to a mixture of love and lust. All he could see was her face, all he could feel was her body and her breath hot on his neck. His hands ran along her perfect skin; her moans and squeaks reached his ears just as always. Everything was perfect in that moment, just like it had been before it all turned sideways. It would have been a strange sight if anyone walked in on him in that moment—there wasn't even a pillow where Kara's body should be—but Marc didn't care.

He had lost her because of Escape, but Escape had brought her back.

"Marcus!"

Marc woke up with a start, his name violent against his eardrums and causing a headache. Seconds later, he realized the headache had less to do with his name and more to do with the beer bottles scattered around his room. Vaguely, he recalled splitting a six pack with Kara, but when he turned over to caress her back, there was no one lying next to him. That was when he remembered that Kara had not spent the night with him, and his headache made a lot more sense.

He split a six pack with himself, and this was just a normal hangover.

"Marcus! Come out here! I know you're there!"

Groaning and setting the heel of his hand against his eye, Marc tried to figure out why the voice sounded familiar, but then he realized it was Lewis screaming from the other side of his door. Standing up and letting the sheets fall away from his body, Marc stumbled over to his dresser as his friend pounded against the door to his apartment. Cursing Lewis for making his headache worse, Marc threw on a loose shirt and grabbed a pair of shorts from his dresser, making his way into the living room.

"Damnit, Marcus, I know you got my messages yesterday! Open up, man!" Lewis shouted, punctuating each statement with another thump against the door. Trying to hop into his shorts and failing, Marc almost fell but caught himself on the bar countertop as Lewis continued his assault on the door. Scowling, Marc wondered if Lewis would go away if he waited long enough, but he knew his friend too well; Lewis would keep going until the police asked him to stop.

"I will break this fucking door down, man, and you know it. Your friendship is worth more than the cost of fixing it, that's for damn sure! Open... the *fuck*... up!" he continued, pausing between words to hit the door, and Marc eventually tired of the whole game. Just as Lewis finished his last demand, Marc opened up the door and his friend barged right past him, coming to a stop by the couch.

"Fucking *finally*..." Lewis said, turning around and breathing out heavily. Lewis was about the same height as Marc, but he looked entirely different. First of all, he was white with blonde hair and—in contrast to Marc's current attire—wore clothes appropriate for an adult. Wearing slacks and a button-up shirt beneath his leather jacket, Lewis had the appearance of a young professional, an appearance Marc should have mirrored.

Instead, Marc looked like he had just fallen out of his bed in college.

"It is way too early to give me this much of a headache," Marc said while walking over to the counter to support himself, but Lewis crossed his arms and sighed.

"You lost the *too early* privilege when they started serving lunch. Marcus, seriously," Lewis said, softening with his friend's name, which was enough for Marc to look at him, "why haven't you been answering your phone?"

"I haven't felt like it," Marc excused himself, but he already felt ashamed of the answer.

"Dude, if you don't come into work, it looks suspicious. I mean—shit, I don't know why I led with that..." Lewis muttered before sitting on the back of the couch. "Are you *okay?*"

"Am I *okay? Really?*" Marc asked, propping his head up with his hand. "What do you think, man? It's only been a couple weeks."

"I... I know, it's just after..." Lewis looked down and rubbed his shoe along the floor. "We worry about you, Marcus."

"You know I go by Marc now," he replied, but his friend scoffed at the name.

"You're *always* going to be Marcus to me, so stop trying. The others can call you Marc, but I've known you way too fucking long," Lewis said, drawing a smile from Marc even under the circumstances. "Way too fucking long, man."

"What, you wanna break up?" Marc asked sarcastically, but once he made eye contact, he could see the joke had not gone over well.

"I miss you, man. Work's not the same, of course, but I miss having you around. More *importantly*, I just—I want to make sure you're okay. After Kara..." Lewis trailed off once he remembered why he was here. "I guess I just want to make sure you're not thinking about trying to see her again."

"What if I am?" Marc asked, causing his friend to look at him with worry. "Is that so wrong? Is it so awful to pretend for a little bit? Make it hurt a little less?"

"Jesus, you already did it," Lewis said, causing Marc to purse his lips and cross his arms. After shrugging, he breathed out heavily and looked to the side.

"So what if I *did? It's my gift to the world,* why can't I use it the way I want?" Marc said before resuming eye contact. "I know it's not real, but... if it's gradual... I think I can handle it better."

"Marcus," Lewis said as he stepped closer, reaching out with his hand and setting it on Marc's shoulder. "*Don't* do it again. I can understand the appeal—I really can—but you're going down a bad road with this. We barely know what's possible under Escape, but I *know* you know this is a bad idea."

"It's—look, man, just for a little bit, I… I get to forget," Marc said, emotions surging and causing his eyes to water up. "Don't I deserve a break from it all? Don't I deserve just a little time where my world isn't falling down all around me?"

"Marcus, I… I *can't* understand what you're going through—I don't know anybody who can—but we're here for you. All the guys, your folks… all we want is to help you get over this, but if you delude yourself, it's only going to make it *worse*. Look at me," Lewis said as he set his other hand on Marc's shoulder, forcing his friend to make eye contact.

"Kara's *gone*. She's dead."

"You think I don't know that?" Marc exploded, knocking away Lewis' arms and retreating to the kitchen so he could point at the ceiling. "You think I don't remember watching her get out from under my arm—laughing about how she could finally *fly*— and you think I don't remember watching her walk over to the fucking ledge and jump off?"

"I know, man—"

"No, you *don't* fucking know, Lewis," Marc interrupted as anger and guilt tore at him. "You weren't *there*. The rest of us… we were *all* fucking there, and none of us did a damn thing. We were all high and experiencing our own worlds, and we didn't even fucking notice when one of our friends decided to go and fall off a ten story building! And that's not the worst part, man…"

"The worst part," he continued, supporting himself on his kitchen counter as tears obscured his vision. "The worst part was trying to explain to her mom why Kara would commit suicide because we didn't want to get thrown in jail for creating a drug that made her think she could fly."

"We buried her, man," Marc concluded, turning back to Lewis and sniffing back tears. "You and me. We made a way for us to escape, and it killed my girlfriend."

"It's not your fault, Marcus. It's *not*," Lewis stated, firm, as he walked around the bar and up to his friend.

"It's no one's fault, we were just—Kara wouldn't blame you. She knew the risks just like all of us and… it may be morbid," he hesitated, looking at the kitchen tiles beneath him. "But it's not a bad way to go."

"A *bad way to go?*" Marc asked, fury building with every word, and Lewis realized he had made a mistake.

"I meant that… I meant that she died thinking she could fly. There was no *fear*. If I had to die, I could think of worse ways," he quickly explained before looking back at Marc and swallowing down his awkwardness. "Of course, I don't mean it was *good*, I'm not trying to—"

"Get out," Marc interrupted, his voice soft and far more calm than his thoughts. Lewis looked up and put out his hands, knowing he had put his foot in his mouth.

"I'm sorry, man, I didn't mean it like that."

"Just get out," Marc repeated, reaching out to grab the handle to his refrigerator as a distraction. "I know what you meant. It's okay."

"Marcus, we care—"

"I know," Marc said, making eye contact and shrugging. "I know it was from a good place, I just can't have you here right now."

"I… alright," Lewis surrendered, backing away and turning to face the door. "Don't do it again, man. You're not going to be able to grieve right until you let her go. It's a mistake."

"Yeah, well, it's *my* mistake to make." Marc crossed his arms as he followed Lewis, coming to a stop at the doorway with Lewis on the other side. "It's a just-for-now thing, man. I just… I need it for now."

"Come back to us, man," Lewis pleaded, breathing out deep. "Work understands for now, but it won't be long before they'll want you to come back. The other thing… well, we can handle that on our own for a while, but I can't make it all by myself."

"And we need *you* back, too," Lewis said before looking away. "It hurt you the most, but we all lost Kara. She was our friend, too."

"I know, man. I know," Marc said, his anger melting away as he saw his friend holding back tears. Stepping forward, he wrapped his arms around Lewis and patted his back, Lewis doing just the same for him. "I do appreciate you coming by. I just… I can't face the world yet."

"Hah, the world," Lewis said before letting out another weary laugh. "Good thing we made a drug where we don't have to live in it all the time."

"Yeah, good thing," Marc said as he withdrew and stepped back into his apartment. Lewis looked at him awkwardly for a moment, but he eventually turned and started toward the elevator. After a few steps, however, he turned around and pointed back at Marc.

"Answer your fucking phone from now on, you hear me? Even if you're… under the influence. I want to know I can reach you." Marc looked at his friend for a moment before surrendering and nodding his head. Lewis returned one of his own before turning back and walking away.

Marc retreated into his apartment and closed the door, but he did not feel like he was home. Without Kara in it, their apartment was just empty space; a mausoleum to a girl who had been alive a few weeks ago. That kind of girl would never have killed herself—Kara would have fought to her last breath—but Marc had deprived her of that. He would never stop feeling guilty for failing to stop her from walking off that ledge.

After sinking down against the door to his apartment, Marc buried his head in his hands before pulling them down his face, stretching his skin in an attempt to wake himself up. Since he was skipping out on work another day, there was not much for him to do. On a normal day, Marc would have just curled up with Kara on the couch and watch a nerdy show, but that was not an option without his girlfriend.

Suddenly, one of those lazy days was all Marc wanted and all the grief and guilt slammed into him like a freight train. He panicked for a moment, whining as his chest started to ache, but then he remembered that curling up with his girlfriend was an option. He didn't have to give her up yet; he had a ready supply of Escape just waiting for him in the other room.

Quickly making his way to the bedroom, Marc threw open the drawer of his bedside table and grabbed a sheet, tearing off a double dose of his own drug, and he did not wait before setting it on his tongue. It was more than he needed for a day of television, but he needed it to set in—and *stay*—for as long as possible. He needed to forget; he needed to delay the inevitable. And so Marc walked over to his sofa and laid down, turning on the TV and waiting for his dead girlfriend to cuddle with him.

Letting out a short laugh, Marcus Wright realized he brought a whole new meaning to denial when it came to the Stages of Grief.

CHAPTER 4

REALITY BITES

Jeremy, please pay attention."

At the sound of his teacher's voice, Jeremy picked his head up from his desk and let his eyes adjust to the harsh fluorescents of the classroom. Mr. Garvey was looking at him behind thick glasses, disappointment evident on his face. Once he was fully aware, Jeremy looked around the room and found all of his classmates looking at him, some of them snickering. Scowling, he pushed against his desk until he was sitting up straight.

"Sorry, Mr. Garvey," he mumbled, but his teacher did not look pleased. With a cluck of his tongue, Garvey put his hands on his hips and nodded at the blackboard.

"You know, we're talking about one of the most exciting time periods, Jeremy. World War II was a watershed moment in history, and you shouldn't be sleeping in the middle of class," Garvey explained, motioning toward Jeremy with an open hand.

"Maybe you shouldn't be so boring, then," Jeremy mumbled, not realizing he had said the words aloud, and he saw anger flash across his teacher's face.

"I'm sorry, Jeremy? *What* was that?" Garvey asked, crossing his arms and walking closer to Jeremy's desk. From the hush of his classmates, Jeremy realized that he had not just thought those words. He gulped down fear as he looked up at his teacher.

"Nothing, Mr. Garvey. I didn't say anything," he replied while avoiding eye contact, hoping it would be enough for his history teacher. After a long moment, Jeremy noticed Garvey back away and then set his finger against a map of Europe.

"Then maybe you would care to explain to us—since I'm so boring—what was so important about Operation Overlord,"

Garvey suggested, and Jeremy realized he was being put on the spot. Feeling anxious, Jeremy looked up from his desk and found that thirty sets of eyes were all staring at him, including two that mattered more than all the rest combined.

Allison was sitting across the middle aisle dividing the classroom in half, and she was looking at him, waiting for him to make his awkward mistakes and whispering just like everyone else. In the real world—*this* world—Allison wouldn't give him cheeky smiles or laugh at his jokes, and Jeremy already wished he was dosing again. It would be hours before he could get back to his house and the sheet of Escape hidden in the puppet, and so he was forced to live in this disappointing world.

"Jeremy? Do you have anything to say?" Garvey's voice broke back in, and Jeremy realized he had been staring at Allison, who was now looking away in sympathetic embarrassment. Suddenly, Jeremy was angry—furious that Garvey had called him out like this—so he turned back to face his teacher at the blackboard.

"The importance of Operation Overlord, otherwise known as the Battle of Normandy," Jeremy began, confidence bursting out of nowhere, "was one of the most important Allied operations in the Western Theater. After deliberately leaking false information about multiple incursions into the mainland to deceive Axis powers, Allied troops landed on the beaches of Normandy, catching the Germans with their pants down," he added, drawing laughs from some of his classmates.

"Because of Operation Overlord, the Allies were able to push forward, defeat the Germans in the Battle of the Bulge, and drive forward to Berlin and cause Hitler to kill himself," Jeremy finished explaining, crossing his arms as he saw Garvey look at him in a stupor. "You could get all that information from watching the History Channel or *Saving Private Ryan*, by the way. Little bit less boring."

"Oh shit," a neighboring classmate whispered, causing Garvey to snap out of his daze and point at the student.

"Hey, no cursing, Warren," he commanded before turning back to Jeremy, who was still sneering at him from his seat. "And you're right, Jeremy, Operation Overlord was important for all those reasons and more. Although you shouldn't be watching a movie like *Saving Private Ryan* at your age."

"It's history, Mr. Garvey. I would think you would want your students to be interested." Jeremy could tell that his teacher wanted to snap at him, but he could also see the surrender in Garvey's eyes.

"You're right, Jeremy, I do want you to be interested. That's why you should try to stay awake during my lessons and I can tell you more about this time period. Okay?" he asked, but it was not a question. Realizing it would be stupid to prolong the confrontation, Jeremy nodded and sat back in his chair, which Garvey took as a victory.

"Alright, class, Jeremy had a good point, but there's much more to Operation Overlord than you can find in a Steven Spielberg film," he began, but Jeremy had already stopped listening. He wished he could have embarrassed his teacher further, but he did not want to get in trouble or—worse still—have the principal call his mother. The satisfaction of ruining Garvey's day did not outweigh the consequences of reality.

Again, Jeremy wished he was back home and under the effects of Escape. In his fabricated world, he could tell off Garvey to his heart's content. If Jeremy wanted to, he could even beat the man to death over and over again, in a thousand different ways, and his history teacher would still be alive and well and droning on about World War II the next morning. The drug was perfect for pretend violence just like it was perfect for everything else.

Remembering how he had loved his experience with his fake Allison the day before, Jeremy turned to look back at the real Allison again. He did not exactly know why—he had already embarrassed himself by staring at her—but he was surprised to see Allison look at him out of the corner of her eye. Immediately,

Jeremy felt ashamed and his stomach dropped, but then he saw the slight tug at the corner of her lips. At once, the shame fell away and his stomach dropped for an entirely different reason, but it was enough for Jeremy to smile as he turned forward.

It meant nothing, he knew it, but Jeremy couldn't help but remember that smile in an entirely different light.

"Nice one, weirdo," a deep voice said before Jeremy was hit from the side, almost causing him to drop his tray to the cafeteria floor. Turning around in anger, Jeremy saw a stocky brute with short black hair looking down at him with a couple friends; all of them seniors, all of them wearing letter jackets for the football team.

"Shut up, Shriver," Jeremy said, trying to walk away from his tormentors. Although he had turned away from them, he could feel all three of them walking behind him, pointing and laughing. "And what's with the jackets? It's not 1950 anymore."

"Fucking photo day, stupid. You think I want to wear this thing?" Shriver hit Jeremy's shoulder from behind and made him stumble, which sent his bottle of soda to the floor. "Ooh, you gotta stop being so clumsy."

"Will you just leave me alone?" Jeremy bent down to pick up his soda, but Shriver got there first and grabbed the plastic bottle. "C'mon, give it back."

"I will, I will. Just wanted to say we liked the show earlier," Shriver said, his taller friend standing off to the side and crossing him arms. This one was skinnier with light brown hair, but from his muscles, Jeremy knew he still put way too much time into lifting heavy objects. Jeremy also knew that he was Roger Blake, Allison's boyfriend.

"Yeah, listening to Garvey is like taking a valium. You tore him down with that History Channel bullshit," Roger said, nodding in approval. "You seriously watch that stuff, though?"

"The History Channel?" Jeremy asked, confused by this new friendliness. Even if he did not know Roger well, Shriver and his friends had spent the last few years tearing Jeremy down, so it was hard for him to trust anything that came out of any one of their mouths. However, since he needed to give them an answer, Jeremy looked away and shrugged. "No, not really. I've just read a bunch of stuff on the internet."

"Hah, that sounds right. You're *way* too nerdy, you know that?" the other senior asked, laughing a little too hard and slapping his shoulder. Jeremy turned to look at the boy—barely taller than Jeremy but his frame packed with muscle—and he wanted to punch out his teeth.

"Look, just because I don't spend my time running around with a ball doesn't mean I'm too nerdy," Jeremy said, earning a scoff from Shriver.

"Yeah, it's all the other stuff, rich kid. Here," Shriver said before shaking the soda in his hand and offering it forward. "Go ahead and drink your soda. Get even fatter and turn into Jabba the Hutt."

"You're one to talk, fucking asshole," Jeremy said under his breath, but he reached forward to reclaim his soda anyway.

Before he could, however, Shriver pulled back the soda and twisted the cap, covering Jeremy completely with carbonated sugar water. Jeremy couldn't even react; he just stood there as Shriver pumped the bottle and sprayed Jeremy all over, wasting his soda, soaking his clothes and embarrassing him in front of the entire cafeteria in one moment. Once the bottle was empty, Shriver dropped it and laughed and pointed at Jeremy, his smaller friend joining him.

"Dude, not cool," Roger said as he turned to his friends, but Jeremy could not hear him. All he could hear were the shouts from everyone in the cafeteria; the whooping laughter, the screams of joy at his misfortune as he stood there. When Jeremy looked down, he found that his burger and fries were soaked through and inedible, and he lifted his head just in time to see Roger arguing with Shriver.

"You went way too far, man," Roger said, but Shriver rolled his eyes and took out his phone, pointing it at Jeremy.

"Who fucking cares, Rog, the kid called me fat."

"You *are* fat."

"Yeah, well, *he* doesn't get to say so," Shriver said before tapping the screen of his phone, a flash of light blinding Jeremy as he stood there with soda pooling beneath him. "And now I have this awesome picture that I'm going to put on Instagram and it's going to have a hundred likes by the end of the day."

"You're such a fucking asshole sometimes," Roger said, but Shriver had already turned around and waved off the statement, leaving Jeremy to his misfortune. Seeing his friends leaving, Roger turned to face Jeremy and looked ashamed as he approached. "Sorry, dude. Shriver's just being a dick."

"Get away from me," Jeremy whispered as the boy came closer, but when Roger put out his hand to touch his shoulder, Jeremy backed away and snapped at him. "Just get the *fuck* away from me!"

"Jeremy, I'm sorry—"

"No, you're *not*," Jeremy argued as he backed away, stopping by a nearby garbage can and throwing his lunch onto the pile. "You guys *never* are. You walk around like fucking royalty, and pick on the guys who can't... who can't..."

"Really, man," Roger started, but Jeremy shook his head and rushed down the hallway leading to the bathroom.

"Just stay away!" he shouted, stomping away from his public embarrassment as the cafeteria continued to laugh at him. He couldn't care that Roger felt bad—he didn't believe it for a second—and it was only made worse because it was *him*. Not only did he have to have Allison, Roger Blake had to embarrass him and ruin his lunch.

It was just more of the same.

"Assholes," Jeremy muttered as he burst into the bathroom, dropping his bag and kicking it across the floor. Frustrated and hurting, Jeremy rushed over to the sinks and braced himself against the counter, trying not to cry and failing. "Fucking assholes…"

This was how it was always going to be; this was his reality. The jocks and the cool kids were always going to be steps above him, taking all of the good girls, living the good lives and ridiculing the people like Jeremy. It did not matter if Jeremy was a good person, whether or not he was funny, it did not matter if he knew more than his teachers; it did not matter that he was another person with feelings.

He would always be the fat kid who would get sprayed with soda for a laugh.

Looking away from the mirror above the sinks, Jeremy tried to recover from his ordeal and walked over to the paper towel dispenser. After waving his hand underneath the red light the machine refused to cooperate, so he slapped the plastic covering with his other hand.

"C'mon, you bastard," he mumbled, and after a few more seconds of frustrated waving underneath the sensor, a solitary paper towel came out. Once he saw this, Jeremy looked at the dispenser and realized it was completely empty.

Chuckling to himself in defeat, Jeremy turned around and placed his back against the wall, sliding down because of the sugar water covering every inch of him. Already it was drying and sticking to his skin, and it just caused him to laugh even harder. It was just not fair; the universe just *had* to be against him, too. Every aspect of reality seemed geared toward embarrassing him and forcing him into a life of misery.

That was when Jeremy looked down and found that his backpack had somehow become unzipped after he had kicked it, and he saw something very curious peeking out of the front pocket. Dragging the bag closer with his foot, Jeremy found a white square of Escape that he had somehow packed away, probably while he was still under the effect.

As soon as he realized what it was, however, Jeremy panicked and pulled his bag closer. Bringing drugs onto school property wasn't just cause for detention, it was a crime, and Jeremy never would have packed Escape in his bag in his right mind. Frantically, Jeremy tried to think of what he should do now and how he could get rid of the drugs, but then he realized that this was not the horrible problem he had assumed it was. Reality had proven itself a harsh mistress and Jeremy had a way to escape from all of that sitting in his hand.

"Shit," Jeremy muttered as he turned it over, forgetting the trouble he could get in if he got caught. Shriver had sprayed him over entirely with the soda and just a few drops of liquid could have ruined the Escape, but Jeremy sighed in relief once he saw his hallucinogen was unharmed. There were four doses in his hand—just a little square that reminded him of a Tetris block—and all of that Escape could break his mind with his current tolerance.

Tearing the square in half, Jeremy stowed one piece in a buried compartment of his bag and then held the other on the tip of his finger. He saw two infinity symbols there; twin symbols promising an escape from his world and his torment. Letting out a soft scoff, Jeremy realized that his bullies would have stolen or bought these drugs from him if they had known, but Jeremy would never let them have it. This was his world, his fantasy, and the jocks like Shriver and Roger did not deserve it.

Placing the piece of paper to his tongue, Jeremy felt much better knowing that reality would not bother him for the rest of the day.

Jeremy set his backpack against the metallic bleachers beside him and looked at the abandoned track field. During the warmer months, Jeremy's classmates would be running up and down that field or, like him, making just enough of an effort to avoid their gym teacher yelling at them. However, it was in the middle of winter, which meant the entire field was deserted.

It was absolutely perfect for Jeremy's trip.

Holding his arms closer to his stomach, Jeremy waited for the Escape to kick in. As much as he had done to mitigate the damage, Jeremy's clothes were still covered in soda and his outer coat could only do so much to keep him warm. Clouds of his breath came out staggered, his body shivered even though it was above freezing, but Jeremy just wished it was ten minutes from now. In ten minutes, he would be in a different world; in ten minutes, the cold biting at his skin would be in a different dimension.

And as he looked at the field and breathed out another cloud of mist, he saw snowflakes forming on his breath.

Smiling, he let the snow build and swirl in front of him, a majestic column of ice reflecting light from the shrouded sun above him. He immediately stopped shivering and pretended he was warm instead, focusing on creating a private spectacle in the air. As he stared into the emptiness, he saw a shimmering Chinese dragon form out of ice and snow, biting its own tail for a moment before moving its long body along a figure eight. No computer could generate something like this; no one could draw what he was seeing. This was an individual, irreplaceable vision meant entirely for him. This was the reality he preferred; a reality he could control.

Growing tired of the shimmering vision spiraling in the air, Jeremy banished the icy hallucination and turned his attention on the field below. In the spring, the grass would be green and vibrant; the nearby tree branches would be heavy with leaves. Then, without another thought, the field burst into life as a way to recreate that vision in his memory. Although he was not surprised that he *could* do this, he quickly realized that he had not intentionally created this new track field.

However, Jeremy was so happy at the sight that he did not care if he had created the field or not. A sea of grass flowed with the breeze, the light turning it from green to blue and back again while leaves burst into existence on the numerous trees. As Jeremy watched, he let those leaves turn to autumn colors, brilliant reds, oranges and yellows, and he even let the smell of cinnamon and pumpkin fill the air.

Breathing in the fabricated scents, Jeremy felt at peace, but he realized he wanted more. This was the first time he had taken more than a single dose, and he did not know the limits of Escape under those conditions. Focusing on the trees, Jeremy let those autumn colors turn to brilliant white and pink, the leaves becoming cherry blossoms that flowed through the air. Before long, the entire track field was swarmed with petals hanging on the currents and made Jeremy feel like he was in another time and place.

But that was just the start.

Before his eyes, Jeremy's visions took hold and he was no longer sitting on metallic bleachers. Jeremy was sitting on an ancient staircase and watching a climactic battle occurring in front of him, hundreds of soldiers wearing samurai armor falling to the attacks of a single, lone warrior with long, black hair. The warrior was dressed in traditional garb—flowing white robes— and he would dispatch every soldier who came against him, coloring the cherry blossoms with their blood.

And as he watched, Jeremy saw the warrior look up at him

with his face; it was Jeremy standing there in some sort of ideal form. This was what he wanted for now; this was what he wanted to be. There was no place in Jeremy's reality for a fat kid who was bullied because he was rich, because he was nerdy, because he was different. This was Jeremy as he saw himself, triumphant as the world came down around him.

"He's quite handsome," a voice interrupted him, and Jeremy turned to his right to see Allison sitting next to him. For a moment he was more than just confused—he had not meant to conjure her—but then Jeremy realized he wanted her here. Just like every one of his other visions, Jeremy wanted Allison by his side.

"He is a little pretty, I'll admit," Jeremy said as his oriental counterpart was surrounded by five men in samurai armor. Before they could advance further, the warrior dashed through all of them in the blink of an eye, each of his strikes complemented by a flash of light. When he stood defiant on the other side, it took a full second before his attackers fell in sprays of blood.

Other people—if they could even see it—might have found his generic stereotyping offensive or silly, but Jeremy did not care. This was his escape, after all, and he could treat this world any way he wanted. Turning to face Allison while cherry blossoms flowed around them, Jeremy realized he could change her, too. He did not have to settle for what he had seen in his history class earlier that day.

Instead of the normal clothes she had been wearing, Allison was suddenly covered in the traditional robes of a yukata, but then Jeremy realized that he did not want that for her. Swallowing down his fear, he let the yukata fall away and replaced it with a long-sleeved shirt and jeans.

"You have a problem making decisions, don't you?" she asked, causing Jeremy to laugh as he looked back at the field. A giant, armored creature had come to face his oriental doppelganger, and Jeremy watched as they traded blows, spiritual flames bursting into existence all around them.

"Yeah, a little bit, but that's okay. I don't really need to make decisions now," Jeremy said, setting his hands on the stone next to him. If he had not wished for it in his mind, he would have been surprised to feel Allison's hand on his fingers.

"I guess you don't. Is this something you always wanted to see?" Allison asked as the armored demon slammed a giant hand down on Jeremy's avatar, the thin man holding his blade above him to ward off the blow.

"*Always* is a strong word," he said just before realizing a great ending for this vision. Letting the demon's hand slide off the blade to the side, the warrior jumped onto the arm before leaping at the helmet covered in flames, grabbing hold of the eye sockets even as blue and green flames poured over him. Pulling hard with all his might and bracing his feet against the demon's torso, the warrior was finally able to remove the demon's helmet after a few seconds. Jeremy could see Shriver's doughy face looking down at the warrior once he landed.

"Oh, so just since lunch," Allison said flippantly, and they both watched as the warrior jumped and then plunged his sword into the bully's open mouth, severing his spine and removing the threat in an instant. After he leapt off the massive body, Jeremy's avatar walked away while the corpse finally fell to the ground, divine fire consuming its body in an instant.

"That was a long time coming, Allison. That's what *that* was," Jeremy said, wrapping his fingers around Allison's hand and squeezing. When she gave him a sidelong glance and a smile, his heart skipped a beat.

"It's too bad it's not real," she said, breathing out the statement, and Jeremy looked back at the field as more of his bullies crawled out of the ground. This was what Jeremy wanted—this was the reality he used as an escape—but his own fantasy had helped to derail his immersion. For that moment before he sank back into his delusion, Jeremy remembered just where he was.

"Yeah, it's too bad."

Although he had skipped all of his remaining classes, Jeremy knew he could not blow off his lessons after school, so he made his way back to the orchestra room once he was finished watching his avatar slice and slash through wave after wave of opponents. With Allison beside him, it had been like taking her on a date to see an action movie, and Jeremy had vastly preferred that fantasy than the real world and the sugar water that had soaked through his clothes. By the time he made it back inside, Jeremy had completely forgotten it was the middle of winter.

He was quickly reminded once he got back into the school building and a wave of heat hit him in the face. It shocked him at first—his body had no way to interpret this clash of information—but Jeremy eventually realized what had happened. Looking at his fingers and letting the illusion fall away, Jeremy realized they were pale, almost blue, and he knew that he had gone too far. If he had spent more time outside under the effects of Escape, he may have succumbed to hypothermia without even realizing it.

Breathing in deep, Jeremy promised he would be more careful when he was dosing. No matter what he saw—no matter what he wanted to see—the real world would still affect him, cold and all. That he dosed at all at school was incredibly foolish, but he had to pay attention to the things that might harm him back in reality. For the moment, however, he would have to forgive himself. There was no harm done—minus skipping class—and Jeremy would just have to be more careful whenever he wanted to escape.

When he finally got to the orchestra room, Jeremy saw it was completely empty except for plastic chairs and music stands. Checking his phone, Jeremy realized that it was much later than he had thought; far too late for him to make it to his lessons. Even the school buses would be gone, and Jeremy would have to find his way back to his house without them. Fortunately, his empty house was in walking distance, but the last thing he wanted to do was lug around a heavy instrument when it was this cold.

Sighing, Jeremy walked over to the storage room and approached his cubby, setting a hand against the wooden frame and appreciating the texture. It was a few seconds before he realized the texture was entirely made up in his mind—his fingers were still too numb from the cold to feel anything—but he shrugged the revelation away. Jeremy had to assume Escape would fill in the details even when he was not trying to imagine another world.

Pushing away his doubts and his theories, Jeremy retrieved the big, black case from his cubby and hauled it over to his usual seat near the wall. After setting it down, Jeremy undid the clasps holding it shut and then lifted the lid, smiling upon the sight of his cello. It was not the most endearing of instruments—he did not get the rock star treatment like a guitar player would—but Jeremy had always loved the sound. Dark, deep, troubled; it was everything Jeremy was put into music.

Picking up the instrument and setting the stand against the floor, Jeremy picked up his bow and placed it against the strings. He tested each string, tuning when necessary, and breathed out deeply, shaking his hand and trying to rid his fingers of the cold. For a moment he wondered what he would play, but then he settled on a prelude to a Bach piece, one of his favorite songs to play.

Except that when he placed the bow to the strings and tried to play, it sounded awful.

"What the fuck is this?" Jeremy muttered to himself, plucking at the strings and trying to figure out if he had tuned it wrong.

After a few moments of scrutiny, however, the cello sounded perfect, so he tried again. Again, Jeremy was disappointed, and he was so frustrated that he dropped the bow back into his case.

Believing it was the cold that hurt his playing ability in such a way, Jeremy leaned back and set his head against the wall. He felt the cool surface through his hair and against his scalp and enjoyed the contrast. Before he knew it, Jeremy was humming the same tune he had been trying to play, his hands moving along in rhythm, and then something wondrous happened.

Just as he was about to close his eyes, an entire orchestra joined him in the song, and Jeremy looked back at the room to find a hundred specters playing along, each of them glowing different colors as the music filled Jeremy's senses. He could only gape at them as the song took on an entirely different life, emotions and light flooding Jeremy's mind and the room. It was a symphony occurring before his very eyes.

"Whoa," he muttered, but somehow Jeremy's voice continued along with the orchestra, his humming reaching a crescendo as it vibrated the room. Before he even realized it, Jeremy had put his cello back in its case and stood up, walking along the lines of ghosts playing just for him. Each of them seemed to be a master of their instrument and they launched into melodies, counter-melodies and harmonies without the slightest hesitation.

Instead of the song he had meant to play, Jeremy found an entire world of music waiting for him because of this miracle drug.

Laughing, Jeremy turned and swayed to the music—a sight to behold if anybody had been watching—and after a few minutes of moving through the ghosts, Jeremy spied his abandoned cello sitting by his seat. Suddenly, the orchestra stopped—his *joy* stopped—and Jeremy realized that he would never be able to create anything so beautiful with his own hands. This kind of wonder, this *exaltation*, could only be achieved through Escape, through his mind.

Anything he could create with that glorified piece of wood and strings would never compare.

Feeling defeated, Jeremy walked over to his cello and packed it away, locking the clasps before picking it up and hauling it back to his cubby. There was no point in bringing it back with him; no point in walking all the way to his huge house with it under his arm. Not when his years of study would never allow him to create something as magnificent as what he had just created in a whimsical flight of fancy.

Once he closed the door to the storage room, the ghosts started playing again, but Jeremy realized the song had become a dirge. Although appropriate, it was not what he wanted, so Jeremy banished the specters back to his imagination and thought up a more fitting tune for the rest of his trip.

And as he bobbed his head to a dubstep track he was making up on the fly, Jeremy tried to convince himself that he did not care about the music he had left behind.

CHAPTER 5

WHAT'S REALLY IMPORTANT

Seventy-two hours, Stafford," Janice Pearson said after the last member of their subcommittee exited the room. Lynn turned from her position by the door, her palm still moist from Congressman Sherman's sweaty handshake, and waited for Janice to make her point. "Seventy-two hours after going to that boy's funeral and you already have a committee."

"The beginnings of one, it seems." Lynn closed the door leading into the hallway, sinc she knew this was about to be a very private conversation. "With Sherman, Gainsborough and Dalley behind us, I think we can at least make it look legitimate."

"Even though it's the furthest thing from it," Janice said with no small amount of venom. Frowning slightly, Lynn approached the table and sat down two seats away from her hostile partner.

"There's very little that happens on the Hill that's legitimate, Janice. Are you still bitter Price put me in the lead?"

"No, I'm past that, though you do need to work on your choices. Dalley got caught with a DUI a couple months back, so we may want to cut him going forward," she explained, turning back to Lynn with a scowl. "I'm more… jealous. You were able to get a subcommittee less than a week after you *heard* about a drug, and little, old me has been fighting in the trenches for years."

"It's sensational, Janice, that's all it is. A circus meant to distract our constituents," Lynn said, pausing and closing her right hand around a water glass. "Just a trapeze act…"

"Meanwhile, I'm left shoveling up the elephant shit when you get to attend candlelight vigils," Janice replied, earning a scoff from her partner.

"Oh, it's not *that* bad. I have the Chris Harmon show tonight, but you have the next appearance on CNN," Lynn argued as she lifted the glass of water off the table. "And we have equal share in the benefit on Thursday, so there's that."

"I've been meaning to talk to you about that, Stafford," Janice said quickly, making Lynn's ears perk up as sipped her water. "I can get reps from three major special interest groups on the line, but we need a better hook."

"A better hook? What do you mean?"

"They don't want to throw any funds at us unless we can prove that we can turn this into a national movement. Right now, it's just us, a regular at Thai lady-boy brothels, a drunk and Sherman's sweaty balls.," Janice sighed as she shook her head. "If we can't get more prominent members on board, they'll probably skip on us."

"Gainsborough likes Thai?" Lynn asked as she contemplated Janice's criticism internally. "Huh, that one went completely under my radar."

"Price has been keeping that secret for a while now," Janice replied with a laugh and a slow nod. "Cashed it in to give you more legitimacy."

"I don't know about *cashing it in*. Lady-boys are the gifts that keep on giving," Lynn said, rocking the glass in her hand so the water would swirl in front of her. "I'll think about some more recruits. We might even be able to convince Price to come forward."

"The only way…" Lynn paused, working through the scenario in her head. "I guess we really need to push the public angle when we conduct our interviews. Really sell it that it's as bad as heroin or meth. Push the idea that it could lead to twenty-first century opium dens."

"Is there any data to support that?"

"Nothing's as good as a few anecdotes and a child's tombstone. You going to be fine on CNN?"

"Of course, I am. I've been doing this a long time, Stafford.

What about you? Do you know who you're speaking against tonight? Last time you were on there, you looked like a lunatic," Janice commented, a smug smile on her face. When Lynn looked back at her in anger, she was surprised to see Janice's eyes flicker with fear.

"I speak to my demographic, Janice. In any case, our tactics are solid. I just want to make sure we can get those special interest groups to take note. Need some sort of sound bite…"

"Some clever way to use *escape*?" Janice asked while drawing air quotes around the word, and Lynn had to hold back her disgusted sigh.

"That's probably the easiest way to do it. Anyway," Lynn said as she stood up and gathered papers and folders into her briefcase. "I'll get working on that and prepare for tonight. You sure you have the benefit under control?"

"Of course, I do," Janice said as she rose to join Lynn. "It'll make your candlelight vigil seem like amateur hour."

"*Shouldn't* it, Janice? After all, you *always* go on about how long you've been doing this," Lynn teased, trailing off as she made eye contact with her furious partner. Lynn knew it was not wise to antagonize her, but she couldn't help it.

"I'm going to kill Price next time I see him," Janice muttered as she moved past Lynn, only stopping at the door long enough to turn back and point at her. "You get national support for us, and I'll make sure our fundraiser makes headlines."

"Thanks, partner," Lynn said with a smile, but Janice left with a growl and a whispered curse. Soon, the clacking of her heels on the tiles of the hallway was swallowed up by other noise, and Lynn breathed out in relief.

It had been one, nonstop assault of information, meetings, interviews and appearances since she had left the Crenshaw's house a few days ago. She had stayed in town only that day—visiting with a local drug rehabilitation clinic before heading to Tommy's candlelight vigil—and she had immediately come back to the organized chaos Janice and Price had left for her. There were already pictures floating around the internet of her mourning the loss of a child, and her partners had been busy in her absence.

"Back to work, then," Lynn muttered as she left the meeting room and turned left down the hallway. It would only be a few minutes before she was back in her office, before Sharon told her about her next appointment, and Lynn was grateful that she had those few minutes before she would have to wear her public mask again.

"Ms. Stafford," a male voice interrupted her thoughts, and Lynn realized she would not even have her few minutes. Putting the mask back on, Lynn turned to find one of her aides catching up, a memo in his hand.

"Mitch, what are you doing here?" she asked, noticing how winded the boy looked. Considering that the sandy-haired boy from Dartmouth was still in college and kept in shape, Lynn had to assume he had sprinted from her office and then around the building a few times just for good measure. After Lynn allowed him a few breaths, Mitchell handed her the memo and tried to explain.

"You weren't answering your phone, Ms. Stafford," he said, halting after her name so he could take another breath. "Senator Price said it was urgent news, and that I should tell you right away."

"Tell me what?" Lynn asked, more to the universe than to the boy walking beside her. Scanning down the memo, Lynn was looking for what was so important when her eyes stopped on two words; just a name that meant a great deal. "Oh, fuck me, running…"

"Ms. Stafford?" Mitchell asked, and Lynn looked to her aide and sighed.

"Call me Lynn, Mitch. The only people who say Stafford are my enemies or people who don't know me," she said, crumpling up the paper in her hand and tossing it into a wastebasket in an alcove to her left.

"Ms. Sta—Lynn, you can't throw away internal memos like that. What if someone—"

"I have more important things to worry about, and it's not like any of that was incriminating evidence. It was just a heads-up," Lynn explained, focusing on the problem at hand and what she could possibly do about it.

"A heads-up about what?" Mitchell asked, causing Lynn to look at him directly, stunned by his innocence.

"What, you didn't read it?" she asked, and Mitchell turned away and shook his head, reminding Lynn of a half-trained puppy.

"Well, no, it was for you, not—"

"You're a sweet kid, Mitch," Lynn interrupted, breathing in deep before looking her aide in the eye. "Senator Price wanted me to know that I will be paired up against Noel Silverman when I go on Harmon's show tonight."

"Oh, I see," Mitchell said softly, allowing Lynn to walk in silence for a moment, but she could actually *feel* him look back at her in confusion. "Who's Noel Silverman?"

"Positively *saccharine* of you, Mitch." Lynn forced a smile for her intern. "You need to pay more attention if you plan to have a political career."

"I thought… you're right," he admitted, looking down, and it pulled on Lynn's heartstrings. Sighing, Lynn laid her hand on the boy's shoulder and caught his attention.

"It's okay, Mitch, it's okay. Let me put it this way: Say you wanted to watch a boxing match."

"Okay?"

"And me? Let's just say I'm Stallone in the first Rocky movie. Nothing to scoff at, right?" she asked, and Lynn could see from his blank stare that he had no idea what she was talking about. "Do you not know the movie?"

"Uh, no, not really. It's a little too old for me," he said, biting his lip, and Lynn buried her face in her hand for a moment. "Pretty much everything before 1980 is a little too... primitive?"

"Well you know the actor, right?" Lynn snapped, pulling her hand away so she could slap it on Mitchell's shoulder. Lynn could see the fear in his eyes—he must have felt like she was disappointed in him—but he nodded eagerly.

"Yeah, I've seen him in those Expendables movies," he said, and it was Lynn's turn to feel ignorant.

"Well, I've never seen those, but you know who I'm talking about. Stallone, big guy, works hard, kicks ass from time to time," she said, drawing a nod from her enthusiastic and boyish aide. Turning from him, Lynn continued down the hallway in a foul mood, forgetting that Mitchell would not get her next reference.

"Well, Noel Silverman is my Apollo Creed."

"Lynn, it's good to see you again," a handsome man said from the other side of the desk, giving a knowing smile to his opponent across the way. If he had not been one of her most vocal opponents, Lynn might have found Noel Silverman attractive in another life.

Then, with a sigh, Lynn realized she found him attractive anyway; it was hard not to see the appeal. With a square jaw clean of stubble, well-kept, light brown hair, calm, blue eyes, and a physique that made him look like he was three seconds from tearing off his suit and exposing his true identity as a superhero, Silverman was everything a man should be. He could have been successful at whatever he wanted to do; just his looks could have gotten him anywhere.

But it just so happened that Noel Silverman was one of the

most intelligent and, more importantly, charismatic proponents for drug legalization.

"My name is Ms. Stafford, Mr. Silverman," Lynn said tersely, making eye contact with the man and hoping to establish leverage in their conversation. If she could possibly make him feel inferior now, he might not be such an intimidating opponent during the broadcast.

"Lynn, come on," Silverman said, tilting his head and looking straight through her. He gave Lynn a disarming smile, but she was able to keep a straight face for the moment. "We've known each other too long for *that*."

"Just because we know each other does not make us familiar, Mr. Silverman," she said, breaking eye contact and looking at the camera fifteen feet away. In just a few minutes, that camera would be showing her image to millions of people, millions of people who had probably not even heard of Escape or designer drugs at all. Breathing deep, Lynn tried to avoid looking back at her opponent. "I expect you to keep this professional?"

"*Professional?*" Silverman asked with a scoff, causing Lynn to turn back, and she immediately wished she hadn't. That man was far too confident, far too comfortable. He looked at her, propping up his chin with a curled fist. "Coming from *you*, Lynn? This whole debacle is only happening because you decided to parade a boy's corpse out in front of the world."

"That's an awful accusation, Mr. Silverman," Lynn replied, trying to maintain her poise. "And I do hope you realize your mistake soon. This drug is harmful, has fallen into the hands of children, and it is our responsibility to make sure that it doesn't harm more people. *Escape* is the wrong word, Mr. Silverman. This drug is a time bomb."

"You know, half of that sounded reasonable, Lynn. You're getting better at this." Silverman sat up and adjusted his suit, still wearing that easy smile. "But here's the ironic part. Us talking about it like this? It's only going to get the kids more interested and it's only going to make it spread. Did you take that into account when you decided to ride the funeral procession to glory?"

"I—" Lynn started, but then the truth of it sank in. He was right, he was exactly right, but there was little that she could do about it now. "I have faith that... that if people know about the dangers of Escape, that we can do something about it."

"Hmm, maybe. I doubt it," Silverman muttered, turning from her to smile at a girl who motioned to him with a comb. When he nodded, she started to touch up his hair as he continued. "Doesn't really matter to me, either way. Never been a big fan of hallucinogens, myself. Get too space cadet."

"Then *why*, Noel?" Lynn asked, unintentionally resorting to using his first name. Inwardly, she cursed herself—she could see the victorious smile on his face—but he was gracious enough not to mention it.

"Devil's advocate and all that business," Silverman nodded at the girl once she finished touching up his skin and then gave a big wave to Chris Harmon, their host for the evening. As he pretended to look happy as the smaller man approached, he kept speaking to Lynn. "You should know how that is. I'm sure you don't believe all the nonsense you spout."

"I have no idea what you're talking about," Lynn replied softly, also waving and smiling at Harmon as he made his way to the desk.

"Don't worry, I'll let you keep up the façade. Just don't let anybody else see through you," Silverman concluded before standing up and greeting their host with a strong handshake. "Good to see you again, Chris."

"Likewise, Noel. Always good to have you on the show," Harmon said before releasing Silverman's hand and continuing to his seat in the middle. Although still reeling from Silverman's insight, Lynn also stood out of her seat and offered her hand.

"Oh, Ms. Stafford, you didn't have to stand up," Harmon said with a nervous smile, but Lynn eased him with a warm smile she stepped forward. When he took hold of her hand, she raised her other to reinforce the handshake.

"I don't have to, Chris; I *wanted* to," she said, with just enough of a gleam in her eyes to make the announcer blush through his heavy makeup. "I didn't expect to see you again so soon."

"Neither did I, Ms. Staffo—" he started, but one look from her made him remember her last appearance. "I mean, Lynn. It's a shame it's over such terrible news."

"I know, Chris, I wish we could get together when there isn't some tragic background," Lynn said, letting go of his hand and stepping back to her seat. "We really should get together for a drink some time."

"Yes, yes, I do think you're right," Harmon replied before sitting in his chair, gesturing for his guests to do the same. After a moment, Harmon turned to Lynn and tried to make eye contact. "I could get one of my assistants to make arrangements?"

"Oh, do that. If they call my secretary, I'm sure Sharon could make some time for us." Lynn looked back at Silverman and hoping to see disgust or anger in that handsome face. Instead, he just smiled and chuckled, and it was not long before someone in the crew yelled and distracted Lynn.

"Airing in thirty!"

"I take it you're both prepared?" Harmon asked, and before Lynn could answer, Silverman gave a soft chuckle.

"It's the same old argument, isn't it? We've rehearsed it before." Lynn glowered at him for it, but she luckily adopted a smile once Harmon turned to watch her reaction.

"I won't stop arguing for safety and health, Mr. Silverman. Perhaps you should find a different field of work if you don't want to perpetuate a drug culture," she said, and she could tell from Harmon's nod that he was already convinced.

"Well said, Lynn. I do find that—" he started, but the crew member interrupted him again.

"Airing in five!"

At that point, Chris Harmon had no choice but to abandon his flirting and look into the main camera, a slight scowl on his face. He was barely more than a parrot, but Lynn had to marvel at his commitment to form. Every weekday, Chris Harmon was on millions of television sets, his displeased face burned into countless retinas. When the crew member waved off the final three numbers in the countdown, Chris Harmon looked like a modern, less reputable Tom Brokaw as he started reading off the teleprompter.

"Hello, and welcome to *Pulse of the Nation*. My name is Chris Harmon, and today we will be discussing the advent of designer drugs. In particular, the drug Escape, which just last week had its first casualty, twelve-year-old Thomas Crenshaw, a boy who was high on the drug when he was tragically killed. With us today are Noel Silverman, spokesman for the Individual Liberties Association, and Congresswoman Lynn Stafford, who is from the same district as the young victim."

"Noel, Lynn," Harmon said, turning to each person as he greeted them. "How are you today?"

"I'm just fine, Chris," Silverman said, nodding slightly and keeping a somber expression.

"I could be better, Chris," Lynn said, shifting the balance and causing both men to face her. This was how she planned it, but now she was on the spot.

"Could be better?" Harmon asked predictably, and Lynn took the opportunity to look back at her camera.

"It is with a heavy heart that I'm back here so soon, Chris. Thomas Crenshaw was a good son, he had parents who loved him, friends and teachers who will miss him. Just a week ago Thomas had a *future*," she said, breathing out heavily and shaking her head. "A week ago, Thomas was given a drug, Escape, and because of that drug, Thomas took his own life."

"A tragedy," Harmon commented, but Lynn was more anxious

to hear what Silverman would say. Instead of looking flustered, or even smiling, Noel seemed to be waiting. Keeping watch out of the corner of her eye, Lynn continued, but she was wary for any counterattack.

"Yes, Chris. This Escape—just one of the newest designer drugs on the market—is a hallucinogen so powerful that it allows the user to see the world they want. It allows them a pure fantasy that is not connected to reality in the slightest," Lynn explained, waving around her hands at the right points. "Because of this, when Thomas imagined he was a superhero intending to save the world, he jumped in front of a bus. At just twelve years old, he could not tell the difference and did not know the danger. A potent, powerful hallucinogen made its way to a twelve-year-old boy, and it caused his death."

"And this drug is legal, Congresswoman?" Silverman finally responded, causing Lynn to falter for just a moment. Fortunately, however, her opponent let her recover and Lynn regained her poise.

"No, Mr. Silverman, Escape is a mixture of different types of hallucinogens, and is thus considered under the same statutes as a Schedule I restricted substance." Before she could continue, Silverman jumped on her response.

"So this drug is already illegal, Congresswoman, is that what you're saying?" Silverman said, gesturing and waiting for her surrender. When Lynn nodded, he turned to Harmon and shrugged. "If it's already illegal, why the witch hunt? Why are we discussing the dangers of an illegal substance in a public forum if legislation is already in place?

"Congresswoman?" Harmon asked as he turned to Lynn, and she had to force herself not to glare at Silverman.

"We are discussing this in a public forum as a way to educate the nation, Mr. Silverman. Unlike you, apparently, I care about what happens to our citizens, what happens to our children, and they cannot defend themselves against a threat they know nothing about," Lynn explained, taking care not to raise her voice. "Most people know the dangers of heroin, of crystal meth, of the other substances flooding the black market, but this is a new threat—a new kind of beast—and it has already claimed its first victim."

"Ms. Staffor—" Silverman tried to say, closing his eyes and ready to deliver a condescending speech, but Lynn did not allow it.

"*That we know of,* Mr. Silverman," she interrupted him sharply before returning to her normal volume. "Thomas Crenshaw was just the first that was reported. How many drug-related deaths are not reported because of fear of legal repercussions? I would bet that there have already been other casualties, that there have been other victims of this... Escapism. With such powerful hallucinogenic effects, it is only a matter of time—an *inevitable outcome*—that more and more people will die under the influence of Escape."

"What proof do you have for those claims, Congresswoman?" Silverman asked, his eyes turning from calm to fierce in an instant. "I would *love* to see your numbers, these reports on the issue. What you have is one poor child who got his hands on a designer drug—just like any determined child could under the right circumstances—and, unfortunately, he was not prepared for the experience. It *is* tragic, it *is* awful, but taking the death of one child by an *illegal* substance and extrapolating a systemic issue from that is irresponsible."

"Irresponsible, Mr. Silverman," Lynn said, looking down at her hands and interlacing her fingers. When she looked back up to the camera, Lynn did her best to summon just a hint of moisture to her eyes. "*We* have been irresponsible. As a culture, as a government, as a *society*... we have allowed these designer drugs, this *Escape*, to spread out among our citizens, among our children. *I* have been irresponsible. I have seen tragedy strike at people who did not deserve it; I have witnessed the pain of too many parents whose children died too young."

"Thankfully, Mr. Silverman, I have found myself in the position to change this. As a Congresswoman—as a person with a voice in your government and a mother who wants the best for my child—I have the ability to stand up for those who cannot. I have the ability to stop the spread of this awful drug, to educate the people, to make sure there is not another Thomas Crenshaw," she said, a single tear rolling down her face as she turned back to Silverman.

"That poor boy thought he was saving the world when he jumped in front of that bus, Noel. In his fantasies, in his heart of hearts—when he *could have been* as selfish as the rest of us— Thomas just wanted to *help* people. He was Superman fighting an asteroid," she said, giving a sad smile before turning back to the camera. "And instead of that boy turning into a grown man—someone who could make a difference—Daniel and Susan Crenshaw now grieve for their child."

"It is a tragedy, Congresswoman, I will not argue that," Silverman repeated softly, trying to salvage some semblance of a discussion. "However, this is *one* death. *One* child who fell through the cracks. You make Escape out to be the next heroin— as the next big evil—when it's just another substance that we do not regulate. It's just another new product for the black market. Escape did not kill Thomas Crenshaw. A black-market drug culture perpetuated by witch hunts *just like this* is responsible. If made legal, if kept controlled—"

"I don't want it legal or controlled, Mr. Silverman," Lynn snapped, some true aspect of herself showing through. "I want Escape off the streets. I want those who created the drug brought to justice. I want to feel safe in the knowledge that my own son will not have a friend give him a dose, that my child will not run into oncoming traffic because he cannot understand the world around him!"

"Whether or not you could make the argument that *adults*

could responsibly indulge in such escapism *makes no difference.* Drugs, alcohol—almost every substance that we consider legal or illegal—will make their way to children even with our best intentions. With strict regulations, with proactive and aggressive investigation, we can at least *limit* the reach of this hallucinogen. We can make it so that even if Escape finds its way to our children, they are aware of the effects," Lynn argued, forgetting how she was supposed to be completely intolerant. "When another child falls down the cracks, I want to make sure that I tried to save them, at the very least."

"Congresswoman, that argument is absurd. This *education* you want to give the next generation could be a byproduct of making the drug legal in the first place. The way you're talking, you may as well completely outlaw guns and alcohol because it would limit their capability to fall into the hands of children," Silverman argued, prepared to list off a barrage of facts. "What you have here is anecdotal evidence, isolated incidents, and the same exact hyper-reactionary behavior you could use when arguing against any civil or individual liberty. There will always be outliers; there will always be freak accidents or correlations to confirm whatever bias you have. The death of one child, however awful, is—"

"One child is enough, Noel," Lynn interrupted softly, not paying attention to the men at the desk or anybody else in the studio. In that moment, Lynn was back with her own son; back ten years ago when he was still smiling, when he was still just a little boy who wanted to be an astronaut when he grew up. When she realized that Silverman had stopped talking, Lynn picked up her head to see everyone staring at her, and she remembered that she was supposed to be acting. Turning back to face her dedicated camera, Lynn did not realize how real tears had fallen from her eyes or how her makeup ran and made her look more genuine than ever.

"One child is enough," Lynn repeated, pausing slightly to

make it seem sincere. "One is already too much."

"I will not stand by and watch the youth of this country fall into a trap; watch them suffer and waste away and die just because I couldn't be bothered to pay attention," Lynn continued, gaining confidence now that she actually believed in the cause. "Even *if* we ignore the tragedy of Thomas Crenshaw, Escape is still out there. It is still stealing the lives of those who use it, gives them instant gratification, gives them everything they want. I know why that can be tempting; I can see the appeal. I can understand why it might even seem harmless, but the real danger of Escape is not bus drivers or back-alley merchants."

"Tell me, Mr. Silverman, what you might think of a drug that would give you anything you want? If a magic little piece of paper with a green infinity symbol could take you directly to the future—to the *life*—you really wanted to live?" Lynn asked, and she could tell that neither Silverman nor Harmon had anticipated this turn. "Why would you ever try again? Why would you ever return back to reality except to earn enough money to buy more Escape? If your reality is so awful that you would take an illegal hallucinogen to run away, why would you ever stop running? Why wouldn't you just give up on reality entirely?"

"Because I know it's not real," Silverman replied, but he was not the same charismatic opponent he had been before. For the first time, Lynn thought the real Noel Silverman was being filmed.

"From what I've heard, seen—what people have reported— that wall between fantasy and reality disappears," Lynn said, turning back to her camera. "Fantasy becomes equal to reality, and even the strongest among us have some weakness, some desire they cannot fulfill. For many, that desire is exactly what drives us forward and makes us become better. That desire is what makes us contribute to society."

"In a society where our youth is already disillusioned and jaded, how can you not expect such an appealing drug to become prolific, especially if we do nothing to stop it?" Lynn asked as she turned back to Silverman, her face hard and analytical. "There is your argument without emotional appeals, Mr. Silverman. That is why I equate Escape to heroin and crystal meth. I can see it not just destroying lives, but entire generations."

"Conjecture," Silverman replied simply, crossing his arms and his gaze boring into Lynn. "All of that is just talk; just empty words. There is no proof for any of these behaviors and there is no way you can make that argument."

"Then don't think of it like an argument," Lynn said, turning back to the camera. "Consider it a warning that if we don't take action now, we will face much worse problems ahead. Daniel and Susan Crenshaw lost their child, and they have given me the strength—the *resolve*—to try to change this future. I want… I want nothing more than for our children to be safe, to grow up, to live in this world, to have the opportunity to change it however they want."

"Political grandstanding," Silverman said, too loud to be a whisper, and it caused Lynn and Harmon to look at him in shock. "You can't say that you're innocent in this, Congresswoman. Do you think this will help you win the next election?"

"Mr. Silverman! What are you thinking?" Harmon shouted, almost rising out of his seat, but Lynn surprised both of them by slapping the desk in front of her.

"I don't care about that!" Lynn shouted, rising to her feet and pointing down at her opponent. "I could lose the next election for this and I couldn't care *less!* Life is about more than my job or my influence. It's about more than a *paycheck*. I care about my friends, my family; every person in my district! I don't give a *damn* if this is my last political act as a Congresswoman—if this is the last important thing I do—because I know it is right. I know that *this* is a good cause. I know that I do not want a dangerous hallucinogen making its way into our schools, into the lives of the next generation, *worming* its way through them and taking them further away from us."

"I care…" Lynn paused, surprising even herself by feeling what she was claiming. "I *care* about Thomas Crenshaw, believe it or not, and his parents. I met with them, I cried with them, and I *made them a promise*. I told them that I would do everything I could so that it would not happen again. I told them that I could not imagine their pain in losing their son, but I *could*, Mr. Silverman. I *could* imagine it and it broke my heart. I never want to experience that while I live. I never want any other parents to feel that pain."

"You call it political grandstanding, Mr. Silverman, and you can go ahead and keep calling it that," Lynn said, shaking her head and sniffing back tears. "But I know what this is. *I* know what I'm doing and why I'm doing it. I'm doing this for my son; I'm doing it for the children—not just in my district but everywhere in this nation. I'm doing this for Dan and Susan; I'm doing this for *Tommy*."

"You two can keep discussing this all you want," Lynn said, grabbing the microphone off her lapel and holding it in front of her mouth for her last words.

"But I'm done *discussing* the *potential* harm of a hallucinogen that helped kill a twelve-year-old boy. I'm done with pretending there's another *side*. A child is *dead*, gentlemen, and it doesn't matter if it's just *one*, Mr. Silverman," she said, turning to her stunned opponent. "One is already too much."

"Lynn, please," Harmon said from his seat, but Lynn looked down at him and shook her head.

"I'm sorry, Chris, but I can't stay here any longer." She placed her mic on the desk and then walked off the stage, staring ahead and trying to look respectable even as tear tracks marred her makeup.

As she left—as she brushed past interns and stunned crewmembers—Lynn realized what she had just done on that stage and what she had given up. Her political career was over after that tirade; it was doubtful she would even finish out the rest of her term. Even the FCC might come after her for the curse word. Still, as she entered the elevator and hit the button for the lobby, finally alone once the doors closed in front of her, Lynn Stafford had to smile.

For the first time in a long time, she had stopped pretending.

CHAPTER 6

LIVING IN THE PAST

ou think you're ready for this, Marc?" Kara asked, curled up on the couch beside him. Before she even opened her mouth, before she looked up at him with those big eyes, before he smiled down at her, Marc knew it was all in his head. This was just the beginning of the trip—his own doubts projected onto the ghost of his girlfriend—and it would not be much longer before he was thrown into another world.

"I think so. I think I need to see it," he answered, his tone more serious than he had intended. Whenever Marc saw Kara, his spirit was lighter, but he had not conjured her on purpose; not this time. It was not entirely in his control—the three tabs of Escape on his tongue had kicked his brain into overdrive—and he tried to keep his wits about him.

"You haven't taken this much in months, dude, you sure you'll be okay? Not since you first started to experiment back when you and Lewis found it." Kara teased him by curling her toes on his bare calves. Feeling the warmth of her skin, Marc only kept himself together because of how she spoke.

There was very little of Kara in those words.

"I know when I did it, Kara," Marc muttered, not expecting the delusion to hear him, but she was a construct of his mind, after all. Nudging him again with her foot, Kara shook her head at him.

"This isn't just so you can feel guilty about me, is it?"

"I—what? Why are you…"

"It's not really me right now, you know that. I'm just the part of you that… well, just isn't feeling it. Thinks you're making a mistake. You know, like *most of your brain* acts all the time," she said before rocking forward and poking him in the forehead.

"You're too hard on yourself, you silly, little nerd."

"I have to be. Otherwise, I'd never get anything done." Marc excused himself with a laugh, but Kara only smiled and shook her head before placing a fingertip underneath his chin.

"Come on, you never get anything done anyway." She turned so she could sit beside Marc, and then she surprised him by burrowing her way into Marc's chest. It gave Marc mixed feelings. It was something Kara definitely used to do, but she would never have done it in the current atmosphere. The conflicting emotions just gave Marc another reason to feel strange; something he did not need, considering what he was about to do.

"I have to do this," Marc said, and the ghost in his arms squeaked briefly before looking up at him.

"No, you don't," she murmured, and Marc realized he was talking to himself. Holding Kara closer, he sighed and closed his eyes.

"I *want* to do this," he said just as Kara's body evaporated in his arms, but it was no cause for alarm. Marc had no intention of taking her with him; this was his time, his pain, and he wanted to face it alone. When he opened his eyes, Marc was no longer in his apartment. All around him were empty desks, a teacher's desk in the corner, and a blackboard at the front of the room. Realizing he had succeeded, Marc let the world build on itself, let it repopulate, and eventually it was just like he remembered.

Breathing in deep, Marc prepared himself for a trip down memory lane.

"Dude, you're tutoring her now," Lewis said, trying to hide the crack in his voice. Letting it slide, Marcus shook his head and doodled in his notebook. It was supposed to be the Midgard

Serpent—a gigantic snake eating its own tail—but it had turned into just a circle as he ran the pen over it again and again.

"Just a little bit. Forty-five minutes after school two days a week. It's really not that bad." Marcus had convinced himself, but Lewis was harder to please.

"Not that bad... Dude, you miss the bus and don't have a car. You have to *walk* home," Lewis stated, tapping the eraser of his pencil against his desk and Marcus shrugged away the comment.

"So what? It's exercise, or something like that. It's not that big a deal," he said, turning to Lewis and finding that his acne-prone friend was staring him down.

"It's a forty-minute walk for you to get to your house, dude. Does she even know that you do that?" he asked, and Marcus shook his head before turning back to his design.

"I dunno. Probably not. I haven't brought it up," he said at a low volume, and he was rewarded with Lewis' hand on his shoulder.

"Marcus. Buddy. *My old friend*," he said, leaning forward until he was just a few inches away. "You are a pussy."

"Shut the fuck up," Marcus said, shoving his friend's hand off his shoulder and pushing him back to his desk. As Lewis laughed at him, Marcus gritted his teeth and shook his head. "I'm not a pussy."

"Dude, you are *totally* a pussy. That girl is using the fuck out of you and you don't stand up for yourself *at all*. Have you even told her that you like her?" Marcus sheepishly looked back at his notebook, creating a new pattern on the other corner.

"I—I haven't had the chance."

"You haven't had the chance? Dude, you just said you spend forty-five minutes with her twice a week."

"That's different, man," Marcus said leaning back in his chair and shaking his head. "That's to help her, and she really needs it. Look, the time just hasn't been right."

"The time hasn't been..." Lewis paused, wiping his forehead

and shaking his head. "*Oh my God,* man, you're fucking hopeless."

"Hey, don't pretend that you're Mister Casanova over here," Marcus said, causing Lewis to look at him with a raised eyebrow. "You haven't even *kissed* a girl, yet. Don't think I need to take advice from you."

"Not even the same, man," Lewis said, rolling his eyes. "I'm totally a late-bloomer. Do you *see* my face? Fuckin' horror show over here. Sucks, I know, but that's why I'm going to do all my hard work *now* when I'm ugly and after all this clears up, girls will see a pretty, rich guy who's super nice and everything."

"You're delusional, you know that?" Marcus asked, serious, but it wasn't long before both of them started laughing.

"Yeah, yeah, I know. It's nice to pretend, though," Lewis replied, sighing in discontent before pursing his lips. "I *think* I might just be jealous."

"Why the hell are you *jealous*?" Marcus asked, scoffing at his friend's behavior.

"*Because* I haven't even kissed a girl yet and my best friend gets to spend two days a week with the girl of his dreams," Lewis said, twirling his pencil between his fingers and then dropping it on the floor. As he bent down to pick it up, Marcus drew an infinity symbol in the center of his page, circling his pen over and over again through the design.

"It's nice, but you don't need to be jealous. She *barely* even knows who I am. That's why I'm waiting," Marcus said, turning to Lewis just as he sat back up. "I want her to like me before I say anything."

"Marcus," another voice interrupted them, and Marcus turned around to see one of their bigger classmates looking at him with droopy eyelids. "Lewis is right. You're a pussy."

"See? Reggie agrees."

"Look, it's just not time—"

"Nah, man," Reggie interrupted, grabbing a worksheet from Marcus' desk without permission. "I know Kara. She likes the confident guys. You just gotta tell her."

"Are you seriously copying off my sheet?" Marcus asked, and Reggie looked at him like he was the idiot.

"Yeah, duh. I just told you how to stop being a pussy. Fair trade," Reggie said before using Marcus' handout as an answer key, writing down the same answers in all his blank spaces.

"I—alright," Marcus surrendered as he turned to Lewis, who was stifling laughter. "I guess I'll tell her today."

"If you don't back out because you're a pussy, of course," Lewis added, unintentionally snorting loud enough for the whole class to hear.

"I'm hearing a lot of talking over there, gentlemen," their teacher said without lifting his gaze from his desk. "Are we doing our work?"

"We're done, Mr. Yeats," Lewis volunteered, earning a grunt.

"And you don't have homework for other classes?"

"Did it already, Mr. Yeats," Marcus replied, and the long sigh coming from their teacher reminded him of a tire deflating.

"If you're lying, you're only hurting yourself," someone replied, but it was not Mr. Yeats. It was higher-pitched, feminine, rougher.

Familiar.

From his spectral position behind his younger self, Marc looked over at his teacher's desk and saw that everything was normal. Mr. Yeats was still looking down at the quizzes he was grading, the young versions of him and Lewis were still chatting, but Marc knew something was off. That had definitely not been his teacher's voice; he knew exactly who it belonged to, but he stubbornly refused to acknowledge it.

Letting the classroom fade away, Marc found himself in another classroom that was a mirror image of the first. However, this time—when he let the people back in—Marcus was alone with his heart's desire.

"Damnit, why can't I get this?" Kara asked, not expecting

an answer from her tutor. Leaning forward, Marcus looked through her work, seeing the different variables and how she had completely screwed them up, and smiled once he figured out where she went wrong.

"Oh, it's simple, you just didn't divide both sides by four so you could solve for X. Remember, you're trying to get X all by itself," he explained as nice as he could, but he was still rewarded with a grunt.

"X can go suck a big, fat donkey dick for all I care," Kara muttered, and Marcus could not help but look at her in wonder. This girl, with her dyed, black hair, her piercings, her ripped clothing, was a unicorn to Marcus. He had never seen anyone who looked like her, acted like her, talked like her.

And somehow, even though he spent most of his days reading through forum posts and seeing horrible things on the internet, that little girl still found a way to shock him.

"What?" Kara asked abruptly, and Marcus realized that he had been staring at her too long. Shaking himself out of his daze, he turned back to the math problem and pointed at the variables with his pencil.

"Sorry, Kara, that was just… something new. Never thought X had a big enough mouth to fit in a *whole* donkey dick." That earned a laugh from his student.

"You'd be *surprised*, Marcus. X gets around. X will *whore itself out* for any number, just like that slut Y," Kara continued, leaning closer and pretending to share secrets. "But you know who's the worst one? The one who puts both those whores to shame?"

"No, who?" Marcus asked, smiling as she leaned in closer to whisper in his ear.

"*Your dad.* He went and got X and Y to gangbang his genetic makeup. Bam! Transitive property, bitches!" she said before giggling, and Marcus had to smile. When he looked back at her, she was giving a huge grin, and Marcus' heart hurt just a little more.

"That's not… Okay, you have the patience to tell an awful science joke that doesn't even work, but you have trouble with *Algebra*?" he asked, cocking an eyebrow, but Kara just shrugged and looked back at her work.

"My awful science joke had gangbanging in it. Besides," Kara said as she leaned forward to scowl at her scribbling. "Math is hard."

"Science is math."

"*Your mom* is math," Kara mumbled, grabbing a bottle from her bag and unscrewing the top before slamming it down on the table for dramatic purposes.

"Very funny, Kara." She laughed as she tried to swallow down neon green soda.

"Dude, you have an awful sense of humor, then. Lucky for you, I'll be here all week. Especially if I keep fucking this up," she said, grabbing her pencil again and circling the X on the sheet. "*There*, found X."

"It's just Algebra, Kara. You're smart enough for this. This is easy stuff," Marcus argued, but Kara surprised him by rolling her eyes and looking at him without her casual confidence.

"Says the guy who's in Calculus in his junior year. This is *your* fucking wheelhouse, dude. *This* is what you know."

"I know other things, okay? I just—it makes sense to me and I'm… I'm trying to help you get there. I don't want you falling behind just because you get frustrated." Kara looked at him pitifully for a moment, but that moment ended when she bent over and started laughing. Marcus waited for her to recover—feeling more foolish by the second—and once she finally started to breathe normally, he let out a sigh and pursed his lips. "Look, I—"

"Dude, no, I'm sorry, I'm sorry. That was just the funniest fucking thing I've ever heard. *I don't want you falling behind just because you get frustrated*," she repeated, mimicking him poorly and waving her hands around. "You barely know me, Marcus, and you're acting like this weird mix between a friend and a teacher and, I dunno, a little Mr. Rogers thrown in there."

"Oh, cool, I'm Mr. Rogers," Marcus said deadpan, rolling his eyes, but he was surprised by a touch on his shoulder. Looking back at her, Marcus found Kara pointing at him in mock anger.

"Hey, don't you talk shit about Mr. Rogers. Anyway," she said, drawing back and picking up her legs, holding them to her chest as she perched on the seat. "It was just funny, is all. Not to say I don't appreciate what you're doing, Marcus. You're a real solid dude, and if I pass Algebra this year it's all because of you. *Thank you* for putting up with my general bitchiness and foul mouth."

"It's... alright. You're welcome," Marcus said, a slight smile on his face. "And I don't mind the general bitchiness and foul mouth. It makes tutoring more fun."

"Yeah, it does! High five, sucka!" Kara shouted, throwing forward her open hand, and Marcus hit it with his own after a moment's trepidation. It didn't make a sound—it was more like he slid his hand against her by accident—and Kara looked at him, to her hand and then back to him. "*Dude. Weak.*"

"I've never been a fan of those."

"Eh, we'll learn you yet," she said, smiling at him over her knees, but then she looked down at her watch and her eyes widened. "Aw, fuck, I gotta go. Keep X warm at night for me!"

"Wait, Kara," Marcus protested as the girl burst into a whirlwind of activity, slamming her math textbook shut with her notebook stuck in the middle before shoving both into her bag, which had metal rings and paperclips pierced through patches for alternative and metal bands. Kara kept moving even though he was talking, and she was just turning to leave when Marcus stood up and put out his hand. "Kara, stop!"

"Hmm?" she asked, turning around in confusion. "What's up, Shouty McShouterson?"

"I..." Marcus hesitated, realizing that this was not the time to tell her how he felt, just like all the other times. However, he had already started, and he would not forgive himself for backing out now. Swallowing down his fear, Marcus breathed in and out, earning a concerned look from the little girl. "I have to tell you something."

"Well, *what?* I gotta *go*, man." Kara pointed her thumb at the doorway, but Marcus shook his head. Clenching his fists, he looked at her and tried to be the confident man Reggie said Kara would like.

"I like you," Marcus blurted out, panicking once the words were out in the open. Kara, that tiny girl who was far too cool to hang out with him, now held Marcus' fate in her hands.

"Yeah, dude, I like you, too," she said, causing Marcus to look at her warily, and only from his reaction did she realize what he really meant. Dropping her shoulders, Kara lowered her gaze to the floor and rubbed her fingers against her forehead. "Shit..."

"*Shit* is not encouraging," Marcus commented weakly, resorting to sarcasm since it was all he had left.

"It shouldn't be, man," Kara admitted, stepping forward so she was just a couple feet in front of Marcus. Looking up at him, she bit her lip and shook her head slightly. "It's not gonna happen."

"I... uh..."

"It's not *you*. You're a cool dude. Real stand-up guy," Kara explained, setting the sling of her bag over her shoulder and holding it with both of her tiny hands. "Though you're a little too normal, I think. I'd scare you eventually."

"That's not true," Marcus tried to make his case, but Kara put out one hand to stop him.

"Even if it wasn't, I'm not in the market. I've been dating Travis for a couple weeks now and it's going really well. We like all the same stuff, go the same shows, watch the same, terrible b-movies from the eighties... you see where I'm going with this?"

"I watch terrible B movies, too..."

"Which is why we'd be good *friends* or maybe *something* *some*day," Kara said, drawing even closer and looking at him from less than a foot away, "but it's not today. It's not anytime soon. I don't like breaking hearts, but sometimes a bitch has gotta do what a bitch has gotta do."

"I... understand," Marcus said, feeling his emotional core stripped away from him piece by piece. As he looked down and tried to avoid eye contact, Kara lifted her hand to the left side of his face and pursed her lips.

"You're a good guy, Marcus. Modern Mr. Rogers. Sorry I had to do this to you." She stood on her tiptoes and pressed her lips to his other cheek, pecking him softly before stepping back and nodding. "I'll find some way to pass Algebra without you. Don't worry about that."

"I can still tutor you—"

"No, you can't," Kara interrupted him, stepping backward as she spoke. "Not saying you were *just* trying to get into my pants or anything like that, but I'm not going to let you do that to yourself. I've barked up the wrong tree plenty of times, myself, and that only ends with falling out of trees."

"You fallen out of a lot of trees in sixteen years?" Marcus asked, bitter at some perceived condescension on Kara's part. Shrugging, Kara shifted her weight to her right leg and looked out the window on the far side of the room.

"Enough of 'em to know it hurts. Enough of 'em to feel like shit if I let anybody fool themselves into thinking my tree is worth climbing. And I sure as shit am not going to profit off that by getting free tutoring from a truly decent guy," Kara said, making eye contact with him again and giving a forced smile. "I'll find some way to find X on my own, I promise."

"If you and Travis don't work out..." Marcus started, but he trailed off once he saw the glint in her eye.

"No promises. I'm bad with those anyway," she said, turning around and heading to the doorway, pausing slightly to look back at him. "Stay Gold, Mr. Rogers."

"Not sure Mr. Rogers was in *The Outsiders*. Seems like the

wrong neighborhood for him," Marcus added, causing Kara to laugh and rap her knuckles against the doorframe.

"You… you're such a nerd. I like it, but goddamn, dude. Can't get one cheesy comment by you without some Oscar Wilde shit," she said, laughing softly before stepping through the door and continuing down the hallway. "I'll see you around, man."

"Yeah, I'll see you," Marcus said, sitting back down at his desk, and then everything froze in place.

As if he had been asleep, Marc gasped in air and looked around him, at the static image of his broken-hearted ghost. For that entire scene—as he watched and fell back in love with the high-school crush version of his girlfriend—Marc had been completely consumed. Instead of maintaining his role as an observer, he had forgotten the present and his reasons for coming back. What was most alarming, however, was that the scene was different from his memory; it had gone down an entirely different path from reality.

There had been no casual joking, no wit when he was a teenager. Ten years ago, Marc had been shy, timid and boring. *That* was why Kara had not gone out with him; she had no reason to spend time with a quiet nerd. She had rejected him outright when he had stammered out his confession, laughing and patting him on the head like he was a lovesick puppy.

And as much as he wanted to believe it, Kara would never have said that she wouldn't let Marc hurt himself; not back then. She was selfish, young—damaged in ways nobody knew—and she would have continued to abuse Marcus for tutoring sessions if he had not been so embarrassed to stop. Then, with no warning, Marc heard her voice again.

I'm not going to let you do that to yourself.

Marc was so surprised by the interruption that he forgot himself, forgot what he wanted, and the world shifted around him particle by particle until he was somewhere else completely, his school a distant memory. At first, Marc was afraid—he did not know where his subconscious wanted him to go—but it was not long before he recognized his surroundings, recognized the people.

And just like that, Marc was right where he wanted to be.

"*Marcus?*"

Although Lewis was laughing right next to him and the chaos of midday traffic was full of blaring horns and a thousand different sounds, Marcus heard that familiar voice and stopped in his tracks. Finding it hard to breathe, Marcus turned around to find a short, white girl wearing a torn white shirt and a black miniskirt running up to him. Before he could fully react, Kara had already leapt on top of him and had wrapped her arms around his neck.

"I *knew* it was you, you fucking nerd!" she screamed, twisting her body and causing Marcus to spin with her dangling around his neck. Although he tried to express his confusion to Lewis, who just watched from a few feet, Marcus eventually wrapped his arms around her back before coming to a stop. Once he did, Kara dropped to the ground and backed away, finally allowing Marcus to see her all at once.

"Kara? Holy shit, it's been… since high school." She gave him an enthusiastic nod, playing with the snakebite piercing in her lip as she bounced in place.

"Indeed, it *has*, Mr. Rogers. I can't tell you how glad I am to see you in the middle of the street, of all fucking places," she said, stretching her arms behind her and torturing Marcus with a direct view of the bra barely hidden by her torn shirt. When she stopped—giving Marcus a reprieve—Kara slapped him on the arm before bouncing again. "How the *fuck* have you been, man?"

"I'm… good, Kara. I graduated and now I'm doing research as a Chemistry TA," Marcus said, setting his hands on his hips before motioning toward Kara, who would not stop moving. "And you? You seem excited about something."

"Hah, nothing's happening for me, Marcus. Nothing at all. Just living, getting that life in, you know, all that stuff," she said before jumping closer and whispering in his ear. "The excitable thing is artificial, by the way. Got acquainted with a certain *white lady* a couple minutes back and just *had* to get outside."

"White lady?" Marcus asked, causing Kara to widen her eyes and frown.

"*Dude*, keep that shit on the down-low," she urged, looking around for anybody who might be listening and only finding Lewis. "Oh, *shit, dude,* I didn't see you there! How you been, *muthafucka?*"

"Oh, you know, fucking mothers," Lewis said, drier than a desert. When Marcus looked at him and mouthed the words "white lady," Lewis set his finger against a nostril and sniffed, making Marcus feel stupid for not realizing it on his own. Luckily, Kara didn't see it because she was turning from one to other far too fast to notice the hint.

"When did you get *funny*, Lewis? Can't remember *that* from back in the day. Only remember something like… know-it-all or something."

"That would have been him," Marcus commented, Lewis giving him a condescending grin before turning back to their energetic schoolmate.

"Only takes a couple years of college to make you realize you were an idiot back in high school. You find yourself."

"Oh, man, I didn't realize I was *missing*! *Or* that I'm still an idiot," Kara said, crossing her arms and rolling her eyes. "Man, that college thing must be *super* enlightening."

"You didn't go? But I thought you got into—" Marcus started, but the girl waved her hand in some random, frantic gesture that only made sense to her.

"Yeah, I did, and I went for a year, but that really wasn't the way to do it. You don't get better at art by listening to how *other people* think you should make art. You do it for yourself, make mistakes, take chances, and then maybe, when you're dead and buried or cremated in a *goddamn Viking funeral pyre!*" she screamed out to the tall buildings surrounding them before settling back down. "Anyway, thought it would be better to just start living, start my struggles, get out in the world and do crazy shit."

"Like getting high in the middle of the day?" Lewis suggested, causing Marcus to turn to him in anger, but Kara laughed and pointed at him before using her other hand to touch her nose.

"Gold star for Lewis over here, but let's be serious," Kara said before setting her hands on her hips. "I get high at *all* times of the day."

"Well aren't you just the poster child for bohemia?" Lewis said, causing Kara to jump over and beam up at him.

"Don't you just wanna squeeze my fucking cheeks?" That shocked Lewis out of his shell and forced him away, which only caused Kara to turn toward Marcus as she pointed back at Lewis with her thumb. "*This* guy..."

"Once you punch through his cool, calm exterior, you'll find that the Lewis Macklemore is just another nerd trying to survive in a harsh environment," Marcus explained in his best British accent, causing Kara to snort and smile at him. "See him now in the throes of fear, a wild girl throwing his delicate world into chaos."

"*Okay*, David Attenborough, it is nice to see that someone is putting in the time to observe such a magnificent creature in the wild." She turned back to Lewis and clasped her hands in front of her before adopting her own British accent. "A shame, though."

"A shame?" Marcus asked, continuing the bit as Lewis looked at both of them.

"Ah, yes, well, you see, the Lewis Macklemore is an endangered species. Natural selection has seen fit to show him that he is not the fittest, nor will he survive," Kara explained, pouting and shaking her head. "Without some sort of intervention, it is likely that this individual will die alone and unloved."

"It is just so unfortunate that those two go together so often, alone and unloved," Marcus commented, drawing a nod from Kara.

"*Especially* for the Lewis Macklemore. It seems the entire world is against him, providing better and stronger opponents who merely have to speak up to draw away any potential mates," she said, turning slightly to look up at Marcus with a grin. "A shame."

"Indeed," Marcus added, and Lewis snapped his fingers to interrupt them.

"What the fuck are you guys *talking* about?" he asked, crossing his arms and sending Kara into a fit of giggles at the same time. When she recovered, she pranced over to him and crossed her arms to mirror him.

"Well, if you were paying attention, you dense, little man, we're saying you're going to be pretty lonely if you keep pushing people away," she said simply, shrugging before heading back to Marcus.

"*You* are going to give me life advice? A self-proclaimed idiot who apparently can't find herself?" Lewis asked, returning back to his snide self after the apparent insult.

"Hey, all I'm saying was that when I first noticed you, I thought you were looking *good*," Kara said, winking at him after giving him a once over. "Though that whole asshole thing you got going on right now isn't really working for you. You'll be a lot more appealing once you start being nice again."

"For your information, I *have* a girlfriend," Lewis declared, which made Kara scoff as she stood next to Marcus.

"*Hokay, sure,* keep telling yourself that. *This* guy..." She nodded at Lewis to let Marcus in on the joke, but she soon abandoned the bit and turned back to him. "And *I'm* okay with not knowing where to find myself, thank you very fucking much."

"Yeah, I'm sure it makes it easy to find your keys in the morning when you don't have any keys," Lewis snapped, causing the other two to look at him skeptically. "Since you can't find yourself…"

"Does that make sense?" Kara asked.

"I can… see where he was going, but that needs some workshop time, dude."

"*Anyway*, what I was saying," Kara said as she nudged Marcus with her elbow and gave him the biggest grin possible. "Is that I'm okay with it, since I'm pretty sure someone *else* had to find *me*."

"Shit, you better keep running around the city, you don't want to miss him," Marcus said, and he could tell from her mock disappointment that Kara already had someone in mind.

"Smartass nerd motherfucker…" she muttered, grabbing a pen from her boot and then yanking Marcus' arm down so she could grab his hand. "Don't get me wrong, it's an improvement from last time, but *both of youse* need to learn some manners."

"Manners, too? Man, you got wise in your life of vagrancy," Lewis said as he approached them, Kara mocking his condescension by mouthing gibberish at Marcus.

"What are you doing?" Marcus asked as he felt the pen dragging across his skin.

"I… am giving you a phone number—specifically *mine*—and a place that you should be at around nine tonight," she explained, biting her lip as she scribbled all over the back of his hand.

"What's happening there at nine?" Marcus asked and, once she was finished, Kara swept the pen across his hand with a flourish and then smiled up at him.

"Just a show, some shitty band that I've been following since they were playing in some dude's garage," Kara said, standing on her tiptoes to whisper in his ear. "It's totally just Travis and his friends. They're *really* shitty."

"Travis, huh?" Marcus muttered, looking away from Kara and feeling like a nervous teenager again. "So you guys are still dating?"

"*Fuck* no, that shit was a train wreck," Kara replied instantly, laughing at her past. "We're just really good friends now, along with all the other guys in the band. You have Lewis; I have the Andy Griffith Sex Change Experiment."

"That's… that sounds funny," Marcus said, trying to pretend.

"That sounds awful," Lewis said, at which point Kara shrugged and threw up her arms.

"It's a little bit of both, honestly. But enough of this fucking awkward shit, I'll see you guys tonight," she said quickly, turning around and starting back the way she came.

"We didn't say we'd come!" Lewis yelled at her back, causing her to turn around and walk backward.

"Please, you went to a fancy college with fancy textbooks and fancy teachers, but I'm pretty fucking sure you need a *life*. I can tell. I can *see* it," she said, putting up her hands and splaying her fingers like some sort of fortune teller. After giggling at her own antics, Kara continued on her way, but not before looking over her shoulder for one last shout. "Come find me, Marcus!"

"…you're fine, Marcus," Lewis said a second after she was out of sight, causing his friend to look at him quizzically. "I understand. You were young. Now, in the prime of our extended adolescence, we can look back at our high school crushes and wonder. Just *what* were we thinking?"

"Exact same thing as last time, but now I'm pretty sure I have a shot."

"You're kidding, right? *Right?* You're not kidding," Lewis stated, supplying his own answers. "What are you *thinking*, dude? That girl walks up to you high on coke in the middle of the day—acts like a *lunatic*—and you want to go see her friend's shitty band?"

"Eh, bonus, I mostly just want to see her," Marcus said, patting Lewis' shoulder as he walked past him and continued toward their original destination. "She's right, you know. You keep acting like an asshole, soon enough it's just going to be me who can stand hanging out with you."

"I can't believe you're considering going to this thing."

"Why not? I was straight-up *in love* with that girl back in high school, and now I get to show her my glorious, new, college graduate self who slaves away for pennies and does his boss' work for him," Marcus said before breathing in deep with satisfaction. "Could be worse."

"You can't expect me to go along with this," Lewis added, crossing his arms as they walked across the street.

"Please, you have nothing else to do. I know for a fact that you were going to watch *Buffy* again just because your girlfriend looked at the DVD case and left it on our coffee table," Marcus claimed, and Lewis did not bat an eye.

"Sometimes you have to go back and watch your favorite series for the thirteenth time instead of meeting a deranged cokehead at a sleazy bar," he replied, but Marcus waved off the comment.

"You act like we never did drugs in college," he said before wrapping his arm around Lewis' shoulders. "And though sometimes you *do* have to reexperience the glory that is Sarah Michelle Gellar staking vampires to the backdrop of 90s guitar riffs, tonight isn't that night. *Tonight*, we're going out to meet my high school crush and her band of misfits, because we *kinda do* need lives."

"And you have to go *find* her," Lewis said, adopting the voice of a village idiot. Instead of getting annoyed, Marcus just squeezed his arm tighter around his friend's neck.

"Sometimes you just have to make mistakes, Lewis."

"Uh, so that… was good," Marcus said, feeling uncomfortable sitting on the ratty, old couch across from Kara's friends. She and Lewis had gone to the bar to get them a round of drinks, leaving Marcus alone with strangers, and he desperately wished he could go back in time and join them.

"You didn't like it. It's cool," the tallest man said, not making eye contact and instead staring at the women standing around in the bar. His arms were covered in full sleeves of tattoos, he had six different kinds of piercings—all of which made Marcus feel out of place—but his open vest was the worst part. Marcus could understand why a lead singer might want to increase his sex appeal, but Travis was the only one not wearing a shirt and it made Marcus uncomfortable.

"It's not that I didn't like it, Travis, I just… I've never really gotten into theory or any of the complexity that goes into writing anything other than pop songs," Marcus said, causing the singer to turn with a sneer.

"Figures," Travis said as he stared at Marcus, but eventually he turned away and resumed his ogling. Marcus was about to launch into another explanation—try to win Travis over—but he was interrupted by the black girl with dreadlocks sitting on the beanbag to his left. After Travis' remark, she put out a hand covered in cheap rings and scoffed as she waved it around.

"Don't worry about it, Mark. Travis thinks he's a genius and ninety-five percent of the time, he's *totally* fucking wrong," she said before taking a sip from her drink, which was mostly ice at that point. After an inaudible curse, she looked back at Marcus and sighed. "And the *other* five percent of the time he's *just* wrong."

"Shut your mouth, Ariana. Don't see you writing any lyrics."

"Of course, not! I'm the drummer, hosscat," she said, turning back to Marcus and seeing the confusion on his face. "What's wrong, Mark?"

"I—my name is Marcus, actually," he said, his shy teenage-self emerging for the moment.

"Ooh, my bad. It's fucking loud in here. Anyway, what's with the *I just bit into a pepper and I think it mighta been a habanero* look you got going on there?" Ariana asked, bobbing her head with each emphasized word.

"That… is the longest way to explain a facial expression that I've ever heard." Marcus laughed at the absurdity, but eventually he recovered and shrugged. "Anyway, it was the… *hosscat?* Never heard that before."

"Oh, that's just Ariana's word, man. Don't get caught up on it. She has this idea that it'll catch on and become the next *dude*," a man replied from his right, and Marcus looked up to see the band's guitarist sitting on the end of the couch. Although Marcus was startled—the man seemed to have appeared from nowhere—he eventually realized that *he* was the odd sight here.

"Alright then. And I'm sorry, man, but I forgot your name," Marcus said, drawing another scoff from Ariana.

"I doubt that. *You* wouldn't forget," the bassist said from the chair to the right, nodding at Marcus slowly in recognition. Once he did, Marcus realized that it was Reggie Nichols, the boy who used to sit behind him in history class.

"Yeah, sorry, man, I just hadn't gotten around to it, yet," the guitarist said before leaning forward and extending a gangly arm complete with long, thin fingers, forcing Marcus to focus on him. "I'm Ulysses."

"Ulysses? Your parents named you that?" Marcus asked as he took the guitarist's hand, but Ulysses shook his head in response, swaying his scraggly, grey hair in the process. Now that he was able to see him clearly, Marcus realized that Ulysses was much older than the others in the band, the wrinkles and crows' feet on his face evidence of at least another decade and probable drug use.

"Nah, man," Ulysses replied, shifting on the arm of the couch and popping his jaw absent-mindedly. "Gave that one to myself. Thought it sounded cool."

"Oh, okay. So you like *The Odyssey* or just a big fan of President Grant?" Marcus asked, causing the older man to look down at him in confusion. As the man stared at him, Marcus could vividly imagine gears in place of his brain, except there was a missing gear so they all spun endlessly without any progress.

"Nah, dude, I just like the name. Fucking *badass*. Makes me feel like I'm some sick guitar player who could fight gods with just the power of music," he explained, fretting an air guitar and bobbing his head to an imaginary tune.

"You… should really look into reading *The Odyssey*. Trust me, I think you'll like it."

"Yeah, sure, man, if you say so. Oh, shit, Kara, you need a hand?" Ulysses said before turning to face Kara and Lewis, who had returned with more than enough drinks. Amusing Marcus to no end, Kara was holding a tray full of drinks like a waiter and moving easily, but Lewis was holding his tray with both hands and looked like he was about to drop it.

"I'm good, hosscat, just lemme *set this down*," Kara said, pretending that the tray was too heavy as she placed it on the table, and then she turned to Lewis and pouted at him before setting her hand underneath the tray. "I got it from here, sweetie."

"So she's got you saying it, too?" Marcus asked, causing Kara to look at him with a silent question. Luckily, he knew how to answer it. "*Hosscat*. Ariana's word."

"Oh! Yeah, that word's awesome. Spread that shit among all your friends when you gather around for your demonic knitting circle." Kara smiled as she passed out shots to everyone gathered around their table, Lewis claiming the seat between Marcus and Ulysses. When Kara handed one to Marcus, she winked before grabbing another for herself and sitting on the couch arm opposite Ulysses, just inches away from Marcus. "So, what should we toast to?"

"How about this guy?" Travis suggested, motioning his shot glass at Marcus across the table. "Guy doesn't like our fucking music, but he's here *anyway*."

"Dude, I don't like your fucking music and I'm here anyway," Kara replied quickly, raising both eyebrows at her ex-boyfriend. Pointing and mock scowling at him, Kara kept eye contact with Travis only a few seconds before turning to Marcus. "Since Travis here is being a huge fucking dick, what's your suggestion?"

"For a toast?"

"No, for his ritual sacrifice," she said sarcastically, and Marcus let out a defeated sigh before looking out at Kara's friends. He did not belong here; these were all strangers and people he would never have met otherwise and it showed. With the exception of Reggie and Travis, Marcus did not know anything about these people, but then he realized that was perfect. It also meant they did not know him, in the past or present, and he had nothing to prove. Raising his glass, Marcus looked at each person slowly and nodded.

"To serendipity," he said, smiling until he realized only two other people in the circle had ever encountered the word. Lewis looked at him skeptically and Travis scowled at him. He could tell from Ulysses' blank stare that the gears were spinning again, but even Kara looked at him with a bite of her lip. Sighing, Marcus lifted his glass again. "To random, fucking chance."

"Ooh, that one I like," Ariana said, all of them lifting their glasses slightly before throwing them back and draining them. After a sharp breath, Ariana nodded at Marcus in approval. "*Serendipity*, huh? Feels good in my *mouf*."

"Yeah, I've always liked it, and it's pretty coo—"

"Oh, shit, Kara, I fucked up his name earlier. Called him

Mark," Ariana interrupted, not letting Marcus explain why serendipity was appropriate.

"Hah, really?" Kara asked, looking down at Marcus in approval. "I could see it. Though it would have to be like a... *Canadian* Marc. With a C and all that jazz; works better with his name anyway."

"I think I'll keep my name for now," Marcus replied, earning a grin from Kara before she rubbed his shoulder.

"But you're our new *pet*, Marc, and we get to name you," she said, acting like she was petting a dog. It was almost enough for Marcus to bark at her, but they were interrupted.

"Why is he *here*, Kara?" Travis asked, causing everyone to look at him before he continued.

"These guys—all offense *intended*, by the way—they don't fucking *belong here*. Just look at them," Travis explained, leaning back and sweeping his hand at them. "They're college people; nerds, fucking straight yuppies."

"Yeah, blame *us* for trying to be real adults," Lewis replied in a snide tone, earning no friends in the process.

"Yeah, sure, I'll blame you, but I think you agree—Lewis, right? You agree that this is stupid; that we have nothing in common, right? Different fucking worlds," he concluded, Lewis nodding and turning to Marcus with a shrug.

"Hey, I *like* these guys, thanks so fucking much," Kara said, gripping Marcus' shoulder and shaking him slightly. "We go way back, even if you and Reggie didn't hang out with them like I did."

"He tutored you, Kara, that's all it was," Travis said, but the situation was momentarily defused by Ulysses standing up and looking Marcus and Lewis over.

"Wait, you guys *knew* each other?" he asked, pointing at them with a crooked index finger. Grunting, Reggie shifted and looked away before responding.

"They're good guys. Marcus let me cheat off his work

sometimes," he added, grabbing his drink from the tray in the center and getting started on his buzz.

"Oh, fucking cool. Alright then," Ulysses said, nodding before reclaiming his seat on the arm of the couch.

"No, *not* fucking cool. They're lame, they're by-the-book, they're straight-laced; they're part of the *fucking system*. Their idea of a good time is watching TV while getting drunk off beer and boxes of wine," Travis said, dismissively sniffing at them while looking away. "I bet these guys haven't even fucking smoked a joint before."

"Hah," Lewis barked, shaking his head in dismay and looking away. When he looked back, he found everyone staring at him. "What?"

"You *smoke*, straight-edge?" Travis asked, forcing Lewis to realize how ridiculous the situation was.

"You serious?" he asked incredulously, turning back to Marcus with a smirk. "Holy fuck, dude, they have no idea who they're talking to."

"You're college students, probably wearing button-ups and ties and all that shit," Travis said, and Lewis leaned forward as he grabbed something from his pocket.

"Dude, we're fucking *chemists*," he said, a patronizing tone filtering through every word. "We make our own drugs."

"Wait, what?" Kara asked, looking to Marcus, who shrugged.

"Yeah, you didn't know? I thought I told you during the show," Marcus said, Kara drawing back and shaking her head to get her bearings.

"All you said was that you're a grad student and you do research in a lab…" she muttered, drawing a chuckle from Lewis as he finally retrieved his hand from his pocket and opened the small piece of folded aluminum foil.

"Yeah, most of the time, but Marcus and I are pretty good at this stuff, so we have extra time and," he said, bringing out a small piece of paper divided into squares, "we're in charge of the storeroom, so we gloss over some inventory numbers for the fun stuff and have ourselves a good time on our days off."

"*Dude*, you brought that *here?*" Marcus whispered urgently, but Lewis didn't see the issue.

"It's not like we marked them yet, relax. Figured that if worse came to worse, we can trip out and salvage the night on our own." He turned in time to see Ulysses just inches away from the white paper, which Lewis stowed away quickly.

"What *is* that, man?"

"Acid," Lewis said simply, turning away from the guitarist to find that every one of Kara's friends was looking at him in childish wonder.

"Travis," Kara said softly, and her ex-boyfriend turned to face her as she lifted her head, "you shut the fuck up. Pretty sure we just became very good friends with these guys."

Almost immediately, the scene froze and flickered like a corrupted VHS tape—the scene warping in shape and color—and Marc realized that he had been absorbed back into his old life and pleasant memories. This time there was no separation between him and the Marcus from three years ago, there was just the one person and that scared him. This was just supposed to be a way for him to revisit his past and see how his life had come to this point, but he was becoming entrenched, each memory making it harder and harder to remember who he was.

Even when he tried, Marc realized he could not make it back to the present, and he panicked as his surroundings shifted and fell apart again, leaving him in a white void temporarily. Once the eternal moments were over, however, the world started to filter back in, false reality filled the void, but it was only made worse once Marc realized where his brain was taking him. He tried to fight it, tried to push it away, but he did not have the strength.

Screaming internally, Marc found himself back there on the rooftop, the moon bright and full above them. Surrounding him were his friends, the closest people in his life, and Kara had already dosed far too much.

"Holy shit, dude, you hit the jackpot with Escape," Ulysses said as he laid in a hammock on Marc's roof, smoking from an ornate pipe once he finished his statement. All of them were there except for Lewis, who was at the apartment putting the last touches on a lab report for their boss.

Watching Ulysses as he breathed out, the memory of Marc manipulated the world so smoke billowed out and became a shifting tapestry showing an ancient battle between giants and dragons. Before his eyes, one of the dragons breathed fire into the tapestry and brought the picture to life, brilliant colors spreading through the air and showing the giants and dragons trading blows. In that moment, *that* Marc was happy leaning against the wall of his rooftop, Kara buried in his armpit, most of his friends sharing the experience with him.

The Marc held hostage in his own memories was mortified and panicking as he relived that terrible night from three weeks ago.

"It's just a blend of the three families, Ulysses. Little bit of lysergic acid, dash of DMT, some phenethylamine, and a couple secret ingredients to bind them together into something stable," Marc explained, even though he should have realized none of them cared. "Was an accident, if you remember."

"Was one of the secret ingredients *love?*" Ariana asked between giggles, and Marc turned to find her grinning at something hovering in the air. "Because I definitely want to marry this drug."

"No, not so much. I leave the love to her," Marc said as he

nudged Kara, predictably saccharine sweet, and Travis groaned from the other side of the rooftop.

"Dude, you lose all of your fucking cool points the *minute* you dose. It turns you into Barney the goddamned dinosaur," Travis said, laughing at his own joke, and then he scooted away from where he had been lying and put his back against the wall. "Oh, man, guys, don't ever imagine—"

"Don't say it," Reggie said, sitting in a lawn chair with his eyes closed. "Don't suggest anything bad to people on Escape. You know that."

"Yeah, yeah, I know the sales pitch. It'll be nice once people know about our shit and we can really start to make money," Travis said, breathing out deeply and trying to banish the imaginary monster no one else could see. "I'm barely making rent right now."

"Hey, making rent is still making rent. We get more connections, we get more sales, we get more product, and then we'll be fucking groovy, hosscat," Ariana explained, making Ulysses laugh as he swayed in his hammock.

"Yeah, dude, once I start using my road connections, we can totally spread this magical, wonderful shit just all over the world," he said, letting out a contented sigh as he turned to face Ariana, who looked like she was trying to make snow angels. "Hey, Ariana, you ever try to imagine a *hosscat* on Escape?"

"I... why the fuck did I not think of that?" Ariana mused before sitting up and crossing her legs. After a shriek of laughter, she put out her hand and ran her fingers through invisible hair.

"Dude, it's pretty fucking amazing, I'll tell you *hwat*," she said, intentionally switching the letters.

"I'll tell you what's *amazing*," Marc added, running his fingers through Kara's hair. "Ulysses *should* have died trying this out. I made that batch up that day and had no idea it was even safe. Instead, the human cockroach rocked on and we have this ridiculous little drug."

"You sure it was *you* who made that batch?" Travis asked, still sitting with his back against the wall, and Marc hesitated before responding. In the throes of pleasure and ecstasy, he had to make sure he was not imagining his own past.

"Yeah, that one was mine, but Lewis definitely tweaked it so it lasts longer and all that. We both made it, really," he said, and Ulysses threw up a hand and shouted.

"Dude, oh shit! I just realized it," he said, turning slightly to gawk at Marc. "You and Lewis created the drug. You're fucking *pioneers!*"

"Uh, yeah?"

"Yeah! So… Lewis and Marc…" he said, waiting for people to jump on it. "Pioneers…"

"Are you trying to say that their names rhyme with Lewis and fucking Clark?" Travis asked in disgust, and Ulysses turned over in his hammock with a whoop.

"Hell *yeah, man!* We got some genuine fucking pioneers into a new dimension!"

"You idiot…" Marc muttered with a smile, too distracted to notice what was happening inches away from him.

Yeah, you stupid fucking idiot, look at your girlfriend! Marc shouted from the ether, but his past self was not paying attention. A dumb, stupid smile was plastered on his face, his eyes were not looking down, not feeling Kara grip his shirt tighter, not seeing her pull at the material.

"This is it," Kara muttered, confusing her boyfriend as he looked down at her.

"What is *it?*" Marc replied, and she pushed herself out of his armpit and looked at him with a desperate smile on her face.

"This is *it*, Marc. This is what I've been looking for all my life," she said, crying as she wrapped her arms around him and squeezed him tight. After a moment, Kara pushed herself to her feet. "I've always… I've always been looking for a way to get out, to escape all this… all this awful shit."

"Kara—what?" Marc asked, looking up at his girlfriend and appreciating how beautiful she looked in his mind. She didn't even change; it was just the air around her that shifted and changed to suit her. "You're beautiful…"

"I am now, Marc. So are you, so is everyone," she said, turning to look at all their friends and laughing. "You're all so fucking beautiful."

"We love you, Kara!" Ulysses shouted from his hammock, and all of their friends nodded in agreement.

"And I love you, too," she replied while walking over to the far side of the rooftop, close to where Travis was sitting. "I love all of you, even when you're being assholes, because you're my family. You're the people I share my life with, and all of you gave me this."

"Gave you what, hosscat?" Ariana asked from the ground, grinning at the small girl who had climbed onto the ledge of the rooftop.

"Freedom. I'm free, guys. Life is what it's supposed to be now, it's what I always wanted, what we all wanted," she said, tears streaming down her face. "I can fly, guys. I can fucking fly!"

"Yeah you can," Ulysses said, pumping his fist in the air. Most of them were smiling at Kara, hearing her words and thinking she was saying something else. However, one of them knew what she meant, opening his eyes just in time to see her on the ledge.

"You *can't* fly, Kara," Reggie said, but she just put her hands on her hips and jumped in place.

"Yeah, I can, Reggie! I'm fucking free now, and I'm going to fly," she claimed, and it was only then that Marc realized what she was saying, knew what she was about to do.

"Kara, no!" he shouted, jumped to his feet, but he was too far away to make a difference. Standing there on the ledge—high on a drug Marc had created—Kara gave him a smile that was supposed to be just another smile.

"I love you, Marc. Thank you for this," she said, turning

around and jumping into the air.

For a moment, Marc thought that he was seeing things, that maybe, *just maybe,* Kara *could* fly, but he heard the thud from the ground below. In disbelief—only Reggie standing up and running with him—Marc made his way to the ledge and saw what he never could have imagined even during the peak of Escape. He screamed then, loud, painfully, so anguished that it brought all of his friends out of their drug-induced stupor.

It was echoed by the real Marc, the man who had tried to escape his guilt and grief by returning to his memories of better days, only to be forced to watch the woman he loved die one more time.

And though he did not realize it, when the real Marc cried out, he was no longer under the effects of Escape. He was not in his memories; he was in his empty apartment. When he cried and shouted, real neighbors heard him; real, living, breathing people were so close, right there to help. If he picked up his phone, he could have called any one of his friends and they would been there as soon as possible. If Marc had called his parents, his mother would have held him as he cried, but he did not want any of them.

Marc had wanted his girlfriend back, and he had lost her all over again.

CHAPTER 7

PSYCHOBABBLE

Jeremy looked around the quiet, mellow room for the hundredth time and wondered if it was organized like this on purpose. Warm, yellow light spilled over everything; over the leather couch along the side of the room, the bookcases and cabinets along the other walls, the amber of the table between him and even the well-dressed, middle-aged woman sitting in a worn armchair identical to his own.

She would have been pretty ten years ago, Jeremy assumed, and he had to admit there was still evidence of that. Dark, red hair framed her face and fell to her shoulders and her thin glasses definitely worked for her, but there were just too many wrinkles for Jeremy. Ten years ago—maybe fifteen—she would have been perfect for one of Jeremy's fantasies, but it was not ten years ago.

In addition, he hated her almost as much as his mother.

"So, Jeremy, what will it be today?" she asked, crossing her legs and dropping a notepad into her lap. She was silent for a moment, looking at him and analyzing his reactions, but she eventually propped up her head with her right hand. "Are you going to yell this time? Complain and rage against the people who have wronged you? Or are you going to stay silent, cross your arms and glare at me? You obviously have *something* in mind."

"It's *almost* like you know me, Dr. Ruby," Jeremy said, crossing his legs along with his arms and feeling uncomfortable in his skin. "I just can't walk in here without a plan, can't I?"

"Can't you?" she replied quickly, earning a glare from Jeremy. "I've been seeing you for a few years now—"

"Four, if we wanted to count," Jeremy interrupted, and he was pleased to see her reaction. For just that instant, he had shaken her, but Ruby regained herself before he could think of anything to follow the interruption.

"Four years then," she repeated while dropping her arm and sitting back in the chair, her hand falling to the notepad on her lap. "Four years, Jeremy, and you fight me every time."

"Some people might say I'm a lost cause," he replied, but he tried to keep staring at her. He was tired of backing down, of seeming like he was scared.

"Who would say that, Jeremy? Why would they say that?" Ruby asked, opening up the notepad and grabbing a pen from the stand near her chair. "Do *you* think you're a lost cause?"

"Bits and pieces, honestly," Jeremy admitted with a heavy exhale. "But it's a popular opinion. Nobody is happy to see me."

"That's not true. Your mother cares about you."

"Oh, *that's* just bullshit," Jeremy snapped. "That woman doesn't care about me. She stopped caring the minute I wasn't useful. She *used* me just like she's using all those other kids."

"You think your mother used you?" Ruby asked, and Jeremy scoffed at the notion that it was just in his mind.

"I *know* she used me. I've seen the pictures back when I was cute and she could use me and my dimples to sway voters," he replied, uncrossing his legs and leaning forward. "I've seen how she's acted ever since my dad left. Have you seen what she's been doing lately? My bitch of a mother is *literally* using a dead kid to further her own agenda."

"Those are some bold claims, Jeremy," Ruby commented, writing in her notepad while maintaining eye contact with him. "But I don't think that's true. Your mother cares about you. Otherwise, we wouldn't have our sessions, and from what I've seen on the news, her feelings on that boy seem genuine."

"Genuine? *Please*," Jeremy said while uncrossing his arms and sitting back in his chair, gripping the ends of his armrests. "Lynn *fucking* Stafford is the furthest thing from genuine. She doesn't care that Escape is becoming popular or that a kid died because he was being stupid. She just cares about what it means for her career. Besides…"

"Besides?" Ruby asked after a few seconds, and Jeremy did not realize he had paused until he heard her voice. Letting go of the armrest and sitting forward, Jeremy interlaced his fingers and propped up his head.

"If she does care… if she does care about that kid," he said, looking away and feeling the tears forming in his eyes. Frustrated and angry that he was actually feeling something, Jeremy forced them back. "It's worse, okay?"

"How is it worse, Jeremy?" she asked, pursuing Jeremy after every admission.

"It means that she cares more about that dead kid than her own. It means that a twelve-year-old boy that she never met is more valuable—more *precious*—than me, alright?" he explained, looking back at his therapist in anger. "It means I'm worth shit to her."

"That's not true, Jeremy, as much as you want to believe it. You're here because she knows that you're hurting and she wants to help."

"You…" Jeremy said, burying his head in his hand and laughing. After a moment of frustrated laughter, he lowered his hand and looked at her skeptically. "I'm not here because she wants to help me. I'm here so that I don't *embarrass* her. I'm here because she doesn't want to waste her time talking to me. I'm here so that if I shoot up a school or OD on something than she can say that she *tried*, that I was *troubled*, that it wasn't *her* fucking fault. I'm a political liability, Dr. Ruby, and she's making sure that she has an exit strategy."

When he was finished raging against his mother, Jeremy sat back in the chair and crossed his arms. Glaring at this woman— who was doing him the courtesy of glaring back without scribbling in her notepad—Jeremy was getting impatient. The twin infinity symbols on his tongue should have kicked in by now, but thirty seconds after he finished speaking, he was still looking at the same, middle-aged woman.

"That's a pretty dark way of thinking, Jeremy," Ruby finally commented, picking up her notepad and setting it on the side table. "Is that how you really feel about your mother?"

"Of course, it is. I said it, didn't I?" he replied quickly, without thinking, but he backed down after a moment's scrutiny. "Well, mostly. I don't think she thinks I could shoot up a school."

"Do you think you *could* shoot up a school?" Ruby asked. It was so audacious that Jeremy looked at her in awe.

"If I had a *gun*, sure, but I don't really want to do that," he replied sarcastically, but his therapist leaned forward slightly.

"But if you *did*. Let's just work through this. If you had a gun—if you had a bad day—would you think about something like that? You've mentioned on many occasions how you hate Barry Shriver and his friends. More than once you've mentioned hating everyone, wishing they would leave you alone," she said, crossing her hands over her lap and looking down on him. "Do you ever think about what you would do in a situation like that?"

"You're… insane," Jeremy said, so furious by her implications that he did not know where to start. "What kind of therapist *are* you? What kind of person are you to even ask me that?"

"Jeremy, it's just a hypothetical situation. I am legally required to—"

"No, that's *bullshit!*" Jeremy shouted as he jumped out of his chair, focusing so much on his therapist that he didn't notice the lights flicker. "I'm not going to shoot up a fucking school just because I think my mother is a bitch! I'm not going to go off the deep end and kill people because I had a bad day."

"I might hate all of my so-called *peers*," he continued, curling his fingers in the air, "but that's because they fucking *deserve* it. The other day Shriver shook up my soda and poured it all over me while every gaping, slack-jawed piece of shit I go to school with laughed at me! And yeah, if I could have gotten away with it, I would have beat the shit out of Shriver, but that's the fucking thing, isn't it?"

"What's the thing, Jeremy?" Ruby asked, calm as she watched his temper tantrum, and it was almost enough for Jeremy to lash out. However, he finally saw the smoke drifting about the room, the furniture warping and changing, degrading as warm light departed and was replaced with ambient twilight coming from outside the room. They were from streetlights stories below, and Jeremy watched as a flying car rushed past a half-opened window.

"The thing is… that I couldn't. In real life, I'm just weak. I'm nothing. *I'm* the piece of shit," Jeremy said, backing away and sitting in his armchair, which had become a plain, wooden chair in his mind. He did what he could to stay in the moment and the conversation, but he was becoming more and more distracted by this new vision. The table between Jeremy and his therapist shattered and the particles rearranged, becoming a simple, sleek glass desk with three holographic displays floating in the air above it.

"You're not a piece of shit, Jeremy. You're not nothing," Ruby said from behind the yellow and orange displays, and Jeremy allowed the middle hologram to disappear and show his new therapist.

Those fifteen years had melted away to show the voluptuous, femme fatale Jeremy had conjured in his mind; dark, scarlet hair crashing in waves onto bare shoulders and a red dress hugging her every curve. A slit rose to her upper thigh on the right side, exposing black stockings and the hint of a garter belt. Held between her fingers was the stem of a cigarette holder, the ember of a dying cigarette filling the room with the smell of scented tobacco.

Jeremy did not know why he had gone so far with the fantasy, but he could not say he did not enjoy the view.

"I am nothing, though, in this world," Jeremy replied, his voice more gravel than words. Bringing up his hand and looking at the calloused, weathered skin covering it, Jeremy realized he was not a teenager in this scenario. It gave him confidence, it gave him strength, and he let himself sink into the role he had created. Lights flickered above him, but he maintained eye contact with the sexual object across the room. "Whatever I do here, it doesn't seem to matter."

"You make it seem like there is another option, Jeremy," the woman purred, and Jeremy thanked his subconscious for the treat. "You keep making the distinction between the real world and... something else. Do you think there *is* something else?"

"Only what we're given," Jeremy said, relaxed as he leaned back in his chair and set his feet on the desk, seeing the dust from his worn, leather shoes disrupting the holograms he had imagined. They were gibberish, in any case, but he appreciated the detail. "It's not much, but it makes the world a little bit more bearable when there's a place to escape to. A place where we can pretend we're not the pieces of shit we are during the rest of our lives."

"Can you take your feet off the table, Jeremy?" Ruby asked, the words sounding awkward through the filter Escape had created. Jeremy knew that she probably sounded annoyed, declarative and authoritative in the real world, but he had left that world behind.

"Nah, I'm comfortable here. Isn't that the point, doc?" Jeremy asked, clasping his fingers beside his head as he leaned back, grinning at his therapist as he tried out the nickname. "The more comfortable I am, the more I'll share, right?"

"You said a place where you can pretend. What do you mean by that?" Ruby asked after a long moment, drawing in a lung full of smoke and making the cigarette ember turn bright.

Soon, that ember consumed the rest of the cigarette—leaving a trail of ashes—and the woman tapped it against the ashtray by the side table. After grabbing a silver case from the table, Ruby flicked it open before setting down her cigarette holder.

Only after gaping at her for twenty seconds did Jeremy realize that she had grabbed her notepad and that this was just a way for his brain to fill in the missing details. Jeremy could not help but smile at the revelation, but he was interrupted by the woman clearing her throat.

"Jeremy?" she asked, and he remembered just where he really was, what he was really doing, who he was really talking to, why he was here. With that wave of information Jeremy realized he may have spoiled his trip—he could already feel his frustration coming back—but he decided to ignore it for now. Looking at the feminine fantasy in the red dress, Jeremy gave a crooked smile.

"Sorry, doc, was just thinking about how I could express it," he said, leaning forward and taking his foot off the table. To his left, a wall turned into a gigantic display showing fabricated news about cybernetic augmentation, but Jeremy tried to ignore the excess detail. "I'm just talking about the movies, the books—all the games that we can use to get away from our real lives. For a lot of kids, that's all we really have. That's the only place where *we* win."

"Where *you* win?" the woman repeated, the headlight of a passing car flickering across the room and the room rumbling from the proximity. As Jeremy watched, Ruby's hair fell across one side of her face, making only one eye visible, and his heart broke just a little bit. He would never get close to someone who looked like that in the real world.

"So that is in contrast to what you feel like in your real life? You feel like you are losing, Jeremy?"

"Losing, *lost*, there's no real difference," Jeremy said as he sat back, rubbing his face against four days of stubble that had grown in five seconds. "I told you I was a lost cause. *That's* how we feel all the time. This world just wasn't meant for us."

"You say *us*, *we*… it sounds like you're including other people. Do you have friends you talk to about these things? Is that where all this anger is coming from?" she asked, and Jeremy had to stifle laughter. It hadn't meant anything—it was just a turn of phrase he had borrowed for the moment—but Ruby had created a whole scenario out of a few mistaken words. Turning back to the gorgeous woman who he now realized was just ornamentation, Jeremy shook his head.

"The anger is mine, always was. Just never showed it to you. And no, no friends," he admitted, looking at the wall of television and seeing a riot break out between law enforcement and what looked like a gang of cyborgs. "They're just people like me, people who saw this world and opted out. Guys who saw the pretty people getting all the opportunities and found different worlds where they could spend their time. Might not seem rational to escape to a world filled with nerds killing the same boss twenty times to get legendary, imaginary boots, but even *that* is better, sometimes."

"So you use video games to escape the real world," she commented, and Jeremy smiled as he felt the numb sensation from the paper on his tongue. "You use these other worlds to escape your feelings, to push them down, to momentarily forget about your real life."

"Sounds dangerously close to a diagnosis, doc," Jeremy replied, almost groaning at her assumptions. Turning, he looked at her in disgust. "But you're barking up the wrong tree."

"Am I, Jeremy? You spent the first half of this session talking about your mother and just when it seemed we would make a breakthrough, really make progress, you deflected it," she explained, her voice reverting to normal even though her body stayed just as provocative. "You turned it into just another way to excuse yourself from the world, another way to blame video games."

"Hey, I didn't blame video games. They're the good guys in this," Jeremy replied, smirking at the flavor of his own words. He must have sounded silly to his therapist, but he felt right at home in his futuristic, gritty fantasy. "And I seem to recall some shitty accusations on your part about shooting up schools. That derailed the topic a bit, didn't it?"

"I was just doing my job, Jeremy," Ruby started, but Jeremy put out a hand to stop her.

"Don't much care about your job. We're not here for *you*, right? We're here for me, to get me past my problems, to make me love my mother again, right? That's the whole point of this, right? To get me to stop blaming her?" Jeremy asked the barrage of questions while shifting in his seat, putting his foot back on the table and crossing his other leg over the first. "We're trying to make me better, doc, and we *might* be able to do that if you don't accuse me of wanting to commit mass murder."

"Jeremy, that's not what I was doing," Ruby claimed, her voice returning to the seductive tone Jeremy preferred.

"No, I'll tell you what you were doing," he said, pointing at her briefly. "You were wasting my mother's money. Just like you do every session, just like you have for the last four years. Because here's your problem, sweetheart. You ain't gonna fix me."

"Sweetheart?" she asked, indignation seeping through from reality, but Jeremy waved it off.

"You *ain't* gonna fix me. It's just not going to happen. This far down the line I'm already broken and nothin's going to help. I already hate ninety-nine percent of humanity—for good fuckin' reasons—and there's no place in this world where I will ever fit in. Those video games are only good until the end—until everybody has the best gear—and then it's just about finding the next world to conquer."

"And eventually, there's not going to be more worlds to conquer, there's not going to be more places to escape," Jeremy said, taking his feet off the table and standing with a groan. Walking over to the window where he could see the expanse of a corrupted and decaying city, Jeremy realized he wasn't just talking about video games anymore.

"And what will you do then, Jeremy?" Ruby asked, and

Jeremy turned back to her and let the fantasy fade away, seeing his disturbed therapist. Sighing, he walked back to his chair and set his hand on the top.

"I really don't know. It's all shit, isn't it?" he asked before heading to the doorway. "And here I thought I had found another way."

"Your session isn't over, Jeremy," she said quickly, hoping to stop him, but then a soft alarm rang from the table next to her. Shrugging and sighing heavily, Jeremy opened the door and walked through.

"One of us is wrong," he mumbled, ignoring the woman behind him and making his way downstairs. For the moment, he allowed the real world to become dominant; it would be pretty suspicious if he walked into a wall or fell down the stairs. He just thought about what he would want once he was alone again.

"Jeremy, please, wait a moment," Ruby said, but he did not listen, walking all the way to the waiting room before she caught up with him. When she set her hand against his shoulder, Jeremy whipped around like he had been shocked.

"Hey, since when could you touch me?" It was easy to see that the question shocked Ruby, but she regained her senses quickly.

"Jeremy, I can't just let you go after all of that," she said, but Jeremy didn't have a chance to respond.

"After all of what?" a woman interrupted, and Jeremy turned to see his mother rising from the couch, almost completely focused on her phone. Jeremy had to assume she was doing something work-related while he was discussing his feelings, but she put the phone away before he could see the screen.

"Ms. Stafford, Jeremy said some very disturbing things in today's session, and in light of his current behavior..."

"Behavior?" Lynn asked, crossing her arms and looking at Ruby skeptically.

"The skipping school, the general behavior toward his teachers, the, well, the way he just acted in our session," she said, her face flushing toward the end. "He was acting very strange, as if he was someone else, and these mood swings and changes in attitude… they could be signs of deeper problems."

"Deeper problems? Dr. Ruby, Jeremy is a *teenage* boy, he still doesn't know who he is," Lynn said, dropping her arms, and made it impossible for Jeremy to stay silent.

"I know who I am, *Mom*, unlike you. Can we just go?" he asked with a venomous tone, but Jeremy looked away as Ruby continued.

"I am well aware of the changes puberty and high school can bring about, Ms. Stafford, but I'm concerned about Jeremy. He speaks with such resentment, such defiance, and these are all recent changes. He's lost weight—"

"He's what?" Lynn asked abruptly, forcing the conversation to a halt as she looked over her son. "Oh, you *are* thinner. Have you been exercising?"

"I dunno," Jeremy mumbled, looking away from both women and staring at the window covered in blinds. If Jeremy had lost weight, he hadn't noticed, but he realized it was possible. With all the Escape he was taking, Jeremy may have just imagined eating.

"He looks like he's lost twenty pounds in the last month," Ruby stated, causing both Staffords to pay attention. "Combine that with these changes in mood, the skipping classes, and the fact that he spends more time playing video games with strangers than with real people, friends, *anybody*…"

"He *has* friends," Lynn scoffed at the statement, but Ruby did not look like she was joking.

"Not according to Jeremy. He says that the only way he can find anybody else like him is to escape the real world. And… I didn't want to say it," she hesitated, looking to Jeremy and clearly deep in thought. He was curious what she meant to say, but then he realized Ruby was more than of an idiot than he had thought. "He mentioned shooting up a school, Lynn."

"You bitch," Jeremy muttered as he backed away. "I didn't say that! You just imagined that whole fucking thing!"

"He mentioned shooting up a school?" Lynn was suddenly concerned, and Jeremy could not believe it. Stepping up to his mother's side, he tried to catch her attention.

"She's lying, damnit, she just sees someone like me and *assumes* that I'm fucked up," he said before turning to the therapist who was currently ignoring him. "And what the hell happened to doctor-patient confidentiality, huh?"

"That stops once people could get hurt, Jeremy," she replied, and Jeremy had to hold himself back from punching her in the face.

"Did he *say* that he was going to shoot up a school, Dr. Ruby?" Lynn asked again, and Jeremy backed away from both of them in shock. It should not have come as a surprise—he knew what his mother cared about—but he could not handle the absurdity of the situation.

"He…" Ruby said, pausing as she looked back to Jeremy. "Technically, no, but—"

"Then he *didn't*," Lynn interrupted, and Jeremy almost thought she was standing up for him. "He's a teenage boy who talks about teenage things, and he's going through teenage changes. As much as you might want to diagnose the next Eric Harris or Dylan Klebold, my son is not the next Columbine shooter just because you put words in his mouth."

"Ms. Stafford—"

"This conversation is over, Dr. Ruby, and depending on how I feel about it later, you may be in touch with my lawyer about your negligent behavior in the very near future," Lynn declared as she placed her hand against Jeremy's back and walked him to the front door.

"Ms. Stafford!" Ruby urged as she walked after them, but she stopped in her tracks once Lynn looked over her shoulder with a dead stare.

"I advise that you stop there, Dr. Ruby, or I might make my

decision here and now," she threatened, and Jeremy's former therapist folded in on herself and watched as the Staffords left her house.

"You really going to sue her?" Jeremy asked as they walked over to their car which was parked on the suburban street, but he had made the mistake of trusting his mother.

"Of course, not. There's no point," Lynn said as she pressed the button on her keychain and unlocked the car, opening her door and falling into the driver's seat before Jeremy even touched his handle. He stared at Lynn, furious for more than a few reasons, but after a moment of this she looked at him impatiently and motioned for him to get in the car.

"And here I thought you cared about the children," Jeremy mumbled, opening his door and throwing himself into the seat. After buckling his seatbelt—more to stop the warning sound than for safety—Jeremy let the world fall away, seeing the expanse of a foreign sea from the deck of a pirate ship. It was more of a distraction than wish-fulfillment, since he had to be ready for his mother's attempt at conversation, but he already felt more comfortable.

"Nice to see that you're doing something to lose the weight, Jeremy, whatever it is," his mother said as she started the car, pulled out of her parking spot and forced Jeremy's pirate ship into motion. Without turning to face him, she said something Jeremy wished was true, even if he knew it was just another empty breath.

"I'm proud of you."

"Don't forget, I have that benefit Thursday night, Jeremy," Lynn said as she turned off the car, the garage door screeching into place behind them. Before she even finished speaking, Jeremy had already unclasped his seatbelt and opened his door. "I'll try to bring home some of the catering, but you should order a pizza or something."

"Yeah, whatever," Jeremy muttered as he stood up and walked to the door. Before he made it, Jeremy heard his mother whistle at him, so he turned to face her in dismay.

"And I saw that note the other night," Lynn said, waiting for him to respond, but she continued once it was obvious that he would not. "You're wrong, Jeremy. I care. Not just about you, but about everyone in my district. It's my job, but I really do care."

"It was easier to believe that *before* you gave up your beliefs and started chasing votes." Jeremy lowered his head before opening the door, unable to see the tears forming in his mother's eyes. "And I stopped believing even before that."

Once he was inside the house, Jeremy walked to his room as the world flickered between dozens of different realities. With the turmoil in his head, in his heart—*all around him*—he could not focus. What he wanted didn't exist in any of those worlds; what he wanted was to be accepted, to be loved, to be cared for, and no amount of dimensional travel could help that.

When he got to his room, Jeremy grabbed his headphones from his desk, shoving them into his ears before turning on an aggressive playlist on his phone. He had created it for when he wanted to destroy the world, and flashes of those apocalyptic scenarios formed in front of him. For a moment, as Jeremy left his room and made his way down the stairs, he almost wanted to see it all crumble away and the world burned to ashes, but he realized he was just lashing out.

Bursting out the front door—figuring that his mother would not come that way—Jeremy started to walk around the house. It was cold, Jeremy knew it even surrounded by hellfire and destruction, but he wasn't in any danger. As he walked around the side of his house, he started to hate this apocalypse in his mind, hated that he was running away like this. As much as he hated other people, as much as he might want to shoot up a school despite his reaction to his therapist's accusation, Jeremy knew he was just lonely. He was ashamed of it, tried to hide it, but he just didn't want to be alone.

Once he realized this, Jeremy switched the playlist to something mellow—something that would not inspire apocalyptic thoughts—and he continued to the back of the house. Their pool had been drained for the winter, but he had no intention of swimming. What he wanted was someone to talk to, someone to care for him, and when his pool came into view, the Escape flooding through his brain gave him just what he wanted.

Allison was sitting there, waiting for him with her feet dangling over the edge. Even though it was winter, she was dressed in shorts and a t-shirt, her golden hair tied back in a ponytail, and she looked like she was basking in sunlight. Opening her eyes, she turned back to Jeremy and, once she realized it was him, beckoned for him to come closer.

"Hey, come here. Water's warm," she said, making Jeremy laugh as he approached. The pool was still empty to him—Allison was dangling her feet over empty air—but Jeremy decided to oblige the fake girl.

Shining, rippling water filled the cement basin, the dying plants of Jeremy's back yard breathed into life, and the clouds above them disappeared. He even went a step further and dressed himself in summer clothes, his fat disappearing along with his winter coat, but he Allison looked at him in disappointment.

"You don't have to wish that away, Jeremy," she said while patting the ground beside her. "I like *all* of you."

"Really?" he asked, forgetting that this girl was in his mind, and the smile she gave him eradicated whatever resistance remained. Jeremy approached her, his true, chubby frame filling out his summer clothes, and he sat down next to her in wonder. "But… I'm gross."

"*People* are gross, Jeremy," Allison said, laughing at him as she shook his thigh. "You're just a little heavy. Don't worry about it."

"But you like… you like people like Roger," he said, losing all confidence and thinking she was the real person, but his fantasy would not let him. Allison lifted his chin with her hand and shook her head while maintaining eye contact.

"He's *nice*, and I like him, but that doesn't mean I can't like you, too," she said, offering a warm smile. Tapping his forehead with a finger, her smile turned into a grin. "Besides, *that* is more important than looks or throwing a ball."

"Could have fooled *me*," Jeremy said, laughing as he turned away from her, choosing to look at the water shimmering in front of him while lily pads formed and floated along a slow current in his pool.

"Jeremy, just look around you," she said, waving her hand from the pool to the sky and to the life surrounding them. "You made all of this from your *mind*. You imagined it, and it became real."

"That's… that's just the drug. Anybody can do that on Escape." He made excuses, but Jeremy felt Allison's hand on his shoulder and he turned to see her looking at the sky, feeling the warmth of fake sun on her skin.

"That's not *true*, Jeremy. Not everyone can do it; some people take it and see nothing except changes to what they know. You've created entire worlds on Escape. You turned your therapist's office into some sort of cyberpunk detective movie," she said, and it caused Jeremy to remember that she was part of the fantasy.

"The real Allison wouldn't know about cyberpunk," he said, feeling even more defeated, but the girl beside him only laughed.

"Her loss, right? She doesn't get to see what I see, to feel what I feel. In your head, in the world you've created, I get to see the real you. I get to see the worlds you make without even really thinking," she said, Jeremy staring at her the entire time. Even if she was made up in his head, his heart melted for her. "When you dose, Jeremy, I get to see every amazing detail, because you want me to be there with you."

"Allison…"

"And that means a lot to me. No matter where you go, no matter what you want to do, no matter what gigantic battles and fantasies you create from nothing, you bring me along. That's why I love you."

"You… you love me?" Jeremy asked, losing his grip on reality as reflected sunlight from the pool flashed off her eyes.

"Of course. Should be obvious by now, shouldn't it? Now make us something incredible. I know you're dying to," she said, looking up at the sky, and Jeremy could not help but join her. The smile returning to his face, Jeremy thought of what to make to impress her, but eventually decided it did not matter. He didn't need to find some situation he could force himself into or find a world where he belonged.

With Allison sitting beside him, Jeremy could explore the universe and belong anywhere.

CHAPTER 8

A PUPPET WITHOUT STRINGS

When Lynn finally got back to her office after exploding on Chris Harmon's show, she really did not know what to expect. She had turned off her cell phone very soon after she had stormed out of the broadcast, but not before sending calls from Senator Price and Janice Pearson directly to voicemail. They would crucify her for this; for cursing on air, for abandoning the script, for being manipulated into exploding on national television. Whatever career Lynn had built had been destroyed in an instant; whatever goodwill this Escape campaign was supposed to garner would not be coming. She had played right into Silverman's hands.

So when she walked into her office, she did not expect Sharon to wrap her in a tight hug and spin her around.

"What—what are you doing?" Lynn tried to pry the woman's arms off her body, but Sharon held her close.

"Giving you the best damned hug I can, you magnificent *bitch!*" she squealed, squeezing Lynn one last time before letting go. When Sharon stepped back and shook her head, a smile on her face, Lynn couldn't shake her confusion. "You deserve some of the *good* liquor for that performance."

"Performance…" Lynn repeated, and her spirit dropped for an instant. "Oh, Sharon, that was—"

"*Fantastic*, that's what it was," Sharon interrupted before heading over to her desk and grabbing her phone. "We're going to get something going tonight, just you wait. I'll call all the people we actually like."

"Sharon—"

"Oh, never mind me or the party, that can wait," Sharon said quickly, holding the phone to her chest and nodding to Lynn's office. "You have people waiting for you."

"I what?"

"Yeah, sorry, was too excited. Senator Price and Ms. *Cuntsicle*," she explained, whispering out the curse word, "are in there. Plus a special guest!"

"Sharon, what the hell are you talking about?" Lynn asked, but Sharon shooed her away before sitting down and giggling to herself. Getting more irritated by the second and confident in nothing but the knowledge that she knew nothing at all, Lynn pushed through the door of her office and found three people waiting for her. She had expected Janice Pearson and Senator Price, who was old, fat, and had a bald spot surrounded by white hair, but there was no way she would have thought the other man would ever be in her office.

There, standing to the side and admiring her book collection, was Noel Silverman.

"Lynn! Lynn, you crazy bitch," Senator Price said as he waddled over, offering a hand with fat fingers for a handshake. Taking it awkwardly, Lynn just stood there as he glowed up at her. "I knew you had *something*, but I had no goddamn clue that was hiding in there."

"What... I mean—*no*," she emphasized, withdrawing her hand and looking at the other three with skepticism. "I'm sorry, but *what* are you talking about?" Scoffing, Janice walked over to the window and crossed her arms.

"You did it, Stafford. You went on national television and you convinced the world that you *cared*," Janice said, turning around so she could make eye contact. "Those special interest groups we were aiming for have all offered their support."

"And *then some*," Price interrupted, backing away so he could sit on the top of Lynn's desk. "We got four more congressmen to back you in the last twenty minutes, we have half a dozen charities lining up to help with the benefit, and your polls are through the fucking roof with almost all the target demos."

"The polls? *What* polls?" Lynn asked, and this time Silverman was the one to respond.

"Oh, you know, the Facebooks, the Buzzfeeds... all the social networks and their relentless pandering to viral trends," Silverman said, grabbing a large book from the shelf and opening it to a random page. "The YouTube video of your rant already has a hundred thousand views and however many *likes*. Comment section is predictably polarized, but you're coming out on top with this one."

"A hundred thousand views..." Lynn said, staggering back to support herself against the doorframe. "And... people liked it... Wait! The *kids* liked it? That makes no sense! I've been unpopular with the youth demographic since before I left *middle school*."

"They still don't like the anti-drug campaign. Don't worry about getting too popular," Price replied, a childish grin on his face.

"But, more importantly, they saw that you cared and that you're doing it for the so-called *right* reasons," he continued, drawing air quotes around the emphasized words. "Which is really more important than your actual stance. What they saw was truth, honesty—someone *human*—and they respected it."

"Good thing we can fake that, right?" Silverman added with a laugh, and Price chuckled as he pointed at him.

"This one! This fucking man! If I didn't have to aggressively campaign against the gays, I'd kiss him full on the mouth!" Price shouted, earning a wink from Silverman.

"Hey, we're among friends here..." he teased, Price dismissing it with a wave of his hand.

"*Why* is he here?" Lynn asked, and Price stopped laughing long enough to look at her, the smile falling away.

"Because he's part of this..." he said, somewhat confused as he narrowed his gaze at Lynn. "The two of you were playing right off each other."

"You were eating right out of his hand, Stafford," Janice added, and Lynn finally realized what role Silverman had been playing. Turning to the man by the bookcase and causing the others to join her, Lynn glared at Silverman long enough that he looked up from the book in his hand.

"Oh, yeah, that. I didn't tell her."

"You *what?* You didn't tell her that we set it up?" Price asked in anger. Janice looked like she was about to start screaming, but Silverman laughed and smiled at them as he closed the book, keeping his finger between the pages as a bookmark.

"Relax, I know how to play Lynn, we've been doing this for years," he explained, his easy tone and smile enough to calm them down. Turning back to Lynn, he seemed to radiate admiration. "I figured the best way to bring out her best was to make her confront her worst."

"It was all..." Lynn trailed off, Silverman laughing before nodding to Price by her desk.

"Devil's advocate, remember? You just assumed it was for the other side," Silverman said before offering the book to her, opening it and pointing at an entry halfway down the page.

"What's this?" she asked, but Silverman scoffed as he backed away and set his thumbs into the pockets of his trousers.

"It's *your* encyclopedia, Lynn. Just thought you'd appreciate the entry," he said with a wink, and Lynn scanned down the page to the entry he had chosen. While she was doing that, the others burst into one-sided conversations, yelling at Silverman for a number of reasons.

"You son of a bitch, we risked so much—"

"Stafford could have fucked up and frozen or, worse, said something stupid! You fucking—"

However, all of that was just background noise for Lynn, since the encyclopedia entry Silverman had chosen was far more engaging than two politicians berating a talking head. She did not even need to read it; she knew exactly who it was. What really meant something was that Silverman had pointed to it and had taken the time to find it in her encyclopedia. All of it was just to make a silent point, even if Lynn did not think she deserved the comparison.

For some reason, Silverman had pointed out the entry for Mother Teresa.

"So… it was just to—it was all just to make me break like that? To show that I cared?" Lynn asked, almost at a whisper, but it stopped the politicians from yelling and caused Silverman to turn to her with a smile.

"Of course. *That's* how you make headlines these days. You have to break the rules, you have to go off-script. You have to do something people won't expect, and forsaking your career on national television in order to protect *children?* That's *gold,* Lynn," he explained, setting his back against the book case and crossing his left leg over his right. "Even if you don't do *anything,* they'll think you're a real person trying to really change the world. Obama built an entire presidency off the word *change.*"

"Brilliant," Price said in wonder. "Brilliant, even if I fucking hate your guts for the risk."

"How did you know I would react like that?" Lynn asked, and Silverman offered her a knowing smile.

"I told you, you don't need to pretend around me. I knew that if and when you blew up, it would be to defend something you cared about," he said, shoving off the bookcase with his back and then walking over to Lynn's side. "Just had to push you in the right direction."

"Well, it worked out, I guess," Senator Price said as he rose to his feet with difficulty, his stubby legs just strong enough to move him around. When he closed the distance and stood next to Lynn and Silverman, he clapped both of them on the shoulders. "Now, I think we should celebrate."

"Celebrate?" Janice asked from the window, and Price turned to her with a frown.

"Why not? We got ourselves a big win here, and I wouldn't

mind grabbing a drink or five. We can't go anywhere public, of course, but if you want to follow me back to my office, we can break into a thirty-year-old bottle of scotch. Started as a twelve-year-old, but... call me patient."

"A twelve-year-old seems in bad taste," Silverman replied slowly, causing Price to back away with a scowl.

"Bad taste? It'll be an *experiment*, Noel! I can give you something better, of course, but this bottle has some significant memories attached to it," he argued, and Silverman set his hand against his chin.

"Memories, too? I—never mind," he said, lowering his hand and sighing before turning to Lynn. "I don't really have anywhere to be, but I can't suffer him alone. You want to join us?"

"So you're all just going to drink in front of me?" Janice asked by the window, and Price stared at her for a moment before continuing through the doorway.

"Only if you want to come and watch us, Pearson, though you can always break your little vow! You two follow when you're ready," Price said over his shoulder, waving at Sharon as he left Lynn's office. Lynn watched the man until he rounded the corner into the hallway and then turned back to Silverman, who was just a little too close for comfort. As he smiled down at her, Lynn almost forgot that she had hated him only an hour ago. When he spoke, she found it difficult to look him in the eye.

"You ready to celebrate a twelve-year-old's death with twelve-year-old scotch?"

"Oh, thank Christ," Lynn mumbled as she staggered into her bedroom, closing the door behind her and immediately falling back against it. Even though she had taken off her heels already, her sense of balance had been completely destroyed by the alcohol she had practically inhaled throughout the night. It had been months, perhaps years, since she had drunk as much. The last time she remembered drinking this much—or remembered the hangover that followed the eventual blackout—was right around the time her husband had cheated on her.

Fortunately, this time she was drinking for good reasons.

"My... kingdom for a bed," Lynn said under her breath, the syllables all merging together. She laughed as she fell down onto the mattress, not even bothering to lift the sheets, and she curled against one of her throw pillows for a moment. When she breathed in through her nose, she remembered his scent and forgot where she was.

Lynn was back in her office, everyone else was gone, and her face was buried in his neck. An instant later, her legs were bare and wrapped around him. When she breathed in again, she remembered Noel's face, the understanding in his eyes, the moments when she felt a true connection. Then, just as she was about to revisit that euphoria, Lynn opened her eyes and realized what she had just done.

Sitting up so fast it made her head hurt, Lynn felt like she would to throw up.

"Oh God," she uttered before that feeling turned into a need, and she rushed over to the bathroom directly attached to her bedroom. After running over to the alcove for her toilet, Lynn quickly fell down to her knees and lifted the toilet lid up just in time for her to vomit a stomach full of liquor, wine, late-night pizza and bile.

For a long moment, Lynn almost thought she would drown on her own vomit, but she did not give into that panic and continued to void the contents of her stomach. When that first convulsion stopped, Lynn almost laughed at her own thoughts—she was too old to be drinking like this in the first place—but then the second convulsion came and she rid herself of whatever remained in her stomach.

After wiping off her mouth with a piece of toilet paper, Lynn fell back against the wall facing her toilet and tried to breathe. The taste of bile still clung to the inside of her mouth, but she was far more disgusted with herself and her behavior. She had declared herself to be a protector of children—Noel had even compared her to Mother Teresa—and then she had spent the rest of the night getting drunk and sleeping with a man she barely knew.

The worst of it all was that Lynn couldn't blame him; she could not say that Noel was an arrogant man who abused or took advantage of her. It had been an entirely adult, reasonable choice, and Lynn had made it with only the slightest bit of convincing. Noel was handsome, charismatic, smart and had seen something in her that had laid dormant for so long that Lynn had forgotten it even existed. Even if she would never do it again in her right mind, Lynn knew that she had wanted it.

That still didn't stop her from feeling disgust.

Picking herself up, Lynn staggered over to her sink and supported herself on the counter with one hand while turning on the faucet with the other. She let the water run for a moment as she regained her bearings, but eventually she lowered her head and started to bring handfuls of water to her lips. At first it was to rid her mouth of the taste of vomit, but eventually she realized she was thirsty and put her lips directly against the water pouring out of the faucet.

After a few gulps, Lynn realized she kept a cup nearby just so she would not have to resort to this behavior, and so she picked herself up and looked for the cup. Once she found it on the other end of the counter by the second sink, Lynn placed it underneath the faucet and decided to pass the time by looking at her reflection. However, once she did so, she found a green post-it attached to the mirror with a message written in felt tip marker. Leaning in closer to see through blurred vision, it took Lynn a little too long to understand what it said.

SAW YOUR BROADCAST. NICE JOB FOR A HYPOCRITE.

Sighing, Lynn drew back from the message and grabbed it with her hand, oblivious that her water cup was overflowing in the sink. She just continued to look at the horrible hand-writing, the spite flowing through every mark. One day, Jeremy might understand, but Lynn realized that it was only a possibility. Every day they seemed to be growing further and further apart, and this was just another symptom of that. As she read the note over again, she turned off the water and grabbed her cup, unaware she was dripping water everywhere.

Crumpling up the note, Lynn dropped it into her wastebasket and walked over to the far side of her bedroom, determined to return to another time. Once she knelt down, Lynn brought out her hand and ran her finger along the spines of her books, every other moment forgetting and then remembering what she was doing. She was just about to give up when she finally touched a white binder and then dragged it out of the bookcase, and then she turned around so she could place her back against the wall.

Opening up the binder, Lynn was greeted with photographs from another era. There were quite a few of her growing up, of her college days, of all the get-togethers and special moments between then and when she met her ex-husband, but she flitted past those with only a few moments of appreciation. She was looking for something else in middle of the night, when she was disgusted with herself and wanted redemption.

About two-thirds of the way through the binder, she stopped and gazed lovingly at a collection of pictures, a child with shining, blonde hair smiling and jumping and playing. A couple of years later and that blonde hair would turn brown, that smile would disappear, a husband would leave and never come back, but Lynn was not looking at *those* pictures. She just wanted to see these; to see the good times, to see when her son still loved her, to remember why she cared so much when other children were at risk.

Lynn looked at those pictures over for an hour, but eventually she passed out with the binder on her lap, her head hanging limp on her shoulder. Her water cup was lying on its side and a puddle was already drying on her carpet, but Lynn would not have cared even if she was conscious.

When it came down to it, water soaking through a piece of carpet was the least of her worries or concerns. What she cared about was the boy in those pictures, the smiling boy who had not smiled in far too long. She had taken out one of the pictures—the boy was holding his hands behind him and grinning up to face the camera—and she held it curled in her left hand. That boy had stopped existing somewhere along the way, and Lynn knew it was her fault. And if she had looked inward instead of distracting herself, Lynn may have realized why she cared so much about a dead child, about the children of other people, why Noel was able to get under her skin.

Whether or not she realized it, Lynn fought so hard for those children because she knew she had already lost her own.

CHAPTER 9

THE FIRST STEP

When that familiar crunch of metal filled the air, Marc opened his dry, red eyes. Sleep had evaded him for days now, no matter what he took, no matter what he tried to do to send himself to oblivion. Sedatives, smoking weed… nothing seemed to deprive him of consciousness or stop the pain tearing at his insides. So, when his phone mimicked a Transformer, Marc merely opened his eyes and threw out his hand, his fingers falling on the back of his phone. Bringing it in front of his face, he turned on the screen to see a text message from Lewis.

Get clothes on. Reggie and I will be there in two minutes.

Marc tried to laugh at the situation—he had not removed his sweatshirt or pants for two days—and he was barely surprised by the rasp of breath that came out of his mouth instead. It had been too long since he had truly laughed, smiled, felt happiness of any kind, so it made sense that laughter would be stolen from him. Marc did not mind. After his journey to the past, laughter seemed extraneous.

Sitting up on his couch, Marc could feel the ache traveling through his limbs, from all the muscles he never used anymore. Escape had made movement unnecessary, and whatever physique he had was gone. Lifting his shirt, Marc found that he was still skinny and his muscles still showed through the skin, but he could tell that he was losing mass. Except for the occasional run to the convenience store or sandwich shop, Marcus hadn't really left his apartment in the last month.

It showed.

Sighing, he dropped his shirt back down and looked at his window, light pouring in and irritating his eyes even more.

Putting up his hand to ward off the light, Marc tried to remember the last time he had truly slept. Escape had never left his system since he had returned from the past; it was just too painful to be sober. As a result, time had lost its meaning, constricting and expanding on a whim. The only constant was the vision of his dead girlfriend.

Noticing that Kara wasn't busying herself in the kitchen, curled up on the couch next to him or jumping on their bed to punk music, Marc realized that he was getting dangerously close to normal. It did not take him long to see the sheet of paper on the table in front of him, and he leaned forward and scooped up the drugs in the same movement. After tearing off two squares, he set the Escape on his tongue and sat back, shoving the rest into his pocket and waiting for Kara's return. Letting his eyes close, Marc was almost relaxed enough to nod off before a stern knock came from his door.

"Marcus," Lewis said from the other side, just as harsh as his knock, and Marc debated on opening the door at all. Lewis could only be here to beg him to come to work or convince him to stop mourning for Kara, and Marc had no desire to give in to either demand. However, when he recalled that Reggie was with Lewis, it caused him to reconsider. Their friend was not one for social calls; he had more important things to do.

"Coming," Marc said, the word feeling strange in his mouth, and he pushed himself off the couch. Stumbling through his apartment, he eventually made it to his door and twisted the handle.

"Do you not lock your door?" Lewis asked, stupefied, but Marc shrugged as he trudged back to a bar stool.

"Didn't see the point," he mumbled, collapsing into the chair and propping himself up on the counter. Nodding briefly at Reggie, who was dressed in his usual black hoodie and matching coat, Marc turned his attention back to Lewis and buried his chin in the crook of his arm. "Why are you here?"

"You look like shit, man," Lewis said, hoping to illicit some kind of reaction, but Marc didn't give him one. "This has got to stop."

"What has to stop, Lewis? My self-pity? My downward spiral? What are you going to tell me that hasn't been said by a motivational speaker?" Marc replied, making his way through each question like it was molasses. Lewis glared down at him the entire time, growing more furious with each word, but he was able to keep himself in control.

"When's the last time you slept, Marcus?" he asked, earning a bark of laughter from Marc before he buried his mouth in the fabric of his sweatshirt.

"Just woke up, kinda," he mumbled into the material, closing his eyes momentarily, but he opened them as soon as Lewis grabbed him by the shoulder and shook him hard.

"Stop acting like a fucking child, Marcus!" Lewis shouted, breathing out hard as Marcus adjusted himself on the stool. "You're killing yourself by doing this."

"Maybe I *should*. Killed Kara. Killed that boy on the news," Marc explained, supporting himself by holding onto the counter with one hand. "Eye for an eye. I got one for each of them."

"*Bull fucking shit,* dude," Lewis said, closing the distance and grabbing his collar, forcing Marc to make eye contact. "You're not responsible for Kara or that kid, and it's time for you to grow up. Everybody gets hurt eventually, everybody loses someone, but life doesn't end there. We have responsibilities. *You* have responsibilities, and when it comes to *you*, you've dropped the fucking ball."

"Is that why Reggie is here? Is that why you're talking to me like some fucking drug dealer who needs money?" Marc asked, his eyes narrowing as he got off his stool and looked Lewis in the eye. "I need to come back so we can make more *product*?"

"Of course, you do, you ingrate. You need to come back to work, to *both* of your jobs," Lewis replied, pushing Marc back and letting go of his collar. "But that's not the worst of it. And you're right. Reggie is here because it affects that part of our job."

"Partly." Reggie kept his hands in his pockets as he closed the door with his foot, stepping back into the room so he was able to see both of them. "Been worried about him, too."

"Yeah, Marcus, you got *Reggie* to worry. Look how placid he is," Lewis said, waving back at their friend. "Didn't bat an eye when I left the door open and started talking about drugs, but you have him *worried*."

"Well, he sees me now and I'm alive," Marc said, turning to the quiet, stocky man in his foyer. "Still worried, Reggie?"

"Sure," he replied simply, not bothering to show emotion. "You look like shit and you're about to lose your job."

"I'm about to lose my job?" Marc turned back to Lewis, who had crossed his arms and was frowning at him.

"Yeah, dude, because you haven't come in for a *month*. Nitterman has been patient—cooler than I thought he would be—but he isn't putting up with it anymore. If you don't come back in the next two days, he's going to put someone else on the program, scuttle your research, everything," Lewis explained, stepping forward until he could sneer down at Marc. "And that means that you're coming in either tomorrow or the next day."

"Or *what*?" Marc asked, mirroring Lewis and crossing his arms.

"*Or* we could go to fucking jail," Lewis replied sharply, stepping back so he was closer to Reggie. "If they terminate you, investigate your research and what you've been using, the next thing they're going to do is take stock of inventory and notice that a bunch of experimental and dangerous compounds have gone missing."

"That's… okay, that's not great, but we moved off-site months ago," Marc replied, lifting one hand to make random gestures. "They couldn't possibly make the connection."

"*Maybe*, but I don't want to deal with maybes," Lewis said, shaking his head, "and I'm still there. Even if we get away with glossing numbers, they're going to look at me next, and they'll notice that I've still been using more than my fair share of bonding agents."

"You're still using the storeroom? I thought we made a deal about that!"

"We did, Marcus, but things took a turn when my fucking *partner* disappeared." Lewis gripped the bar counter with his right hand. "You handled a good part of that, dude, and when you left, I had to get creative."

"God, are you fucking kidding me? I leave for a month and you turn into an idiot?" Marc asked, but he could see the fury almost explode out of Lewis.

"You're calling *me* an idiot?" he snapped, pacing around the open kitchen and making wild gestures before slamming his hands on the sink. "I did what I *had* to do, Marcus, and I'm not the one making bad decisions, here! I'm not the one who started up a drug operation, built a network of dealers out of his girlfriend's junkie friends and then left a giant fucking, blinking sign for the authorities saying *look at me* after someone jumped from the roof of his building!"

"We're not friends, Lewis?" Reggie asked after a moment. Lewis attempted to start up an apology and resorted to scrunching up his face and forgetting how to speak, but he abandoned the effort once he heard Marc forcing out ragged breaths. Marc had clenched his fists so tight that his dark skin was turning white, but Lewis only turned to meet him with gritted teeth.

"Might not be the only friend you lose today, Reggie," Marc said, his tone murderous, but he could not move a muscle. He only continued to glare at Lewis—at his supposed *friend*—as a blood vessel burst in his left eye. "Lewis is doing a pretty damn good job of cutting ties."

"The time of being a good friend—of consoling you and trying to make you feel better—is *over*, man. It's time for tough love. I'm sorry about Kara, we all are, we all miss her, but this has got to stop."

"Because it hurts your ability to make money, right? Because you want to keep making drugs and you don't want to get in trouble because you were too stupid to shop somewhere else for bonding agents," Marc said, his nostrils flaring. "I have to make up for your mistake, so it's time for you to start disrespecting my girlfriend and call it *tough love*. It's time for you to bring it all out into the open, how you hated her, how you think she changed me for the worse, how you now get to say *I told you so* and it's all fine because you're just trying to *help*."

"He *is* trying to help," Reggie commented, forcing Marc to abandon his staring contest with Lewis. "He's right. You need to stop. We don't want to lose you, too."

"Reggie… you," Marc said under his breath, trying to find some way to talk to his stoic friend, but another voice destroyed all of those thoughts.

"You *do* need to stop," Kara said, and Marc turned to see her by the window, the light coming from the window above her drowning out her features and turning her into a silhouette. Although shocked at first, Marc recovered himself and acted like he was turning away from his friends out of anger. Even though Kara continued to speak, he acted like he was not listening. "It is hurting you. Ever since we got back, when you saw me die again."

"It's destroying you, Marcus," Lewis said, forcing Marc to face him, but Marc was still painfully aware of the ghost on the other side of the room. "It's destroying who you were, who you've become, and you better fucking believe that I care about that the most."

"Yeah, sure," Marc said, bringing up his hand to his chin and looking at Kara out of the corner of his eye.

"Yeah, dude, that is what I care about. We've been best friends since high school and I don't want to give that up," Lewis said, oblivious that Marc was only half-paying attention to him. "This isn't an *I told you so*, because I was fucking *wrong*."

"Wait a second, you're admitting… you were wrong?" Marc turned in shock, and he found Lewis looking at him with sympathy.

"*Yeah*, dude, I was. When you were all obsessed with Kara, I told you to stay away. When you saw her after high school, I thought you were insane for chasing her all over again. But I was wrong. You guys were *great* together, and it was obvious to everyone but me until I found the two of you curled up on *that* fucking couch," Lewis said, smiling as he pointed at the furniture, causing Marc to look from the couch and then to the girl standing by the wall. "And you guys were watching *Mystery Science Theater* and adding your own crappy jokes."

"Hey, Raul Julia had no business being in that movie," Kara said while pointing at the TV screen, and Marc realized it was just a memory and what that meant. Marc's tolerance had already increased, but he did not have the time to focus on it. Turning from the memory, Marc found that Lewis had lost his smile.

"You made Kara better and, to my incredible surprise, she made you better. You weren't a shy nerd around her; you weren't an academic shut-in. Kara brought you out into the open, made you into the person you were supposed to be, and I'll admit it. I was jealous. Three years with her, and she had already done more for you than I ever did," he admitted while looking away, and Marc realized how much his friend was hurting.

"Lewis, that's not—" he started, but Lewis lifted his head and shook the tears from his eyes.

"And the rest of them are my friends, too, even if they're not like us. Reggie is a steel trap and I can count on him for anything. Travis will curse you out for the slightest mainstream thought, but that man would fight to the death for any of us. If she sees you having a bad day, Ariana will make cupcakes and give you a strong glass of whiskey while you slaughter immature teenagers on Halo. They're all great in their own way, and meeting Kara and all of them has made both of our lives better," he said, drawing closer and setting his hand on Marc's shoulder.

"We're asking you to come back, man. Yeah, I screwed up and I need your help so we don't get arrested, but we need you to stop living out this fantasy, we need you to stop running away. Give up the Escape and live your own life. Kara would want it that way," Lewis said, almost convincing Marc, but Kara's name brought him back to his pain. Looking at the girl at the window, Marc shrugged off Lewis' hand and shook his head.

"Kara wouldn't care." He walked into his living room and stood next to his dead girlfriend. "Kara never wanted to be here. She didn't want to live. This world was cruel to her, ruined her, damaged her, and she wanted to be anywhere but here. When we gave her Escape, we gave her the perfect way to kill herself. We gave her a way to end it all without knowing it, without making the choice. We gave her a way to not feel scared. We *gave* it to her."

"That's not fucking true," Lewis said, but Marc turned to the ghost looking up at him.

"That's not your fault, you didn't know," Kara said, but Marc did not get the chance to look at her for long. His shoulder was yanked back around until Lewis was looking down at him and pointing a finger into his face.

"That's not fucking true and you need to stop blaming yourself! Kara fell off that roof because she thought she could fly, not because she wanted to kill herself! She wasn't running away from you. She wasn't unhappy!" Lewis' voice trembled as he shouted. "What happened on that roof was not your fault!"

"You weren't there! You didn't see her!" Marc yelled, pushing away his friend and sweeping his arm across his body. Pointing up at the roof, Marc did not realize he had banished Kara from his perception, did not see Reggie appear where she had been standing.

"I was," Reggie said, grabbing Marc's wrist and dragging it

down to his side before backing away, standing by the coffee table. "I was there, Marc, and she wasn't trying to die."

"Reggie, you heard her," Marc squeaked out, but Reggie shook his head slowly.

"I did. And you're right. I can't tell you what it was like to know her in high school, to see the bruises. We all ignored it for her, but we saw it and she knew we saw it," he said, doing his best not to mumble. "She talked to us on the rooftop like that because she knew we would understand. She knew you would understand."

"Reggie…"

"She wanted to live, Marc. You and Lewis made her want to live. Made her want to see the next day. What happened was an accident. It was fucked up, but it was just an accident," Reggie concluded, speaking more to Marc and Lewis than he had during most of their friendship. His face was empty of emotion, his eyes were dry, but Marc knew there was more under the surface.

"I—I still," Marc said, pushing his way past his friends and standing next to the bar. Kara formed in his kitchen, sitting cross-legged on the stove and, even though she was smiling, it only made Marc's heart heavier. "It's still my fault."

"Fine," Lewis muttered, walking past the couches and to the stool next to Marc. "We'll work on it. We'll let you hate yourself for the time being, but don't think we'll ever stop, Marcus. No one blames you for her death—and eventually we'll change your mind—but you can't keep going like this. We need you to come back. We need you to be sober."

"Why do I need to be sober?" Marc asked, avoiding eye contact and choosing to look at Kara dangling her legs in front of the oven door.

"He doesn't want to be the boring one," she said, and Marc immediately saw it as just another verbal jab from their shared past.

"Because I need you to help me with our next order, and you

can't work while dosed on Escape."

"Next order? What are you talking about? We had at least seven thousand doses in the storage unit," Marc said while crossing his arms in hostility, but Lewis shook his head and nodded at Reggie, who was sitting on the back of the couch.

"No, not anymore, not after Ulysses," Lewis said, and a migraine formed in Marc's head with the name. Suddenly, he remembered that Lewis had not mentioned the older man in his heartfelt speech, so he fought through the pain and ground the heel of his palm against his temple, which Lewis noticed. "What's with you?"

"Just a... headache," he said, forcing his hand back down and looking at his friend, even if his eyes felt like they were about to explode. "What happened with Ulysses?"

"Ripped us off," Reggie answered, causing Marc to focus on him. "Left a note saying he would be back, but our inventory is gone. We still have enough raw materials to make enough for our current orders, but we need to prepare enough for five thousand doses by Friday."

"Five thousand? That's ridiculous!" Marc shouted, crossing his arms and looking back to Lewis. "We don't have the scale for that. Even if both of us worked non-stop, we would be done by—"

"Dawn Friday morning," Lewis interrupted, his hands in his pockets. "We might be able to push the meet a little bit, but not for long. And if we don't deliver because we admit that one of our dealers stole our inventory, it's going to look real bad on us."

"Then it'll look bad on us, who cares? We're still the only ones making it," Marc commented, but he could tell from the way Lewis looked away and covered his face in his hands that it was not that simple. Turning to Reggie and finding him at the end of a long sigh, Marc realized that someone must care very much about appearances.

"Mob connection. We promised. They want their product.

It needs to get to them," he explained, and Marc was angry with Reggie for the first time in his memory. Rushing forward, he grabbed Reggie by the collar and tried to pick him up from the couch. He was too heavy for Marc to succeed, but he got his point across.

"What the fuck are you doing making deals with the mob? *What the fuck were you thinking?*" He shook his friend, but Reggie just stared back before reaching up and removing Marc's hands.

"It's the next step, Marc. With the mob behind us, we can expand, gain more connections, have protection. The mob would make our lives easier. Our current problem..." Reggie paused, standing up to his full height and towering over him. It surprised Marc—Reggie slouched so often that he had forgotten how tall he was—but it did not make him any less angry. "Is that we don't have the product we promised them. Now you and Lewis have to make it."

"Make it yourself," Marc growled, stepping back to his foyer and looking at his friends. "I'm not getting caught up in that mess."

"You're already caught up in it, whether you want it or not," Lewis said, standing next to Reggie and crossing his arms. "But we can solve this problem, Marcus. You sober up, you come back, we work our asses off, and our connects won't know at all. We'll get to Ulysses when we get to him, we'll make you forgive yourself after *that*, but you *can't* just give up now. You can't throw in the towel. We're depending on you, and you're coming back to work tomorrow."

"You just get to decide that, huh?" Marc asked, so frustrated that he did not notice that Kara had disappeared from his kitchen and reappeared next to the bathroom door. "You just get to tie my hands, throw me into business with the mob, and you think I won't be mad?"

"No, I *know* you'll be mad—I know you'll be angry with me until this is over—but that doesn't fucking matter," Lewis said, stepping closer as visions of Kara formed between them, which dissipated as he walked through her ghosts. It confused Marc at first, but eventually Kara flickered into the empty space beside the couch, leaving Marc to focus on his friend who was only a foot away.

"It doesn't fucking matter, because we're going to grow up, we're going to make this batch of Escape, and you'll be clean and sober and not spending all your time in your head."

"What if I don't want to, Lewis? What if I don't care if the mob comes after me? What if I don't care if I lose my job? What if I don't want to make five thousand doses for you? What if I don't mind spending the rest of my short life high off my ass on Escape?" Marc asked, pushing his friend with each question, up until the point Lewis was right next to Kara. "What if I kick you out of my apartment and then dose myself as soon as you leave?"

"More than you've already dosed?" Reggie asked, shocking Marc into backing into the foyer.

"Ooh, busted," Kara said, but Marc was staring directly at Reggie.

"Already dosed?" Marc asked, drawing a shrug from his friend.

"It's obvious." Reggie yawned before reclaiming his seat on the back of the couch. "You're acting like a customer."

"You're high right now, Marcus?" Lewis asked, looking at him in disgust, but Marc did not get a chance to answer.

"Only a little," Reggie interrupted before looking down at the floor. "His tolerance must be catching up to him."

"How much are you taking, man?" Lewis asked, stepping forward and forcing Marcus to retreat toward his door. With every step, his gaze hardened and his tone deepened. "How much are you on *right now?*"

"What's it fucking matt—"

"How *much*, Marcus?" Lewis shouted, and Marc's back hit the wall at the same time.

"However much I want!" He tried to shove Lewis away, but his friend surprised him by forcing him against the wall and pushing his feet off the ground, Marc's throat held in his right hand. Before Marc could react, Lewis made a grab for his chin, but Marc struck out with his knee and sank it into his friend's gut. That caused him to wince and double over, but Lewis kept hands on him.

"Reggie!" he urged, and the other man closed the distance fast, assisting Lewis in keeping Marc against the door.

"Stop it," Marc protested, but between the two of them, he was held up against the door and they opened his mouth. He tried to stop Lewis from going further and snapped his teeth, but Reggie squeezed hard on his jaw and forced it open, allowing Lewis to dig his finger into Marc's mouth.

With a quick movement, Lewis dragged his finger along Marc's tongue and the Escape came with it, and he let go of Marc soon after that. For a moment, Reggie continued to hold Marc against the door, but Lewis eventually patted him on the shoulder and that was enough for Reggie to release Marc and him slide down to the ground in a coughing fit. When he recovered enough to look up at his friends, Marc found both of them looking down at him with pity.

"Two doses, Marcus? You're already at two and it's not enough for you? How did you let yourself get like this?" Lewis asked, but Marc was not going to entertain them.

"Get out," he muttered, pushing himself to his feet and slapping away the hands that came to aid him. Lifting his head, he glared at Lewis for a moment before turning to Reggie. "Get out of my fucking apartment."

"Marcus…"

"Get the *fuck*," he screamed, slapping Lewis by the arm and grabbing a handful of shirt, "out of my apartment now! Get the fuck out!"

"Marcus, just stop—" Lewis tried to say, putting up his hands just in time to ward off a flurry of weak attacks.

"Get out, get out, *get out!* You're *not* welcome!" Marc shouted, pulling and pushing Lewis and trying to force him out of his apartment, but a hand settled onto his arm after that.

"No. We're not leaving," Reggie said, and Marc was so angry that he threw a punch into Reggie's jaw, staggering his friend back onto the couch. After the frenzy left him, Marc realized what he had done, saw the blood trickling out of Reggie's mouth. However, Reggie just pushed himself off the couch and stood up, wiping the blood off his face with his sleeve.

"We're not leaving."

"What?" Marc asked, confused by the statement, but Lewis backed off and stood beside Reggie, crossing his arms defiantly.

"We're not leaving, man. You need us. You need this more than we thought. We're going to help you get clean," he said, looking to Reggie with the last statement like it was a question, and Marc could see the relief on his face when Reggie nodded slowly.

"I'll call the cops, you assholes," Marc threatened, but it only made Lewis laugh at him.

"You're going to call the cops when you're the creator of the new hit drug? When you probably have Escape and other drugs all over this apartment? *Please,*" he scoffed, turning slightly and waving a hand at the couch behind him. "Just come over here, take a seat on the couch. It'll suck, but we'll help."

"I'm not taking a seat on the couch with you. I'm not getting clean. I'm not going to help you, you fucking dick," Marc said, turning to the clutter on the counter and grabbing his keys. "I'm going to leave, and when I get back, you better be fucking gone."

"Marcus!" Despite Lewis' protests, Marc grabbed the doorknob and yanked hard—giving into a temper tantrum as the door resisted him—but eventually he twisted the knob and pulled the door open, turning to face Lewis with a scowl.

"That's not my fucking name, anymore," he said before

setting down the hallway and slamming the door behind him. It resonated through the entire hall, waking up a dog in one of the other apartments and setting off a chorus of barks, but Marc did not care. His last refuge had been taken from him—the last place that truly felt like home—and it had been his friends who were responsible.

He could not believe Lewis, Reggie, or even Ulysses. Between the three of them, they had ruined their fledgling operation and put them all in danger, and Marc knew they blamed *him* for it. Their compassion and understanding about Kara's loss only went so far—went until it put their money at risk—and now they had kicked him out of his own apartment. He could not dose and feel comfortable; he could not escape to his fantasy world anymore.

And as another vision of Kara flickered in front of him and disappeared into the door of a closed elevator, Marc knew it would not be long before she disappeared for good. With his tolerance the way it was, his personal supply would not last long. Sooner or later, he would have to deal with Lewis and his other friends just to get his fix. Otherwise, he would never waste away another afternoon with Kara or roll around with her on the bed again.

Getting killed by the mob almost seemed like a better fate.

When he stumbled back to the door of his apartment and retrieved the keys from his left pocket, Marc realized he would have to surrender. To see Kara, to feed his addiction, he would need to make more Escape. Lewis was not going to give it to him and without a job he would not be able to acquire the raw components or tools, so his choice was made for him. If Marc wanted to keep living and maintain his blissful disregard for

Kara's death, this would be his last night of freedom for some time. And after spending the last few hours of daylight with flickering remnants of Kara, all Marc wanted to do was dose one last time and spend the night with her.

Fumbling with his keys, Marc got frustrated as they evaded him, but he eventually got his thumbs to cooperate and shoved the key into the lock. When he turned it there was no resistance, and Marc cursed Lewis for leaving his apartment unlocked. Sighing, he twisted the doorknob and opened the door, crossing the threshold and dazed by the light greeting him. After raising his hand to protect his sensitive eyes just like he had done that morning, Marc's eyes adjusted to the light far too late.

Reggie, Lewis and Marc's parents were staring at him from his living room.

"What the hell—" Marc started, but then he felt something strong hit him from behind and force him into the apartment. Whipping around and ready to fight back, Marc was halfway to throwing a punch before realizing that Travis was looking down at him. The realization stopped him mid-swing, and Marc was so surprised by everything that he could only step back into his kitchen, almost jumping when the oven door slammed behind him. Turning, he found Ariana standing up with an oven mitt on her hand, holding a fresh pan of cupcakes.

"What the fuck is this?" Marc was unable to escape, and Travis moved to put his back against the wall of his apartment, scowling at Marc and crossing his arms.

"Intervention, you jackass," he said, sniffing and propping his foot up against the wall, smudging it with his boot, but Marc did not care about that. Turning from the tattooed man—who was thankfully wearing a shirt underneath his vest—Marc found Lewis standing by the television, one hand in his pocket, the other one motioning to the couch.

"Have a seat, man," he said, but Marc slammed his hand against the counter and shocked Ariana into dropping her pan onto the stove with a clatter.

"Are you fucking *kidding* me, Lewis? After all we've been through and all we've done, you're fucking giving me an intervention?" Marc shouted, so angry that spit gathered at the corner of his mouth. "My girlfriend dies and you give me an *intervention*? What's *wrong* with you?"

"Marcus, Lewis cares about you. *We* care about you. Everybody in this room loves you," a declarative voice interrupted, and Marc turned to look at his father, who was standing next to his mother with a hand on her shoulder. They looked like they always did— his dad in khakis and a sweater, his mother in khakis and a nice blouse—and it killed Marc for them to see him like this, to finally know the truth. Broken, tweaked out and an addict to his own drug, his parents were seeing him for the true failure that he was.

With just one act, Lewis had betrayed him worse than he had thought possible.

"You bring my parents into this…" Marc muttered, bracing himself against his kitchen counter. "What gives you the right, Lewis? What gives you the right to do this to me?"

"You did it to yourself," Travis replied, earning a glare from Marc. Instead of backing down, he pushed off the wall and stepped into the kitchen a few feet away from him. "You went down this road and got addicted to running away. You're the one who was too cowardly to deal with it."

"Too cowardly?" Marc rushed forward, grabbing Travis' vest with his hand and pulling him down to eye level. "Too *cowardly*? You don't get to say that, man. You don't feel what I feel."

"Yeah, you're fucking right," Travis said, turning and then pushing Marc into the hallway. Following after him, Travis shoved him into the living room as he kept talking. "I don't feel what you feel, because I feel something else. I get to feel angry that I didn't stop her. I get to replay the scene over and over in my head and watch as my ex-girlfriend jumped off the roof."

"Yeah, and imagine—" Marc tried, but Travis pushed him

harder against the couch before pulling him back and gripping his collar with both hands.

"I don't *need* to imagine, Marc, I was there!" Travis shouted, cigarettes and whiskey flavoring every word. "I saw your heart breaking, I saw you fucking lose it, and I understand! I fucking understand, you asshole, because I could have *stopped* her! I could have jumped up, grabbed her waist, her hand—I could have done a shit ton of things instead of looking at the fucking dinosaur in my own head—but I *didn't.*"

"I didn't, Marc." Tears ran down his cheeks as he let go of Marc, backed up against the wall and looked down at him. "I didn't save her. I was still in love with that girl and I just sat there. And my fuckin' heart broke—just like your heart broke—and we don't get to see her again. I understand, Marc, I fucking do."

"But I let her go," Travis said as he wiped snot from his nose with the back of his hand, sniffing back the rest and pretending to be alright. "I let her go, because that's what we're supposed to do. We're supposed to move on, you fucking asshole. We aren't supposed to keep her ghost here."

"Travis, it's not... it's just," Marc said, his anger evaporating momentarily, but Lewis cleared his throat and brought it back. Turning around, Marc saw Lewis motioning to the couch again.

"Just listen, man. You're not here to talk; you're here to listen to us," he said, and Marc bristled at his audacity.

"I'm *not* here to listen to you. I'm here because this is my *apartment*, and *you* are trespassing," Marc said, pointing at Lewis before turning to his parents. "Mom, Dad, I'm sorry he called you here, but this is all just a mistake. He doesn't know what he's talking about."

"Yes, he does, Marcus," his mother spoke up, her hands folded in front of her. "Lewis told us everything, about Kara, about the Escape. We're going to stay, and you're going to listen."

"Oh, he told you everything?" Marc repeated, turning back to his best friend. "Just *what* did you talk about? Just *how far* did you go to explain why they're here? Did you talk about the drugs? Did you talk about *where* they came from, Lewis, huh? Did you do that?"

"He told us *enough*, Marcus. He told us how you created the drug in the lab and how you got hooked after Kara," his father answered, forcing Marc to look back at him in shock. "That's not why we sent you to college."

"You told them…" Marc breathed out the words as he set his hand on a stool to support himself. Lifting his head, he looked at his parents and broke. "Dad, I'm sorry—"

"Don't be sorry to me," his father replied, wrapping his arm around his wife's back. "Be sorry to your mother, your cousins, to your friends. Look at them if you want forgiveness. I need more than that."

"Dad, I—"

"I need you to stop, Marcus," his dad said, breathing out deep. "I need you to throw away whatever drugs you have. I need you to be clean and show back up at work. Once you've gotten yourself out of this mess and you're back on your feet, *that's* when you can come back to me with an apology."

"Jason," his wife said, but Marc's father did not back down.

"He knows what he did, Karen, and he knows what that means. We can care about him all we want, but he needs to make a change. He won't get there if we hold his hand," he explained, but Karen pushed away from him and shook her head.

"He lost someone he *loved*, Jason. Would you want someone to talk to you like that if you lost me?" she asked, scowling before facing her son and her disappointment turning to concern. "What your father means is that we're here to help you get better, Marcus. We're here so that you can move on. Grieve for Kara the right way—the *healthy* way. The only way to do that is if you let us help you."

"No, I know what he meant," Marc said, looking at his mother for only a moment before staring at his father. "I know exactly what he meant."

"Marcus, he just doesn't—" she started, but Marc put out a hand and talked over her.

"He's disappointed, Mom. He's looking at me and he's seeing a son who wasted his money and his time," he claimed, maintaining eye contact with his father throughout, and Marc could see anger flash across his face. His mother tried to reach out and place her hand on Jason's arm, but there was nothing she could do to stop them.

"*Damn straight* I'm disappointed, Marcus," Jason stated, crossing his arms and glowering at his son. "I gave you the best opportunities I could. I gave you a nice, white neighborhood where you could grow up without having to worry about getting shot. I paid the full tuition for the college you wanted even though you had scholarships for a dozen other universities... Hell, Marcus, I didn't bat an eye when you said you were dating Kara, and she had *troubled kid* written all over her."

"Don't you talk about her like that," Marc growled, ready to leap forward and attack his father, but Jason shook his head and sighed. He resumed eye contact only after swallowing down something else he wanted to say.

"I'm not here to insult Kara, Marcus. My point is, I gave you all of that, I gave you the life that my parents didn't have—that a lot of my friends would have killed for—and you decide to *make drugs*? You *couldn't* have been more sheltered, Marcus, but you threw away your education just to run back to the streets and get kids hooked on the next *poison*," he said, breaking eye contact and looking at the window. "So yeah, I'm disappointed."

"You act like it's a new thing, Dad," Marc replied, and his father looked at him with a raised eyebrow.

"I beg your pardon?"

"You've always been disappointed, Dad. Doesn't matter what I did, it never meant anything to you. I breezed through school, got all those awards, but you never bothered to look away from the TV or the paper long enough to care. You made it clear that the only thing you wanted from me was to get through college, get a job and keep quiet. I had to be a good, black son who wouldn't embarrass you," Marc said, emotions surging through him as he stood tall under his father's scrutiny. "If I didn't—if I stood out *at all*—I was going to be a failure in your eyes. You never cared about what *I* wanted."

"What are you *talking* about? What did you even *want*, Marcus?" Jason asked, laughing at the questions, but Marc did not smile back.

"I don't *know*, you asshole!" Marc yelled, clenching his fists. "I never got the chance to know! You just told me to keep my head down and choose something reasonable for a major, something that will get me a job. I never got to explore, to figure myself out, I never got to realize what I wanted until it was too late! I was all the way through college and I had no fucking clue what I actually wanted to do with my life, and you were expecting me to grow up and be an adult and have a job right out the gate!"

"I am *so* sorry, Marcus, but are you *listening* to yourself?" Jason shouted back, meeting his son head-on. "What you're saying is *ridiculous*. Of *course*, I expect you to grow up and be an adult. You're twenty-six years old! I gave you this—"

"*Yeah*, Dad, you gave me this," Marc shouted over him, throwing out his hand and slamming it into the stand holding his DVD collection and sending it to the floor. "You're the one who never let me find out who I am, who gave me a quarter-life crisis, and then looks down on me because I'm not perfect. Thanks for the *gift*, dad!"

"You ungrateful little…" Jason muttered, perfectly content with beating sense into his son, but his wife stood between them and fanned out her arm.

"Don't you dare, Jason," she warned, turning to look at Marc over her shoulder. "Marcus, we're just here to help."

"You know who helped?" Marc said, laughing in dismay

before looking back at his parents. "*Kara*. When I was with her, I was *me*; I wasn't Jason Wright's son. I wasn't a chemistry student, which I only *started* because you told me to get a real career. She brought out the real me, the one who actually wanted things, who wanted to *do* something, who was more than just another person sleepwalking through life."

"And now she's dead," Marc said, turning away from his parents and shoving his hands in his pockets. Once he did, he felt the sheet of paper he had put there that morning, and the absurdity made him smile. The only reason he had returned to his apartment was to get enough Escape for one last trip, but it had been in his pocket the entire time. Letting the smile fade away, Marc realized what he truly wanted. "And she took the real me with her."

"Marcus, that's enough," his mother commented, her stern tone reminding Marc of when he had been caught drinking on his seventeenth birthday, and he turned to look at her one last time. "You're hurting and you're lashing out, but enough is enough. We cannot help you if you don't admit that you have a problem."

"Enough *is* enough, Mom. I *do* have a problem." Marc lowered his head and walked to the doorway, trying to hide the tears threatening to undermine him. "But none of you can help me. Escape can't help me. The only person who can help me is dead."

"We're here, Marcus, and we can help you if you let us," Lewis said, speaking up for the first time since Marc's parents had started talking, and it was enough cause for Marc to face him. Standing there by the television with DVDs scattered around his feet, he seemed ridiculous. Marc wanted to hate Lewis, wanted to yell and hurl things at him—blame him for everything from Kara's death to using his parents like this—but Marc could see the pain in his eyes. For all his betrayals, Marc could see that Lewis was trying to bring him back from the edge.

Unfortunately, Marc went over the edge the second Kara jumped from his rooftop.

"I know you want to help, Lewis," Marc admitted, but he still turned away. "But I don't want you to."

"I'm not going to let you leave," Travis said as he barred Marc's path, and Marc had to wonder why. From the very beginning, Travis had a made a point of hating him, but even *he* was trying to help Marc. It was enough for a tear to fall from Marc's eyes, but Travis could not stop him.

"I'm not asking, dude," Marc said, confusing Travis for a brief moment before he slammed a fist into the man's gut, doubling him over and forcing the air from his lungs. With no mercy, Marc raised his knee into Travis' crotch and pulled back on his shoulders, which was more than enough for the man to crumple to the floor. His audience was so shocked that Marc had enough time to jump into the kitchen and grab a butcher knife from the wooden block by his stove, startling Ariana into falling and putting her back to the refrigerator.

"Sorry, hosscat, didn't mean to scare you," Marc said, backing away from her and waving the knife at the rest of his friends and family. "Intervention's over. Go home. No one is going to follow me."

"Marcus, no, stop it," his mother pleaded, tears in her eyes, but Marc could see the anger coming from his father. Just as he broke eye contact, Marc saw Reggie rising from his place on the couch. Slowly, his friend made his way past Marc's parents, past the scattered DVDs, and then came to a stop by the bar counter.

"Don't go," Reggie said, straight to the point, and Marc's will almost broke. Even though he didn't say anything and didn't show any outward sign, Marc could tell that Reggie understood. He knew what Marc intended, even though he had only made the decision seconds ago. In that moment, Reggie had succeeded where the rest did not; for that split-second, Marc did not feel alone.

"I have to," Marc said, backing away to the door, and he

watched as Reggie lowered his head and sat on the back of the couch, defeated. Marc did not want to hurt him like that—did not know he *could* hurt him like that—but he was tired of fighting. Marc could not stand another minute of this, so when he got to the door, he opened it and passed through the threshold, holding a knife to keep his loved ones at bay.

Within a few seconds of letting the door close, Marc turned his knife so it was pressed against his arm, hiding it in the sleeve of his sweatshirt, and rushed over to the elevator. As it took far too long for it to get to his floor, Marc thought about how poetic it would be to go to the roof and jump like Kara, but he realized it would be too easy. Someone like him deserved to suffer and, once the door finally opened, Marc passed through and pressed the button for the lobby, anxiously waiting for it to close.

Once it did, Marc brought out the Escape in his pocket and looked at the remaining doses. As he finished counting out the infinity symbols, Marc realized there was a camera recording him from the corner of the elevator, but he shrugged away the consequences when he realized it did not matter. With fifteen little squares in his hand, Marc knew his plan would work. Once he had gotten far enough from his friends and family, he would take all of them at once, and an elevator recording would mean nothing.

Either the Escape would kill him, or the real world would find a way.

CHAPTER 10

COGNITIVE DISSONANCE

J.eremy looked to his right along the sand of the arena and saw a Mongol warrior screaming his heart out— all the more appropriate for the pulsing heart in his hand—and for a moment Jeremy wondered why he had imagined it. When the warrior took the heart in his hand and tore a solid chunk of flesh off with his teeth and spat it out in a spray of blood, Jeremy was not surprised. He was bored by the man's antics, by the way he pumped his chest or spun his sword around in complicated, dangerous movements no sane man would attempt. When Jeremy tried to improvise and allowed a white tiger to pounce on the warrior from behind and clamp powerful jaws around the meat of his shoulder, he thought it might make it more interesting.

It just felt hollow.

"Jeremy!" an irritated voice broke through, and Jeremy allowed the desert arena to fall away so the real world of Mr. Garvey's classroom could take its place. Turning to his left, Jeremy saw his teacher standing above him, one hand on his hip and the other on Jeremy's desk.

"Yeah, what do you want?" Jeremy asked, forgetting his place, and Garvey balked at his tone.

"What do I..." he muttered, stunned for a few seconds, but then Garvey remembered he was in a position of authority and cleared his throat. "Jeremy, you've been staring at that wall for five minutes. I called your name four times and you would *not* stop staring. What's so interesting about those cinder blocks, Jeremy?"

"I dunno, blank canvas?" he said, sniffing loudly and crossing his arms. Once he let out a deep breath, Jeremy yawned at his teacher. "Why are you still looking at me?"

"Do you not understand how disrespectful you're being, Jeremy?" Garvey asked, stepping back and waving his hand over Jeremy's classmates. "Not just to me, but to your class? You're acting like you're doing us a *favor* by being here."

"I'm pretty sure these guys don't give a shit if I stare at a wall, Garvey." A hush fell over his classmates as his teacher blinked in shock.

"Jeremy, mind your language," he said, whatever authority he had absent from his voice. "You cannot speak like that in school."

"Why not? First Amendment, right? You teach history, you should know that," Jeremy said, letting the cinder blocks of the wall turn into windows to other worlds. It was almost like watching a dozen different channels, but Jeremy knew he would lose his patience soon. However, for the moment it distracted him, and he did not notice his teacher walking up to him in anger.

"I know what the First Amendment is, Mister, but you are walking a very dangerous line right here. If you keep up this behavior, I'll have to send you to the principal's office," Garvey threatened, but Jeremy just laughed in his face.

"Oh, God, *please* do that. Send one of your best students to the principal's office because you're such an awful teacher that you can't keep our interest for five minutes," he said, causing Garvey to retreat to the backboard and set his hand against his chest.

"Jeremy, *what* has gotten into you?" he asked, and Jeremy almost wanted to stick out his tongue and show the four, blurred infinity symbols. Deciding that was too much, Jeremy just shrugged and scratched his nose.

"Pair of brass balls, Garvey," Shriver said from the other side of the room, and it made Jeremy turn to him in annoyance. Once he did, Jeremy noticed that every student was staring at him, including Allison. She wasn't *his* Allison, but it still made his heart drop into his stomach when Jeremy saw her watching him. He only broke eye contact because Garvey threw his hand out and pointed at Shriver with a knobby finger.

"Watch it, Barry, you don't want to get in trouble, too," Garvey said, breathing in deep and puffing out his chest before turning back to Jeremy. "Jeremy, you need to stop—"

"Or what, Garvey?" Jeremy interrupted, closing the windows to his other worlds and getting out of his seat. The world shifted around on him, becoming a dozen different fantasies and giving Garvey another identity every time, but eventually he settled on a reality where his teacher had become an oversized koala bear. "What are you going to do if I don't stop?"

"I can give you detention, young man," he said, but that only made Jeremy snort with laughter.

"God, Garvey, like I care! Do you know what I'd be doing if I wasn't in detention? Sitting around doing nothing!" he shouted, supporting himself by leaning on his desk. "It's not like I ever do your homework anyway, or any of the homework in my other classes. That paper I turned in two days ago? Plagiarized the whole thing."

"Jeremy! How could you?" Garvey sounded like he was actually hurt, but Jeremy just waved it off before sitting back in his chair and grabbing his pencil.

"*Because I can get away with it*. Because even if you caught it, you're not going to touch me because I'm a congresswoman's kid," he said, pressing the pencil against his notepad so hard that it broke off the tip. Once he did that, Jeremy tossed it at the trash can by the door and shrugged when he missed and it fell to the floor. "Just the way the world works."

"That's not how the world works, Jeremy, and your actions have consequences no matter who your parents are," Garvey said as he walked up to Jeremy and motioned for him to stand up. "Get up. You're going to the principal's office."

"Ooh, scary..." Jeremy kept looking at his notepad, but Garvey ripped it away from him and flung it at the wall behind him, which made Jeremy look up in alarm. "Hey!"

"*Hey, yourself,* Jeremy. Now get up, gather your things," Garvey said, waiting for Jeremy to put his book in his backpack, and he only stepped back once Jeremy was standing. "We're going. Now."

"You can't do this," Jeremy replied, but Garvey only knelt down and picked up the notepad before walking back over and placing it in the open compartment of his bag.

"On the contrary, Jeremy, I'm your *teacher* and you are being disruptive in my classroom. I am going to escort you to the principal's office, and you'll be lucky if you end up getting suspended," he explained, zipping up Jeremy's backpack before looking him in the eye. "You're not *untouchable*. You're just a *kid*, and you need to respect your elders."

"Mr. Garvey—"

"*Move. Now,*" Garvey commanded as he walked over to the door and held it open for Jeremy. As he waited for his insolent student, Garvey looked back at his students with a sigh. "While I'm gone, look over chapter ten. There will be a pop quiz about what you read last night."

"What, but…" Shriver complained, but one look from their teacher was enough to silence him.

"I'm not hearing it, Barry. Now you," he said while turning back to Jeremy, who was standing next to him. "Get a move on."

"Fine," Jeremy grumbled, holding onto the shoulder straps of his backpack with each hand. As he walked through the hallway, he replaced the walls with magnificent paintings of magical warfare, but he did not stay in his fantasy long before Garvey was walking beside him.

"This is disappointing, Jeremy," he said, not bothering to make eye contact. Jeremy resented the tone and the very fact that he was being escorted to the principal's office, so he tried to figure out a suitable punishment for his teacher. After five or six changes, however, Jeremy realized they were not satisfying at all, that it did not punish Garvey. It was all in his head and—because of that—there was no true revenge to be had.

"You and me both, Mr. Garvey," Jeremy admitted, choosing to let the real world dominate his perception. They walked in silence for a few moments, making their way through the prison-like hallways, but eventually Garvey cleared his throat.

"You're a good kid, Jeremy. You're smart. You know what you're talking about, and until recently, you never made any trouble," he said, sighing through the words. "You don't need to act out like this."

"I'm not... acting out," Jeremy replied, seeing the office come into view once they rounded a corner. "I... never mind."

"If you need someone to talk to, Jeremy, we have Mrs. Kensworth, your guidance counselor. You can even talk to me if you're really desperate. I know I'm no first choice, but that might be why I understand," Garvey said, causing Jeremy to look at him skeptically. "I think I know what you're going through."

"No offense, Mr. Garvey, but you have *no* idea," Jeremy said, drawing a laugh from Garvey, and it was obvious his teacher did not believe him. Smiling, Garvey shook his head in dismay until they were just outside of the school office, and he only stopped when he put his hand on the door handle and looked back at Jeremy.

"Oh, Jeremy, we all thought *that* at one point. I think you'd be surprised, though. I know what it's like to be the *odd man out*," Garvey said as he opened the door, and Jeremy almost wanted to berate him further.

"Yeah, I'm sure you got sent to the principal's office a lot," Jeremy muttered, and he could tell from Garvey's silence that his sarcasm was deserved.

"I—well... no, I didn't," Garvey admitted, and his attempt at conversation had to be abandoned. After waving at the receptionist on the phone, Garvey led Jeremy through the office, past guidance counselors and administrators, and eventually came to a stop at the last door, knocking three times and waiting.

"Yes, who is it?" an irritated man said from the other side, and Garvey took it as permission to open the door halfway. "Oh, Clint, what's going on?"

"I have a troublesome student here, thought you could have a chat with him," Garvey said, waiting a moment before nodding and then pushing the door open. Once it swung open, Jeremy was able to see the balding man with a red beard sitting behind the desk.

"And who is this, Mr. Garvey?" the principal asked while crossing his hands over his desk, and Jeremy felt Garvey's hand guiding him into one of the cushioned seats. Angry at the touch, Jeremy violently shrugged off his hand, but he made his way to the chair and sat down, trying to avoid eye contact with the principal.

"This is Jeremy Stafford, Principal Hendrick. A good student, but he was being disruptive in my classro—"

"Stafford?" Hendrick interrupted, and Garvey stopped to awkwardly look at his boss. "As in Lynn Stafford?"

"Uh, yes, sir, Lynn Stafford is Jeremy's mother," he said, standing up in alarm as Hendrick sat back in his chair.

"Ah, well, I see," Hendrick stammered, new beads of sweat falling and collecting at his brow. Although the principal tried to keep his poise and twirled a pen in his hands, Jeremy could see the effect of his family name. He could almost smell his mother's influence in the air.

"He spoke disrespectfully toward me, cursed, and talked back to me even when I warned him to stop," Garvey explained, but Hendrick did not turn to Jeremy with a stern expression. After catching his breath and considering the situation, the principal turned back to Jeremy and reclaimed some sense of authority.

"Well, Jeremy, what do you have to say for yourself? Did you speak up against Mr. Garvey?" he asked, twirling the pen nervously, and Jeremy felt bad for both of these men. Garvey was trapped with disrespectful students who would not listen, and Hendrick was held hostage by Jeremy's connection to his mother, a woman he despised most of the time. He couldn't let them suffer like this.

"I did, Principal Hendrick. I've been having a rough time lately," Jeremy admitted, turning to look at the window so he could make up a lie without any distractions. "My… dad is having another kid. I don't know… I just—It's complicated. I'm sorry I acted out."

"That does sound complicated, Jeremy. I understand. That can be tough," Hendrick commented, nodding even though Jeremy was not watching. "So you talked back to Mr. Garvey because you were upset, huh?"

"Something like that," Jeremy muttered, staring out the window and envisioning a massive homage to the Tower of Pisa out of precious stones and swords, just to do it. It was as pretty as Jeremy could imagine it, but it felt as useless as this conversation, so he let it crash to the ground and shatter into nothingness.

"Well, if you need someone to talk to about it, Mrs. Kensworth can—"

"I have a therapist," Jeremy interjected, putting his hands in his pockets and shrugging. "I just need to deal with it on my own."

"Hmm, well, if you change your mind, our doors are always open," Hendrick said, setting down his pen and breathing in. "So from now on, do you think you can behave in Mr. Garvey's classroom?"

"Dan—" Garvey started, hesitating when his boss nervously glanced at him, "Principal Hendrick, I think we should consider giving him detention and speaking to his mother…"

"I don't see why, Mr. Garvey," Hendrick said, turning back to face Jeremy. "For something like this—in light of his home situation—I think we can make an exception for Jeremy here. Provided that he does not make any more scenes, of course. Do you think you can help with that, Jeremy?"

"I…" Garvey muttered, but eventually he surrendered and folded his hands in front of him, his willpower emptying out of him in seconds. Jeremy felt bad for Garvey and how the principal had undermined him, and it was only made worse when he realized they had more in common than he had thought. Garvey was being pushed around by a bully, forced to deal with unforgiving, ungrateful and miserable little teenagers who did not respect him in the slightest.

It was almost like Jeremy was seeing his own future.

"Do you think you can behave in class, Jeremy?" Hendrick repeated, and Jeremy turned back to him with a nod. In his mind, he resolved that he would not be just another miserable victim, but he would play the part for now.

"I'll try to do better, Principal Hendrick. I promise."

When the final bell rang, Jeremy picked up his bag and climbed out of his seat just like every other student in his class. Conversations exploded, the teacher protested and reminded them of homework, but it was all just noise to Jeremy. None of their words mattered; none of *them* mattered. Almost none of his classmates would ever amount to anything—would ever be anyone worthwhile—and Jeremy was starting to realize he was going to end up the same way. In his chaotic fantasies, Jeremy always had a position of power, but it was all just surface decoration. When it came to the real world, his mother was the only reason he wasn't at the bottom of the food chain.

It only made Jeremy more frustrated.

Pushing his way past slower students—moving inches at a time when he could not—Jeremy was having a difficult time choking down his rage. They moved like cattle, just meat for the slaughterhouse, and he was trapped with them. The thought manifested itself because of the Escape in his system and Jeremy was soon surrounded by the smell of bloody carcasses and rotting flesh, the sounds of dying animals resonating through him.

"Shut up!" Jeremy pushed his way past a small heifer, and he only remembered that he was in public after moving to the next flight of stairs, where he let the real world filter back in to show a chubby girl staring at him in disbelief. Faltering only for the moment, Jeremy turned away from her and continued down the stairs, sinking further and further into himself as he went. He thought he heard the girl complaining, but her opinion was worthless anyway.

Finally making it to the front door, Jeremy walked into the winter air and breathed in deep, feeling the cold take the fire from his lungs. It was refreshing after such a long day; just what Jeremy needed to get past his anger. Once he calmed down, Jeremy started walking to the lot for the buses, but he slowed down once he saw Allison sitting on a bench.

She was wearing different clothes than earlier in the day, her hair was tied back and she did not have anything with her, which were the only reasons Jeremy slowed down at all. Knowing there was still Escape in his system, Jeremy had to wonder if he was imagining her or just imagining the world change around her, but he could not tell. His subconscious had taken control, lately, and he did not know whether he could trust his own eyes. When Allison turned and noticed Jeremy, his breath caught in his throat, but then she raised her hand and smiled like nothing was wrong. It was simple—nothing but a gesture—but it meant more than that to Jeremy.

In his addled state, it made him think it was *his* Allison.

"Hey, what's up?" Jeremy asked while drawing closer to the girl, and he did not notice her body language as she turned. He did not see the confusion.

"Not much, Jeremy," Allison said, almost looking around for

KEVIN KAUFMANN

an escape. "Are you okay?"

"Yeah, I'm fine, just a long day," he said, sitting down next to her and causing Allison to scoot back, which he did not notice. As soon as he had thought it could be his Allison, his mind filled in the gaps, making her seem more like the girl in his fantasies. When she scooted back and put distance between them, Jeremy's mind just showed her in the process of getting more comfortable.

"You do look tired, Jeremy," she said, and Jeremy saw Allison tilt her head and smile at him. "What was that with Mr. Garvey today? Did he give you a bad grade or something?"

"Him? No, there's nothing wrong with him. I just don't feel like caring anymore. You understand," Jeremy said, oblivious to how little Allison understood him. "I spend every day with these people, and I get to see how much they don't matter."

"How much they don't matter? Jeremy, where is this coming from?" she asked, and that was when Jeremy finally realized that this was not *his* Allison. His Allison would have agreed, joked around; she would have asked him to create something from his mind. She would already know the answers to these questions.

Now, looking at her and seeing the hallucination fall away, Jeremy realized that he was speaking to the actual girl of his dreams.

"I—I don't know," Jeremy said, losing confidence by the second, but he couldn't just leave. When he had first thought it was his Allison, Jeremy had not worried at all and had not given his behavior a second thought. Seeing the real Allison looking at him with concern, he realized that he could try; he could at least *attempt* being a real person. "It's just one of those things. Like watching ants in an ant farm."

"You think people are like ants?" she asked, and Jeremy had to shrug and break eye contact.

"They're… well, no. It's just similar. There are all the ants who work hard every day, building tunnels to nowhere, and I guess that most of those ants don't know they're wasting time.

They don't know that their entire lives are just little tunnels of sand which mean nothing but… it all means nothing, really. And they'll never know," Jeremy said, stumbling through his explanation and shaking from a mixture of cold and nervousness.

"Okay, I think I get it," Allison said, rubbing her hands together to keep warm. "So most of the ants are, like, basically wasting their time. And you think that people—most of the people you know—are like those ants. I guess that's *kinda* true," she admitted, looking to Jeremy uneasily. "It's pretty dark, but I can see it. So you think you're, like, one of the king ants or something?"

"I… well, ant colonies don't have kings," Jeremy said, unable to stop himself from correcting her. As he thought about the question, Jeremy realized that this real Allison was losing her appeal, but he tried to push the thought out of his head. Turning to face her, Jeremy shook his head. "But no, I'm not part of it. I'm one of the humans who *watch* the ant farm."

"Oh, so you think you're better than regular people," Allison commented, and Jeremy could see her looking down on him. "I guess you would, wouldn't you?"

"It's not that I'm better, I'm… I'm just outside the system. I'm an ant looking at you from outside the glass," he said, realizing that he was being more honest than he had intended. After today, seeing his mother's power at work, he had his doubts about being superior. That thought led to another, caused him to think about her second statement, and Jeremy turned back to face Allison with a furrowed brow. "And wait, what was the *you would, wouldn't you* for?"

"Oh, well, you know," Allison said, waiting for him to supply his own answer, but she sighed and put her hands between her thighs. "Because of your mom, right? You get to throw around her name and nobody will touch you. Like Mr. Garvey, today. *I* couldn't get away with what you did."

"I… didn't get away with it," Jeremy said, feeling guilty as he looked away, but then he realized he did not like the assumption, even if it was true. Turning back to Allison, Jeremy gave a firm shake of his head. "Trust me, my mom doesn't make me feel better than everyone. Just the opposite, actually."

"She seems to baby you in those speeches, though," Allison replied, and Jeremy was filled with all kinds of animosity. He was not surprised about the anger toward his mother for putting him in that position, but he was starting to feel frustrated with Allison, as well. The real version of his dream girl—once she started speaking—was nothing like the girl who shared his fantasies. That Allison was proud, strong, smart, compassionate and interesting and everything he wanted. This one was shallow and her intelligence left much to be desired. She was nice enough to talk to Jeremy, but there was no way to reconcile this girl and the Allison in his head.

The real Allison was just *too* real.

"It's all just talk. It's all just an illusion," Jeremy muttered, more to himself than to the girl beside him, but Allison replied while he picked up his things and prepared to leave.

"Yeah, must be rough to have a famous mom. At least you get out of problems with teachers." She smiled at him with the repetition, and Jeremy forced himself to smile back at her. She had been nice, so he could at least return the favor.

"Allison! What the hell are you doing talking to that loser?" Shriver's voice interrupted them, and Jeremy turned to the entrance to see Shriver approaching with two of his interchangeable friends, Roger walking beside them.

"Thanks for talking with me, Allison. Sorry to be so weird." Jeremy rushed through his goodbyes, and he was walking away from the bench and to the buses before Allison responded at all.

"Bye, Jeremy. Hope you feel better," she said after him, and Jeremy almost wished he could still like her. Escape had ruined his expectations, but the girl really *was* nice. He was just about to feel good about talking to her when Shriver ruined any chance of that.

"Oh, c'mon, Jeremy, come back!" he shouted, and Jeremy turned to find Shriver beckoning for him to come closer. "We ain't gonna bite! You don't have to stop talking to Allison just because of *us!*"

"Dude, just let him go," Roger said, holding just one strap of his bag as he stood next to his girlfriend. Jeremy had already turned back around to walk away, but he stopped once he heard Roger continue. "The guy has issues."

"Yeah, he does, *mommy* issues," Shriver replied, letting out a laugh that shook Jeremy to the core. "Guy grows up with a senator mom and he gets to act like he's better than everyone."

"She's not a senator and it's not like that," Allison entered the conversation, and Jeremy's stomach flipped. Before he could turn—before he could stop her—she told them what Jeremy had said in confidence. "He feels like he doesn't belong. Like he's watching all of us get to have normal lives."

"Of course, he doesn't *belong!*" Shriver said, propping himself up on his shorter friend's shoulder. "He's Jeremy fucking Stafford. Even if he wasn't a pretentious, fat, little piece of shit, he's practically autistic. The guy is too weird to live."

"Too far, man," Roger said, but Jeremy's blood was already boiling. He had already turned—already started walking back—and he focused on the bully who had tormented him for two years.

"Too far? Fuck that noise. That little brat made me fail a pop quiz today just because he wanted to make fun of the teacher," Shriver said, scoffing at Roger's comment.

"It was *easy*, Barry. If you had read the chapter for homework, you would have been fine," Allison said, but Shriver grabbed his crotch and pulled up.

"*That's* what I think of reading. Who fucking reads anymore except pussies like Jeremy *my mom's the president* Stafford," Shriver said, nudging his friend with his elbow and high-fiving the other, but eventually he noticed Jeremy walking back. Turning with a smile on his face, Shriver pointed at Jeremy and laughed. "Hey, look who the fuck it is! Did you miss your bus, Jeremy?"

"I didn't miss anything, Shriver," Jeremy said under his breath, his fingers curling into fists, and he let the Escape build off his anger. The sky cracked open, blood-red crags burst out of the ground, lightning crackled around them, but their surroundings were not the only thing that changed.

Shriver had become an ogre with skulls around his neck, his unmentionables barely covered by a ragged loincloth. Next to him were two sniveling and screeching trolls—their limbs grossly extended and their mouths permanently held open—hunched-over and reminding Jeremy of hyenas. Even Roger changed, becoming a gigantic warrior in black armor, and Allison was covered in yet another pink gown, but Jeremy did not care about either of them. It was all there to fill in the gaps and complete the illusion.

Because in his mind, Jeremy had turned into a muscular barbarian, his only goal to beat his opponents into a bloody, red pulp.

"Walking pretty hard there, Jeremy," the ogre murmured, punctuating it with a belch, but Jeremy did not care. He just stomped forward, the links of his chain metal rattling against armor. When he was within a few yards of the ogre, Jeremy dropped his bag onto the ground, which cracked from the sudden impact. "Hey, you dropped something."

"I'll drop *you*," Jeremy promised, closing the remaining distance in a short run, leaping into the air and aiming to slam his hand into the ogre's ugly, fat face.

"Whoa, what the fuck?" the ogre said, his voice mixing with his real-world counterpart, but Shriver sprung into action and shoved Jeremy's chest with both hands, sending him back to the ground and causing Jeremy to stagger and then fall. He had not expected Shriver to push him back like that, but the sight of the ogre looking down at him was enough for him to climb back to his feet. "*What* are you *doing?*"

"I'm not taking it anymore, Shriver!" Jeremy shouted, his voice deep and intimidating in his fantasy. Sweeping his hand across his body and lightning spreading through the air around him, Jeremy believed he would win. "I'm going to kick your ass, and you're going to leave me alone!"

"Oh my god, holy shit," the ogre said, backing away in fear, but that was just the Escape trying to compensate. After a few breaths, the ogre launched into raucous laughter, the trolls mimicking him, and Jeremy was left standing there confused. Eventually, once the ogre wiped a tear from his eye, he looked back up at Jeremy with a sigh. "Oh, man, you can walk away now and there won't be any hard feelings. Jesus, that was good."

"It's not a fucking *joke!*" Jeremy screamed, several volcanoes sending magma into the air around them in sympathy for his cause. "I'm fucking tired of this! I'm tired of you assholes getting to do what you want and making fun of me! I'm tired of seeing you *win!*"

"One day—just *one* day—I want you to lose. To feel like I feel," he concluded, clenching his fists tighter, but the real world filtered in for a moment and Jeremy saw Shriver walking up to him with his friends on each flank. The moment was gone quickly—the ogres and trolls took their place after a second—but it shook Jeremy's confidence.

"If you want to fight, loser, we can fight, but you're not going to win. You're pudgy, small, and any *one* of us can *fuck* you up," the ogre said, leaning down to tower over Jeremy. "You're fucking worthless, dude, and your mom isn't here to save you."

"Shriver, stop," Roger said from the side, but the ogre shook his head and brought it closer to Jeremy's face.

"I didn't start it, Rog. Jeremy just needs to remember who he is. He needs to remember he's a weakling and a coward, and this will be over. It won't even be worth talking about," Shriver said, and Jeremy could not take anymore. Throwing his head forward, Jeremy intended to break Shriver's nose, but between the Escape and his lack of experience, he missed completely and met foreheads with his bully. It dazed him and forced him back, but Shriver spent most of his extracurricular time getting tackled by athletes, so he recovered quickly.

It was not the fight Jeremy wanted.

"Fucking asshole," Shriver said as he planted his fist deep in Jeremy's gut and ripped the fantasy away from him. As Jeremy stepped back and pain spread through his torso, he could only see the real world. Just as he let another fantasy take its place—back to his samurai themes—one of Shriver's friends stepped in and hit Jeremy with a right hook which sent him to the floor in a heap. One of his teeth was knocked loose by the strike and blood sprayed out of his mouth once he landed, but Jeremy did not have time to focus on the red spray pattern in front of him.

"Come on, rich fucker," Shriver said as he picked Jeremy up easily, setting him on his feet just in time for his friends to hold each of Jeremy's arms. Barely able to think through the pain, Jeremy was forced back into the real world and his real body. Once he was secured, Shriver aimed blow after blow into Jeremy's ribs, his fat rippling with each strike. "Oh, he's fucking *soft*."

"Shriver, stop it, *now*," Roger commanded as he grabbed Shriver's shoulder, but the bully shrugged it off and pointed to Allison.

"You take her home, how about that, Rog?" he asked, and Jeremy's world shifted again, showing the underbelly of some advanced city. Shriver turned into a fat, bald, brute without a shirt, his arms and legs covered in a rudimentary exoskeleton. Jeremy did not have the strength to look at the bullies holding him, but he looked at Roger and Allison, who were covered in form-fitting leather cat-suits, and he wondered if they would help him.

"Barry, he learned his lesson, alright?" Allison asked, her

eyes glowing with neon blue light, but when she turned back to Jeremy, her face was filled with disgust. "He's just special, is all."

"No, he's not," Shriver said, his childlike face stretching into a grin. "He's not special at all. He's just another sad, little, pathetic nerd who would be better off killing himself."

"No, I meant in the head—"

"I *know* what you meant, Allison," Shriver snapped, jerking his head to glare at her with beady, black eyes. With a cruel smile, he turned back to look straight at Jeremy. "But he's *not*. He's fucking weird—I'll give you that—but Jeremy *knows* who he is. He knows how the world works. Jeremy knows *what* he is, and he knows that it's *nothing*."

"Shriver, stop right now, or I'm going to—"

"Going to *what*, Rog?" Shriver asked, advancing on Roger so fast that Jeremy's mind turned him into a hybrid creature of snake and man. Leaning over Roger, who had reverted back to normal, Shriver's black tongue flickered in and out with interest. "You gonna rat on me? You gonna choose that fucking freak over one of your friends? Over one of your teammates?

"Barry, seriously, he's had enough," Roger said, faltering slightly, and that was enough for Shriver to think that he had won. Slithering back over to Jeremy and his cronies, Shriver cracked his knuckles and tilted his head from side to side.

"You and Allison go on ahead, Rog. Unless you want to watch, of course," he said before slamming his fist into Jeremy's jaw, and the pain was enough for the real world to come back entirely. Shriver continued like that for a while, every blow just shy of knocking Jeremy out, but eventually Jeremy heard a scuffle in front of him. He couldn't see through his left eye—it was already swelling shut—but when Shriver's cronies dropped him to the ground, Jeremy was able to see Roger dragging Shriver back.

"You can't do that, Barry!" Roger shouted, pulling Shriver away and their friends following them, but eventually Roger let go and let Shriver stand. The brute was fuming at him, but he stopped shy of throwing a punch and gestured for his friends to do the same just as Roger continued yelling. "What the fuck were you thinking?"

"I was *thinking* that little rich boy was getting the ass-kicking he deserved," Shriver argued, but Roger pointed back at Jeremy as he continued.

"Did you fucking forget, dude? His mom is in *Congress*. What do you think happens when a congresswoman's kid gets hurt, huh? You can kiss your fucking scholarships goodbye, that's what," Roger argued, Jeremy just barely understanding his words. He was bleeding from a few places, his ribs felt like they were broken and his eye was swollen shut, but what hurt most was his pride.

Even though he had wanted to win—even though he had believed in himself—reality had triumphed.

"Fuck, well… shit, what am I supposed to do about it now?" Shriver asked, and there were hushed whispers after that. Jeremy couldn't care what they were saying and didn't want to know what they intended. All he wanted was for the pain to stop and for the tears to stop flowing. He was weak, worthless—a constant source of shame—and he didn't even have the willpower to stop crying. This, Jeremy knew, was how it felt to be a failure.

"Hey, uh, Jeremy," Shriver's voice came from above him, and Jeremy lifted his head to see his bully looking at him with his hands in his pockets. "I got carried away there and… well, shit, man, I'm sorry."

"You're *sorry*?" Jeremy asked, unable to comprehend the sheer gall of his classmate.

"Yeah, man, and I'm sorry about all the name-calling and bullying. It wasn't right. I got some things to work on," Shriver continued, and Jeremy shook his head in dismay. This was more than just ridiculous; it was impossible. For a moment, he thought it might be the Escape in his head again, but when he stood up and looked back at Shriver's face—saw the sheepishness and the false compassion—he realized what was going on.

"You just don't want me to tell my mom," Jeremy stated, his words warped by the fat lip Shriver had given him. Seeing the reaction on the bully's face, he knew he was right, and Jeremy decided that he could compensate for his weakness from before. "Why *shouldn't* I?"

"Look, Jeremy," Shriver started, his jowls quivering as he panicked, but that was all Jeremy needed to see. With just that look of fear on Shriver's face, he was satisfied, and so he put up his hand and shook his head.

"Don't worry, asshole," Jeremy said, turning around and grabbing his bag. "I'm not going to tell her."

"Thanks, man, really." Shriver sighed in relief, but Jeremy was already walking away. "Though, I mean, why not?"

"Barry!" Allison whispered, but Jeremy wasn't offended. He turned back around, waited for them to acknowledge him, and then spat blood out onto the concrete. After breathing in and trying to ignore the pain in his ribs, Jeremy shrugged.

"This was *my* fight, not hers. I won't tell anyone," he said before turning back around and cradling his ribs. As he walked away from his bullies and tried to salvage some dignity, they could not see the tears that fell no matter how much he hated them; they could not hear Jeremy admit the truth. Giving voice to his pain, Jeremy's confession leaked out of him with no one to hear it.

"No one would care, anyway."

CHAPTER 11

WELL-DRESSED SAVAGES

ynn! My god, you look fantastic!" a heavyset man said as he pushed himself through the crowd, a female server barely escaping from his path. The server hovered there once the man in the oversized tuxedo noticed her existence and—already red in the face—he picked up one of the glasses of red wine on her tray before waving her off. Turning back to face Lynn, who was in a form-fitting white dress with silver etched into a floral design along her left side, the man drank half the glass before he staggered forward.

"Senator Bertrum, how good to see you! Though you need to stop flirting with me in front of your wife," Lynn replied, winking at the woman following behind the large man. Letting out a guffaw, the senator reached behind him, pawing at the woman's arm and finding her just out of reach. "Hello, Nancy."

"Lynn, this really is quite lovely," the woman replied, standing beside the senator and pretending she was not embarrassed by her husband's behavior. "You've outdone yourself."

"Yes, really quite nice, this place. With the streaming whats-its and the... the... oh hell, you know what I mean," Bertrum said before raising the glass to his lips, set on draining it all. Before he could, however, his wife grabbed his hand and pulled, forcing him to take just a sip.

"Hah, well, I'd love to take the credit," Lynn said, smiling as she noticed Mrs. Bertrum's attempt to stop her husband, "but Janice Pearson is the one responsible for organizing this benefit. She's been doing this a long time and I would be lost without her."

"Just words and lies, that one," Bertrum said, waving around his glass and somehow not sloshing it all over his suit. "You'd be just fine on your own, Lynn, and you know it. That stuffy woman has been associating with those angry mothers so long that it's rubbed off on her. Doesn't know how to throw a party without making everybody feel guilty about drinking."

"She *does* represent an organization against drunk driving, Senator," Lynn replied, trying to remain neutral in such a public place. "When raising money to protect children, we don't really *need* to be drinking, do we?"

"No, but it certainly helps!" Bertrum joked, emptying his wine glass before placing it on the tray of a passing server. After grabbing another—his wife only momentarily trying to stop him—he turned back to Lynn with a goofy smile. "Alcohol makes everyone a little bit looser, little bit more fun… a little bit more willing to sign *big, stinking checks.*"

"Honey, can you please—"

"Nancy, don't you worry about me, I know how to handle a little drinking and a little schmoozing," Bertrum talked over his wife, looking at the wine in his glass, and Lynn could see the senator's mind working slowly as he tried to focus on the wine. When he lowered the glass, he looked at his wife with a warm smile. "See? I can stop. This one is just for looks."

"And the other ten?" Nancy asked, drawing a chuckle from the senator before he turned to Lynn.

"Well, those were for *me*," Bertrum said with a wink, setting his hand on Lynn's arm for a brief moment. "Very nice job so far, Lynn. We'll get you on the Senate floor soon enough, I think."

"Well, that's up to my constituents, isn't it?" Lynn asked, the senator chuckling softly at the remark before gathering his wife with his free arm.

"You just keep up that act, Stafford. You just keep up that act," he said, smiling as they walked past Lynn and to the next political figure a few feet behind her. Although she smelled the wine on his breath, Lynn knew that Bertrum could play the game and manipulate the system. That he approved of her meant quite a good deal; a man like Senator Bertrum would be a strong ally.

Breathing deep, Lynn took in her surroundings and tried to find other potential allies; she did not get dressed up in an uncomfortable, tight dress for nothing, after all. Still, it made her look elegant, distinguished, and that was what she needed. The glitz and glamour of it, the streaming lights hanging from corner to corner, the crystalline decorations scattered throughout the hall; all of it was there to dazzle and distract her guests and confuse them into making promises. For some, it was just to cement deals already in place. For others, it was to use free food and liquor and shiny baubles to make political alliances.

Spotting Janice Pearson speaking with two men she did not recognize, Lynn realized she might need to introduce herself.

"Janice, who are these dapper gentlemen?" Lynn asked once she was within speaking distance, and all three turned to face her. Lynn could see the murder in Janice's eyes—she clearly did not want Lynn there—but the men seemed to appreciate her company. The tall one, whose hairline was receding but was otherwise fit and healthy, looked up and down her body without hiding his interest, but Lynn pretended not to notice. She was so busy not noticing that she barely looked at the older, black man before he started speaking.

"Oh, Ms. Stafford, I was hoping to speak with you. My name is Bill Erwin, and next to me is my partner, Jordan Merrimont," the man said as he extended his hand, and Lynn brought up hers to meet it.

However, instead of shaking her hand, Erwin turned it over before leaning down and kissing the back of Lynn's hand. Momentarily stunned by the archaic act—and his moustache hair pricking her skin—Lynn only recovered her poise by the time he stood back up.

"A pleasure, Mr. Erwin," she said, but the man raised his palm and shook his head.

"Bill is just fine, Ms. Stafford."

"Only if you call me Lynn," she replied with a smile. At the familiarity, Erwin rose his glass to salute her.

"I think we can make that happen," he said before lowering his glass, leaving Lynn to turn to his associate and offer her hand.

"And Jordan, was it?" Lynn asked, the man stepping forward and—unlike his partner—shaking her hand.

"That's right, Ms. Stafford," he said, a little too eager, and once Merrimont let go of her hand, Lynn tilted her head and set a hand on her hip.

"You can use my first name, too," she said, but he just shook his head and swirled the wine in his glass.

"I think I prefer Ms. Stafford for now. Maybe once we get to know each other," Merrimont said, the smug smile on his face telling Lynn all she needed to know. Teasing him with a smile of her own, Lynn looked at him out of the corner of her eye even as she turned to Janice.

"I hope that's soon," Lynn said before making eye contact with Janice. "And just how do you know these gentlemen, Janice?"

"We've represented a few cases for the women at MADD, Ms. Stafford," Erwin answered for her, and Lynn turned away from her spiteful partner to face the short man. "Oh, I'm sorry, and you just told me to call you Lynn."

"I think I can forgive it just this once," she replied, grabbing a glass of red from a passing waiter. "And you said cases? And Jordan here is your partner?"

"They were responsible for the Anthony settlement, Stafford," Janice interrupted, and Lynn turned to face her with a smile. "They were able to prove negligence on the part of the school system, and because of these two, our classrooms are safer."

"Well, thank you for that, gentlemen," Lynn said, noticing the scowl on Janice's face as she took a sip of wine and turned back to the lawyers. "And you're certainly welcome to stay and enjoy the refreshments. Have you thought about donating?"

"Oh, more than that, Ms. Stafford," Merrimont said, drawing Lynn's gaze. "We were talking to Janice about representing the

Crenshaws for this whole Escape debacle. A nice, high-profile case would do a great deal to promote awareness to a new level."

"That would be fantastic, Jordan! I'm glad you want to help," Lynn said, false appreciation flowing through her words before she gave him a skeptical look. "But just who would you take to court? The police haven't said anything about catching the drug dealer."

"Oh, we can figure that out later," Erwin answered, waving away the details with his free hand. "Local law enforcement, the schools... whoever seems the most negligent in front of the camera. Honestly, we don't even need to win."

"Right, it's just... exposure," Merrimont added, delaying on the word just enough to make Lynn uncomfortable. "You pay us enough to cover the court fees, we get you more time with the news. We all win."

"Unless you succeed, and then whoever you take to court will suffer," Lynn said, crossing her free arm over her stomach and clutching her elbow. "And if you sue the city for this big payout, *everybody* suffers."

"Necessary collateral damage." Merrimont replied before draining the rest of his glass and swallowing it with a sigh. "Besides, in that speech of yours, you said everybody was at fault. Unless you've changed your tune?"

"That's... I think I understand," Lynn said, taking a sip of wine so she could stall. Once she considered the idea for a moment, she turned to Erwin and pursed her lips. "It's more about the message than it is the money."

"Exactly, Lynn, exactly," Erwin said, nodding with his glass before turning to his partner. "Though we have to pay for our beach property somehow!"

"Says you! I like the mountains," Merrimont said before looking at Lynn out the corner of his eye. "Big fan of skiing, and I'm always looking for someone to go with me."

"To each their own," Erwin said with a laugh, reaching

forward to clink glasses, but then realizing with alarm that Merrimont had an empty glass. "Oh, what are you doing, Jordan? Let's get you another drink so we can do this right."

"Excuse us, Janice, *Ms.* Stafford," Merrimont positively *oozed*, and they were swallowed up in the crowd within a few seconds. Giving them enough of a head start, Lynn kept her smile in place for a moment before turning to Janice.

"I'm sorry, Janice, what the hell was that?" Lynn asked, the smile faltering only slightly as she fumed beneath the surface.

"This is how it's *done*, Stafford," Janice said, crossing her arms and making her purple dress even frumpier. "You bait the news, you start a case, you build up support over the months and stir the pot for more controversy. As much as I hate to admit it, you got us off to a good start, but I can take it from here."

"Take it from here?" Lynn asked, biting her lip to keep herself from slapping the woman. "Janice, what do you think will happen if your lawyers seek damages from the city and win? The way we're manipulating this thing, they might be able to drum up enough sympathy to convince a jury."

"So? Then we have legal precedent, we can push legislation through and the Crenshaws would get a nice payday to make up for the loss of their son," Janice ran through the list of reasons, seemingly unable to comprehend the consequences.

"And if I am associated with a case against a city *in my own district*, Janice, how do you think that will reflect on my chances to win my next election?" Lynn asked, and from the way Janice smiled at her, she could tell that her partner had most definitely considered that possibility.

"That's not my problem, *or* the committee's problem, or Price's problem, or the Crenshaws' problem," Janice mused, looking back at Lynn with malice in her eyes. "Seems like your problem, Stafford."

"We're going to have a talk with Bill about this," Lynn replied, the smile disappearing from her face, but Janice gave a contented sigh before she followed after the lawyers.

"Oh, Stafford, it was *his* idea." Then she left Lynn with her thoughts.

In the space of one, small conversation, Lynn's night had turned from enjoyable into a political nightmare. When she had made her speech on Harmon's show, she had been speaking from the heart and outside reason or rational consideration for her career, but it had somehow worked. It had not taken long for Lynn's associate to abuse and twist it around, but she could accept it for the greater cause.

But now that greater cause had backed her into the corner.

Lynn stood there for a moment contemplating her next step, but then she noticed most of the people in attendance were slowly moving to the entrance, swarming and fighting to see what was going on. Only then did Lynn hear the shouts and the chants, and she followed the herd to the entrance, unable to hear the words. Once she was at the edge of the crowd, Lynn was finally able to understand what was happening and it only made her night worse.

"Stafford is just an opportunist! Just another political rat! She's raising money in there to fund her political career, not to wage a war on drugs!" a strong tenor yelled through a megaphone, and Lynn cursed under her breath. She didn't even need to hear what they had been saying beforehand; it all had the same meaning. It was something she should have expected, but she had been riding high on the feeling of doing something worthwhile and so they had caught her by surprise.

"Excuse me," Lynn said to the man in front of her as she lightly pushed him to the side. Once the man recognized her, he swept his arms in front of Lynn, setting off a domino effect among the attendees. Before long, Lynn had a clear path to the entrance, and she breathed deep before walking forward, her head held high. Seeming weak and backing down now would only give her opponents more credibility, so she pretended to be dignified, nodding at each guest along her way.

"Lynn Stafford is a sham, a political stooge! She doesn't care about kids, or even drugs! This is all just a—" a shout greeted her once she exited the building, but the voice fell silent as Lynn made her way down the steps and to the curb, coming to a stop just a few feet away from the line of protestors who had gathered just for her. There were signs plastered with slogans and pictures in some hands—none of them very pro-government—but many of the protestors were just there to yell and provide another body. Now, each one of them, ranging from idealistic teenagers to middle-aged perpetual adolescents, was staring at her in shock.

"This is all just a...?" Lynn asked, crossing her arms and waiting for the ringleader to come forward. After just a moment, a young man in his early twenties pushed through the picket line and stood three feet away from Lynn, a megaphone in his hand.

"You have a lot of nerve coming out here like this," he said, but Lynn only cocked her head to the side and met his angry gaze.

"It's a public street, sir, and I'm part of the public. Just like all of you," she said, gesturing her hand over the gathered crowd, "which is why you're allowed to protest... well, just what *are* you protesting? I'm seeing a lot of different signs. Reminds me of the Occupy movement..."

"We're protesting you and your opportunistic, bottom-feeding political agenda," the leader said, pointing at Lynn with the megaphone. "You're what's wrong with the system—another cog in the machine—and we're not going to stay silent!"

"What's your name?" Lynn asked, remaining calm and uncrossing her arms, instead folding them over her midsection and clasping her hands together. She hoped the less-hostile stance would change the atmosphere. "You seem to know me pretty well for someone I've never met."

"*My* name doesn't matter. None of *their* names matter," the man said, gesturing to his supporters. "We're the *American*

Fucking People and we're tired of seeing this gross misconduct!" Cheers rang up with the last statement—just like Lynn assumed they would—and she let them die down before responding.

"I'm tired of seeing gross misconduct too, *American People*," Lynn said, lifting her gaze and looking at each person in the crowd as she turned her head. "The political system is flawed—I admit it—and I can tell you that there are certainly individuals who have and will continue to abuse that system. Favors change hands, votes can be bought; there is a lot of external and internal pressure."

"But what I can tell you," Lynn said, stopping herself before she started naming names, "is that you are protesting the wrong thing. I understand that you're angry, *frustrated*, but this is one of the *good* causes. This is one of the issues that matters, that is not corrupted for some political agenda. This is an issue that affects us all."

"Lies!" the leader said, turning to his group of protestors and bringing up his megaphone. "Just more words to shove down our throats! Lynn Stafford is *not* an angel; she is *not* some crusader for good!"

"A week before she started to abuse the memory of a dead child, our *representative* was demonizing marijuana," he said before turning back to face Lynn, the megaphone still blasting his voice into the air. "Arguing and talking, that's all Lynn Stafford is good for. Leading us around the berry bush and introducing legislation we don't need!"

"Legislation that we don't need?" Lynn asked, doing her best to stay calm. "You think legislation that will prevent the death of children is something we don't need?"

"It's not about the children, you hack!" he shouted, bringing the megaphone away from his lips and waving at the crowd of politicians and representatives crowding the entrance to the building, his supporters cheering him on. "It's about *them!* It's about trading favors and making money and pacifying the masses! It's about making us think a good drug is as bad as heroin and making sure our prisons are full!"

"You think Escape is a *good* drug, then?" Lynn asked, dropping the nice pretense completely and scowling at the protestor. "You think a drug that led to the death of a child is *good?*"

"Why not? Have you ever taken it? Do you know how it feels?" he asked, smiling at her. "It's *harmless*, just like most drugs! Our bodies are *ours*, and you shouldn't limit *us* because you want to use the death of a kid to further your own career! As long as you're not an idiot about it, Escape or any other hallucinogen won't kill you."

"*As long as you're not an idiot?*" Lynn asked, bristling at the statement, and she could see this leader was already starting to lose support from the crowd behind him. "As long as you're not an idiot, you can take Escape, is that right? Since Thomas Crenshaw was an *idiot*, he deserved to die before he made it out of middle school."

"No, that's not—"

"As long as you're not an *idiot*, you get to take drugs that alter the world around you. As long as *you* are not an idiot, you can dose on Escape whenever you want, waste away your life however you want," Lynn continued, raising her voice so everyone could hear. "As long as *you* are not an idiot, the mothers and fathers who lose their children to people high on Escape are not your problem, because *you* weren't the idiot. Just because *some* idiot took Escape and got into a car and ran through a red light because he thought he was riding a flying chariot, just because *that* idiot killed a father or a mother and created an orphan, that doesn't really matter, because at least *you* weren't the idiot."

"That's not what I said, you—"

"When we make laws, young man, we don't make them for *just* idiots, we make them for everyone. We don't discriminate against *idiots*, because everyone is equal in the eyes of the law. And when there is a substance that can completely alter someone's perception—when that drug can fall into the hands of a *young boy*—there is a problem. A problem that we must address, even if it does not lead to legislation," Lynn said, shaking her head in disappointment.

"That's not what this is..." the man said, his confidence deserting him along with his supporters, and Lynn knew she was close.

"That *is* what this is, young man. This benefit is to raise awareness against a drug that has already claimed victims. This benefit is to prevent further pain and suffering. You are protesting a fundraiser to save children, I hope you realize that," Lynn explained, but her opponent was stubborn, unable to understand he had been defeated.

He was just a bit of an idiot, himself.

"You are using them all. This is all just political theater. You are abusing the memory of that kid," the leader said, pointing at her with the megaphone after every statement, but he did not get any further along his tirade.

"Please leave," a gentle voice came from Lynn's side, and she turned to find Daniel and Susan Crenshaw standing next to her, Daniel's arm wrapped around Susan's shoulders. Rubbing his wife's upper arm with his hand, Daniel looked like he was on the verge of tears. "Just go."

"She is *abusing* the memory of that kid—" the man shouted, but Daniel did not let him continue.

"That *kid*," he interrupted, gritting his teeth slightly, "was my son. That... *idiot*... was my boy Tommy, and the only one abusing his memory here is *you*. Please.... just leave."

"I—I'm sorry, sir, but she can't be allowed to keep going with this farce. This is ridiculous, it's terrible—"

"She's trying to help, you... you..." Susan said, losing her nerve before she could insult the man. Instead, she breathed deep and shook her head. "She wants to make it so parents like us... so that..."

"So that there won't *be* more parents like us," Daniel saved her, rubbing Susan's arm and consoling her. "Protest something that matters, protest something else, but don't protest against the memory of my son."

"I..." the man said, backing away, and when he turned to his supporters, he found them already scattered, walking away from him with their signs pointed to the ground. When the leader turned back, he found Lynn staring at him like he was a monster, and it was not much longer before he followed after his fellow protestors with his head hung low.

"Daniel," Lynn said, turning to face the parents, but Daniel shook his head slowly and tried to smile.

"You're doing a good thing, no matter what they say, Lynn. Thank you for what you're doing," he said, clinging to his wife, and Lynn realized that they were holding each other up. "Just... thank you. Thank you for caring."

"Daniel, Susan, it's not enough," Lynn said, surprising herself by meaning it, but Susan put up her hand.

"It is for us. You give us faith, Lynn," she said, sniffing back tears and trembling in her husband's arms. "And I think that's enough for us tonight. It's time for us to go home."

"Are you sure? There are still people inside who might—"

"No, we've lasted about as long as we could," Daniel said while walking past Lynn, pausing briefly to set his hand on her shoulder. "You take it from here, okay?"

"I will," Lynn promised, setting her hand on top of Daniel's, but the moment was over within just a few seconds, the grieving parents moving past her and down the sidewalk and leaving Lynn by herself in the street.

She looked after them for a while, emotions and thoughts clashing against each other with no clear victor, but eventually she turned to go back inside. Once she did, applause echoed through the air, and it took Lynn a moment to realize that the crowd gathered in the doorway had watched every moment and heard every word. Breaking into a smile and waving at her cheering audience, Lynn gave herself to the moment, to the satisfaction of her moral and political victories.

Because after what Janice had just told her, Lynn knew she would have to compromise one of them in the very near futur

"Lynn, you just keep on surprising me," Price said, and Lynn turned away from a departing philanthropist to find the stout senator looking at her in appreciation. "Every time I think I have you pegged—have you boxed in—you go and throw all my plans out the window. Hell, sometimes, I think you *believe* what you say."

"Maybe I do, Bill, maybe I do," Lynn said with a sigh, finding that most of her patrons had gone.

Serving staff were packing up and throwing away the remains of the benefit and the relatively-sober guests were carting off those who had too much to drink. Spotting Senator Bertrum and his wife, Lynn smiled once he saw that it was Nancy who was staggering and having a general problem with balance. However, it was all inconsequential; the man holding Lynn's fate in his hands was standing in front of her.

"Belief… almost as dangerous as pretending, you know that?" Price said, sitting down in a plastic chair and motioning for Lynn to take the seat next to her. "Both of them are pretty risky in this game, but you get hurt more if you care."

"I know, Bill," Lynn said as she joined him and set her elbow on the table, propping up her head. "And I've heard that you're planning to make me pay for it."

"Yeah, from who?" Price asked, tilting his head. "I only talked to Noel about *my* plan."

"Then it must have spread from him," Lynn said, too tired to feel anger. "Janice told me about the lawsuit."

"*What* lawsuit?" he asked, and Lynn realized Janice had been playing her.

"Janice told me you had suggested a lawsuit for the Crenshaws to seek damages against the City, which would have caught me between a rock and a hard place. *Is* that news to you?" Lynn watched the senator's face for any sign or hint of manipulation, but he seemed sincere when he shook his head and puffed out his cheeks.

"Yeah, not so sure about that one. It's not *bad*—we could work with it—but it would shoot you in the foot…" Price looked at Lynn and popped his jaw, but he scoffed once he realized the situation. "Oh, I get it. Pompous, crazy bitch, that one. Useful, but Jesus, she just isn't content to take a back seat."

"So you didn't give her the idea?"

"I would think after building you up like this that you wouldn't think I would throw you down *just* when you were getting a reputation," Price said folding his hands over his ample midsection and sighing. "Even if I didn't like you, you're an investment. One that's paying off like a penny stock of Microsoft."

"Aww, you're just saying that," Lynn said as a smile crept across her face, and the senator met it with a shrug.

"Sometimes you throw out a few pennies, sometimes you get back a nice chunk of change," Price said, breathing out slowly. "But no, the end of your career wasn't my plan. My plan was to get you to take lead with tomorrow's congressional hearing about restricted substances. Have you push that there's not enough oversight or investigation when it comes to drugs like Escape."

"You… want me to lead a congressional hearing?" Lynn asked, lifting her head and sitting back in her chair. "You want me to go on the record about this?"

"Why not? You're already a public figure, you crusader, you," Price replied, sitting up and pushing off his knees so he could stand. Once he was upright, he seemed to glow with pride for her. "You'll go up there, you'll hem and haw, you'll reignite that once proud flame of hating youth culture and good times. From there, you can ride this tragedy onto the senate floor. Maybe even past it…"

"Bill," Lynn said as she stood with him, shocked at the sudden turn, but she was still taking it in when the senator offered his hand.

"Just remember your friends, Lynn. This could be the start of something big," Price said, and Lynn took his hand warily, fearful that she was imagining the whole situation. Once she felt his palm against hers, doubt crept in and she took a sharp breath.

"But wait, I don't really know much more about the drug than those briefing materials you gave me. I can't lea—"

"You'll be fine, Lynn. What you know is already enough, but I'll have someone write up the questions and send it to you in an email. You can spruce it up—make it official Stafford language—but it'll be a good start. We'll take care of you," the senator promised, releasing Lynn's hand before turning and walking away. After a few steps Price stumbled to the side, catching hold of the back of a chair, but he waved it off once he regained his balance.

"Shit…" Lynn said under her breath, barely able to understand what had just happened, but then she realized she could not stay much longer. With everything that was going on, she needed to be prepared, she needed to sober up. She needed to head home and *try* to sleep. Cleaning up after the party was the last thing she needed to be doing.

After gathering her things and saying a few words to one of the caterers telling him to speak to Janice about finishing up, Lynn left out of the back entrance of the building. Even while dressed in a matching white pea coat, the winter air tore through her and her thin dress, but Lynn was willing to bear with the cold since it was only a few minutes of walking to get to her parking garage. Just a momentary discomfort when it was all said and done.

Lynn's mind was in chaos while she walked across the street, the parking garage in front of her, and she almost did not notice the man standing under the street lamp between her and the entrance. Smiling, Lynn nodded at the man dressed in a brown hoodie, but he did not return the nod. Lynn thought it was odd as she passed by, but she did not expect the sudden prick against her neck or the pressure in her vein.

Trying to turn and failing, Lynn was already losing her strength when strong arms wrapped around her. She couldn't speak—something had stolen her ability to say anything intelligible—but she could still think as a white van screamed around a corner and then jerked to a stop in front of her. Panicking, fear drowning out any rational thought, Lynn could only keep her eyes open as the door slid open and the man carried her in, other hands taking hold of her and pulling her in.

"No…" she whispered, what was left of the adrenaline coursing through her allowing her the one syllable, but the door closed, the van pulled away from the curb, and four men wearing black masks looked down at her.

"Lynn Stafford, we will not hurt you," a familiar voice said, but Lynn could not recognize who owned it, not with whatever it was flowing through her veins. "It was just a tranquilizer, a way to keep you from struggling."

"This," the masked man said before bringing out a small square of paper and turning it over inches in front of her face to show four green infinity symbols, "is what you're demonizing. What you're fighting so hard to keep out of the hands *of the children*. This is the wonderful, terrible potential that hides in all of us. *This* is Escape."

"And now," he said as he set the paper against Lynn's tongue, "you see why we needed to tranquilize you. Can't have you spitting it out before you get to feel the effect. What you have on your tongue is four whole doses, enough to last a virgin like you somewhere around a full day."

"I envy you, actually," he said while sitting back, and Lynn finally realized who it was. She had spoken to this man; he had just traded a megaphone for a mask. "That kind of experience is something you can only have once. It'll be special."

"Wh..." Lynn uttered, but it took everything from her. Darkness surged from the edges of her vision and what she *did* see was already fading away. Looking back at the man, losing focus and all concept of sense, she could see him smiling with his eyes.

"We'll take you home, Congresswoman, don't worry. You'll be back to ruining lives soon enough."

Then Lynn Stafford passed out from the tranquilizers, four doses of Escape on her tongue.

When she opened her eyes, Lynn saw a handful of stars scattered in the cloudless sky, and she realized that only the strongest and brightest could break through the light pollution around her home. Turning her head, she saw her front yard and the grass that had died during the winter. Frowning, she wished that it was still vibrant like it was in the late spring, and she smiled as light poured over her lawn and showed healthy grass spreading out in front of her.

Laughing, she turned her head to look at the sky again, and she was surprised to see a whole universe had formed in the seconds she had turned away. It was better than any planetarium she had ever seen—she could see the clouds of nebulas and the bursting of supernovas—and for a moment she just marveled at the sight. This was something she had always wanted to see with Jeremy, just like all those ancient ruins she had never gotten to explore, like all those cities she had wanted to visit. To see something like this sky, she would have had to run away to Alaska or some other barren country.

And as soon as she thought about Alaska and the aurora

borealis shimmered in her suburban sky, Lynn finally remembered what had happened. Suddenly, lying down outside her front door was unacceptable and Lynn jumped to her feet to find that she was still dressed in her white dress, her coat still wrapped around her. Grabbing her purse from the ground, Lynn saw that everything was still there—nothing had been stolen—and she breathed a sigh of relief.

That relief turned to panic once she remembered what those men had done, and she brought a trembling finger up to her mouth and stuck out her tongue, hoping it was all just some elaborate dream. However, when she dragged her finger down her tongue and felt something clinging to her skin, Lynn realized it was not a dream.

Holding her finger in front of her, Lynn saw four green splotches that used to be infinity symbols, and the protestor's voice came back to her memory. With his voice came a vision to her left, and Lynn turned to see the protestor shaking his head at her and pointing at the sky.

"Don't imagine *me*. Just enjoy your trip," he said, fading away as Lynn realized that she had conjured him, that the Escape in her system would stay with her for the next day. However, before he disappeared completely, Lynn's subconscious gave him one last act of revenge, one last statement to send her spiraling into despair.

"Good luck with the hearing tomorrow. Should be fun."

CHAPTER 12

FULL OF TERRORS

Marc was walking down the street when he got that first tingle in his brain. His tongue had gone numb twenty minutes ago and his muscles were already tense, but he didn't notice anything was different until that itch started in his brain. Looking away from the park to his right, Marc craned his neck to see the shining splendor of a hotel sign, thousands of light bulbs warming a city dead from winter. Marc turned to face the hotel—drawn to it like a moth—but he did not anticipate the light spreading out from the sign and stretching into the night like brilliant plasma.

Waves and shimmering columns of golden, liquid energy issued from the sign until Marc realized that he was responsible, and he gave into childish temptation in that moment. The energy changed color, becoming neon pinks, greens and blues—every shade and variation of crayons he had loved as a child—and it was not long before those streams of light collided with other objects. When they did, it was like Marc was painting with his mind; he watched as a bus stop was splattered with a dozen different colors.

It made him forget his troubles momentarily, but then Marc remembered why he was tripping. As he lifted his finger to feel the Escape crowded on his tongue, the light disappeared and left Marc alone on the sidewalk. There was more than enough Escape to send him into shock and shut down his body—that was the whole point—but Marc had a moment of doubt as he stood there feeling the paper on his tongue. It was not too late; he could turn back now. He could beg for forgiveness for drawing a knife on the people who cared about him.

Once he remembered the blade hidden in his sleeve, Marc

realized he had tied his hands. His friends might forgive him, his parents might send him to a psychiatric hospital, but that was not the real issue. Marc would never be able to forgive himself. After killing his girlfriend and threatening all of them, Marc did not have a choice. He had to put an end to this—he had to *suffer*—and Marc realized that Escape may have been too light of a punishment. Drawing the knife from his sleeve, Marc flipped it around so he could look at its edge.

"Don't you dare," Kara said, and Marc looked behind him to find her leaning against the stone column of the rock wall surrounding the park. An open gate was to her left, iron hinges complaining in the wind, but she was staring at him with her arms crossed and her right foot propped up against the column. Although he knew Kara was just a product of his subconscious, Marc could not resist approaching her. He could not abandon the idea of saying goodbye one last time.

"I deserve it, Kara. After what I've done, I deserve it. And I…" Emotion stole the words from him, but he was able to continue after letting out a resigned breath. "I don't want to be here anymore; I never really did. And I definitely don't want to keep going if you're not here."

"That's *stupid*. You're *fucking stupid* for a nerd sometimes, you know that?" Kara said as she lowered her foot and stepped forward. Her arms were still crossed as she looked down at the knife in his hand. "You took *all that* Escape and you're just going to slit your wrists in the middle of the fucking street?"

"Why *shouldn't* I? There's no one here to stop me. *You* don't count," Marc said, waving around the knife through his hallucination. Kara's ghost broke apart and reformed once the blade was through her. "I was a coward to try and overdose. I should face my death head on, right?"

"Oh, so your parents can deal with the nightmare of finding you here *bleeding* out? Or so the cops can find your body—write you down as a fuckin' *junkie*—put you in a morgue and then nobody you care about will even know you're dead for a few days? Which option sounds like it'll hurt them more, Marc?"

"Or is this all so that someone *can* find you?" she continued, stepping back until she was standing outside the gate.

"Is this just some cry for help? Just *poor, widdle* Marc whoring himself out for attention? Tell you what," Kara said, holding out the inside of her arms, faded ridges scattered up and down her wrists. "Cut sideways. That always worked for me."

"Stop it!" Marc stepped forward and knocked her arms away, not realizing how solid they felt. "That's not what I'm doing! I need to be punished and I need to die… *that's* why I took all that Escape. So I *couldn't* back out!"

"Then prove it," Kara said, stepping on her tiptoes so her face was inches from Marc's. Even then, he wanted to kiss her and force her lips against his, but Kara backed away before he could react, instead standing by the open gate. "Take a walk with me."

"Kara…"

"And leave that thing there," she said, pointing at the knife and then to the rock wall. As soon as she dropped her arm, Kara passed through the gate, but she looked back at him as she walked. "If you want to commit suicide, we're going to do it right."

"I…" Marc started to argue, but he did not have the willpower. One look at the knife was all he needed, and he set it down on the wall with a heavy breath. He backed away, staring at it for a moment, but Kara was right. For him to atone for his crimes, he could not take the easy way out.

It was only seconds before he was through the gate, but Kara was already much further down the path than he had expected. Marc ran after her—not realizing that his mind was responsible for his ruined expectations—and it seemed like Kara was getting further away no matter how fast he ran. It felt like he was sprinting for five minutes, running over bridges and even taking shortcuts through the grass, but she was always out of reach.

Eventually Marc was able to catch up with her, but he was

out of breath by the time she looked down at him in disgust. Gasping in air and bent over, Marc was in pain as he took in his surroundings, the lights of the city not strong enough to penetrate this deep into the park. Shadows frantically encroached along the edge of this clearing, the light of the full moon putting up little resistance. Still, Marc was able to see Kara, which was all that mattered to him.

"Why did you go… so fast?" Marc asked before he recovered fully, forced to gulp in air midway through the question. With a sigh, Kara walked over to a nearby bench and sat down, patting the wooden planks beside her.

"I didn't, dude," she said as Marc took his place by her side. "You made that happen. You made yourself run all this way."

"What—I didn't," Marc said, but then he remembered the Escape on his tongue. In just a few seconds, Kara had convinced him that she was real, but now she was doing just the opposite. Regarding her with suspicion, Marc looked ahead and propped up his elbows on his legs. "So I wanted to come to some deserted spot, huh?"

"For some reason," Kara said before looking up at the sky. Marc followed her gaze and saw clouds filling half the sky, but the moon was bright, or as much as it could be with all the light pollution. Still, it gave Marc light he desperately needed. "It's pretty, huh."

"Maybe. Maybe it's just in my head," Marc said, punctuating it with a heavy sigh. "Why am I here, Kara? Why, in these last moments, is my brain showing me a full moon? Why am I sharing this with you?"

"It's actually full, you asshole," Kara replied softly. "You didn't make up the lunar calendar and you didn't make the clouds. It's just one last, little moment of serenity before it starts."

"Before it starts, huh? Before my brain shuts down and leaves my body to rot, it wanted me to look at the night sky. Seems like a waste," Marc said, looking down, but Kara slapped him on the knee before pointing back up.

"It's not a *waste*. Whatever time you have isn't a waste," she said, nodding up at the moon before dropping her hand onto Marc's knee. "You forgot that, Marcus. You forgot what really had value. You dumped so much of your self-worth into Kara that you *forgot* you are someone without her. And now—because you're a fucking *idiot*—you're trying to get rid of all the time you have left."

"Marcus… Kara hasn't called me Marcus since the night we found each other." Marc looked at the night sky and watched as clouds swirled through the air. It would not be long before Escape flooded through his mind and destroyed him.

"It's because I'm not Kara and you know it," she said, squeezing the hand on top of his knee. "She's gone and she's not coming back. I'm here, like this, because it makes you comfortable. Because in your final moments, you wanted a guide. Someone to talk to you while you're dying."

"Sounds about right," he muttered, watching as the clouds turned into various shapes without his intent. There was no point in directing the transformation or imagining another world. Marc had already resolved to let his mind wander and see where it took him. "You're my Virgil, leading me to the Inferno."

"Fuck you. You're no Dante," Kara said, and Marc laughed as he stared at the clouds bend and fold, becoming a tribute to his youth. Video game characters, gods and beasts from mythology, even action movie stars formed out of the darkness. It was almost enough of a distraction that he smiled, but he remembered himself soon after.

"No, I'm not, and Kara was no Beatrice," Marc said, placing his hand on top of the imaginary hand on his knee, but then he saw something terrible emerge from the clouds.

At first it was subtle—the faces of his childhood heroes became thinner and their flesh withered away—but eventually their skin disappeared completely. One after another, every man, woman and creature turned into skeletons, the rapid decomposition shocking Marc into trying to imagine something else. Anything he could think up would be better than to see these things die and crumble away.

Except that when he tried to change them back, nothing happened.

"What the—why are they staying the same?" he asked no one, the clouds stubbornly refusing to transform even when he focused on them.

"You're not in control, Marcus," Kara said, and Marc looked down at the girl to see that she was becoming thinner and her cheekbones stretched the skin of her face. When she turned to him, Kara reminded Marc of a concentration camp victim.

"*Why* am I not in control? That's not what Escape is supposed to be," he stated, furious that his mind would allow Kara to change like that. Turning back to the clouds above him, Marc put out his hand and squeezed on invisible threads, exerting tremendous willpower over his own imagination. However, it only seemed to get worse. Jaws fell off of heads, forearms dropped away from elbows, and a shadow grew along the horizon, solid darkness rising about the trees.

"You don't know what Escape *is*, Marcus." Kara's voice was deeper than before, and Marc turned to find she had decayed further.

Flesh was missing from the left side of her face, skin peeling back from the hole in her cheek, and her right eye had disappeared from its socket. Nails had been torn off some of her fingers, bone peeked through gashes along her arms and legs, and Marc scooted back on the bench as far as possible. He was horrified, but Kara continued to look down at him just as she had before she had turned into a rotting corpse, as if nothing had changed.

"This is… this is impossible," Marc said, forcing a laugh out of his zombified girlfriend.

"Which is why it's happening, dude. You made a drug that made people see what they imagined, which is already enough, but you have no *clue* what you got yourself into. I mean, just look at that," Kara said, pointing back at the skyline. Marc could not stop himself from turning and watched as the shadow reached its breaking point. Before Marc's eyes, the membrane of darkness tore away to reveal a gigantic skull, bits of muscle and skin clinging to the bone as its jaw yawned open.

"The fuck is that?" Marc asked, watching as the skull rose into the air, a spine following after it, the rest of the torso coming into view after that. "Why is that happening?"

"It's a skeleton, you idiot," Kara said, drawing Marc's eye with a shake of her head. "But it's happening because you tried to overdose on an experimental drug. You never did any real tests, Marcus, but you decided that taking fifteen doses of Escape would overload your brain and kill you. And who fucking knows, right? You *could* end up just fine. This *all* could have been for nothing."

"No…"

"*Yes,*" Kara said, smiling as she shook his leg with a rotting hand. When she let go, Kara leaned back in her seat and crossed her legs. "Though I don't know—probably because you don't— but I do know one thing."

"What's… what's that?" Marc asked, looking at the sky and finding the colossal skeleton had emerged completely from the shadow, breathing in air that whistled through the gaps in its ribcage. As it looked up at the moon and reached up, Marc realized what it was going to do.

"That you're not in control. What's happening right now is that Escape has destroyed the walls between your conscious self and the rest of your mind. And you fucked up, Marc, because you took it in a very impressionable state. You're killing yourself with it because you feel guilty for her death, because you don't want to live anymore," Kara explained as the skeleton grabbed onto the moon and sent cracks along its surface, pulling it down even though Marc knew that was impossible.

"I know. I did this," he admitted, but he could hear Kara laughing on the other side of the bench. Turning back in anger, Marc found that Kara had disappeared and he immediately jumped to his feet. However, no amount of frantic searching around the clearing revealed where she had gone, and it was not long before Marc realized that he was alone. As dread filled his every fiber, Marc lifted his head to the sky, watching as the gigantic skeleton brought the moon above its jaws. He could not look away even as Kara spoke through the ether.

"All of those feelings of guilt, resentment and anger... it only opened the doors. Until the end, your mind will give you everything you think you deserve. It will throw all kinds of horrible things at you. It will give you pain. It will dig deep. You're in Hell, Marcus, and you put yourself there," Kara explained, the skeleton opening its mouth wide and poised to swallow the moon whole. Marc's breath caught in his throat as seconds became eternal, but then Kara's voice ushered in a nightmare.

"Ah, that's right. You used to be afraid of the dark."

Before Marc could move, run—do anything—the gigantic skeleton dropped the moon into its mouth and banished everything into darkness. Marc was blinded in an instant, and he screamed as he staggered backward, trying to find the bench where they had been sitting. He thought that if he found something concrete—something *stable*—that he would be able to handle the darkness, but he could not even see his fingers let alone a bench.

Hyperventilating, Marc dropped to his hands and knees and tried to feel the texture of gravel or grass or anything at all. When he felt blades of grass between his fingers, Marc breathed a sigh of relief, but he felt something warm on his skin after just a moment. Marc was confused at first, then afraid, but he did not expect the pain that followed after the warm, wet sensation. Whatever it was he had touched, the nerves of his fingers were now screaming at him, and Marc hunched over as he heard cries of agony and terror.

It was almost too much to take. Marc forced his eyes closed as his fingers burned and shoved his wrists against his ears to try to block out the sound, but that only made it worse. Rocking back and forth while screaming out in pain, Marc had been absorbed into the darkness and his Hell. Only after a few minutes did he notice the light shining through his eyelids, and it took a few seconds after that for him to realize that he was no longer in the dark.

Relaxing slightly, his fingers still on fire, Marc opened his eyes to find that he was still in the middle of the clearing, dim, red light allowing him sight in this new world. The sky was still dark—shadows covered almost everything but the forest path—but Marc could see. It allowed him to think, but the pain in his fingers resurfaced and he removed his hands from his ears so he could see the damage. Out of nowhere, Marc was surrounded by white light, but it brought no comfort.

His hands were covered in blood—dozens of gashes ran along his fingers—and Marc looked down to find that the grass that had given him so much relief was not grass at all. Tiny, razor-sharp blades had grown out of the ground, blood now dripping along the edges, but that was not the worst of it. As the screams continued, Marc looked back to his hands to find that his fingers did not belong to him. Each cut had turned into an open mouth, complete with teeth covered in his blood.

Marc fell away from his own hands in a panic—his back hitting something hard within just a few seconds—and he did not know what he could do. However, as soon as he was out of the white spotlight, the cuts in his hands instantly healed like nothing had ever happened. Marc looked at them for a long time, turning them over and back and expecting new terrors, but he was completely fine. Marc was momentarily relieved, but then he remembered that he had backed into something and jumped to his feet, ready to see the next nightmare.

It was just the bench.

Breathing out even heavier, Marc put his hand to his chest and felt his heart beating, smiling as he felt it pumping away, but then he heard a growl from his left. The smile fell away, his eyes opened wide, but Marc could not move. Fear took over everything—destroyed even his ability to yell—and he turned his head slowly to see where the growl had come from.

The trees and bushes were quite menacing in the red light filling his last hours, but Marc knew there was something waiting beyond the foliage. He watched the darkness, his eyes focusing on every gap in the trees, and he turned the rest of his body to face the threat. Holding his breath and wishing he could stop the sound of his heart beating, Marc started to back away. He was able to take one step, then another—gravel making far too much noise under his feet—and he wondered if it was all a trick, just his ears hearing something that wasn't there.

Then a pair of yellow eyes opened in the darkness.

"Shit," he muttered, almost clapping his hand to his mouth because of his idiocy, and his curse was met with another low growl. As he kept backing away, Marc saw another pair of eyes join the first, then another from five trees away. Whatever it was, it had found Marc, and he didn't want to be in this clearing when they decided he was food. Once he was past the bench, Marc decided that he would just have to run for it, so he took a deep breath and turned, hoping he could escape.

When he turned, he found a hundred yellow eyes looking at him from the darkness of the other path.

"Oh, God," Marc said, turning back to see even more eyes had joined the first few, and he heard something breaking through branches from another direction. Whipping around—not even trying to hide himself anymore—Marc saw a gigantic, skeletal foot crash through the trees. Rational thought abandoned him as he ran away from the monsters, past the bench and into the darkness of the forest.

Branches and bushes gave him resistance—some of them tearing into his face and his neck as brambles caught his sweatpants—but Marc could not care. All he wanted was to be as far from the skeleton as possible; to be as far from his hunters as he could run. His lungs burned as he tore through foliage, not even pausing after landing wrong on a bunch of rocks, and it was a wonder that he did not break his ankle.

As he limped through the shadows, the light barely enough to see where he was putting his feet, Marc realized that he was not going to escape. They would eventually catch him, especially since he did not know where he was going. Pain came at him from every direction, and even his fear was not enough to push him further. Surrendering, Marc leaned up against a tree and sucked in air, tears streaming down his face.

"I thought you wanted to suffer."

Surprised by Kara's voice, Marc looked around and saw that the red light was gone, replaced by will-o'-the-wisps that bathed his surroundings in green and blue light. The trees had changed, too, becoming gnarled, twisted things, and barbed vines wrapped around them and hung from branches. Seeing a particularly nasty one that would have taken his head off if he had continued, Marc's mouth opened in shock, but then he remembered who had been speaking.

"Where are you? What's happening?" Marc asked, stepping into the middle of the trees and looking for any sign of his girlfriend. All thoughts of the monsters pursuing him had been banished—all he cared about was seeing Kara again—and he breathed frantically as he looked for her. He thought he heard her laugh and whipped around to face her, but only shadows greeted him.

"You wanted to die, Marcus," her voice came from behind him, and Marc turned and discovered a tall, stone cross had formed between the trees. A mound of earth was placed before it, and Marc had no choice but to approach the cross in fear. He was drawn to it, and he realized when he got closer that the soil had been moved recently. Someone was buried under there—that was obvious—but he had no idea who it was.

"I did want to die," Marc answered softly, stepping forward until he was standing over the grave.

"Then why did you run?" Kara asked, and Marc did not have an answer for her. He looked at the stone cross—almost as tall as him—but there was nothing written on the slab. Kneeling down, Marc turned his attention to the soil in front of him. "If you wanted to die so bad, why didn't you let the monsters eat you?"

"I don't know," he said, leaning forward and tentatively setting one hand on the dirt. Contrary to his expectations, it was warm and beckoned him to venture further. Without another thought, Marc dug fingers into the soil, feeling it yearn for him, and he picked up a handful of dirt.

"If you wanted to die, why didn't you just stand there? Why didn't you let them rip you apart?" Kara asked, but Marc was in a daze. He only shook his head as he threw the dirt away and then dug into the soil with both hands.

"I don't know," he repeated, throwing the dirt to the side before diving back in. Once he sent a shower of earth to his right, Marc gave up holding back. In the ambient light of the will-o'-the-wisps, Marc went about destroying the mysterious grave. For minutes he tore into the soil and threw it away, not noticing how the mound wasn't getting smaller.

"Do you think it might be because you want to live? That maybe it's not just instinct? Instinct gave you this nightmare. Your subconscious threw you into this hellhole," Kara said, causing Marc to pause and sit back on his knees. "This is *you*, Marcus. What you're doing now is under your control, and you ran away."

"I ran away," he repeated, looking up to find that the cross was no longer a blank surface. His own name was etched into the stone—along with the year he was born and a hyphen followed by a snake eating its own tail—but nothing else.

"You tried to live," Kara said, her disembodied voice faltering. "You didn't want to die. Some part of you knows that you're not supposed to die like this. That I didn't want you to kill yourself."

"Kara…" Marc said, looking back at the funeral mound beneath him. The cross had his name on it, but he was on the wrong side of the dirt. If this was his grave, someone had made a mistake.

"Just tell me, Marcus," Kara pleaded with him, fear and desperation seeping through. "Just tell me that you don't want to die. I don't want you to die, so don't! Just tell me!"

"I…"

"*Please*," Kara said, and Marc finally saw her appear to his left. She was still decayed—skin and muscle peeling away or entirely absent—but she was not looking at him like before. Tears streamed from her eyes, even the missing one, and she seemed in genuine anguish. "Don't die for her, Marcus. She wanted you to be happy."

"I'm not—"

"Just tell me," she repeated. "Admit it to yourself. Admit that you don't want to die."

"I…" Marc said, looking back to his grave, back to the cross, and he finally realized the truth. This cross *wasn't* meant for him; he was not finished. However much pain was in his heart, there was something keeping him here. When Marc lifted his head to the sky and saw light appearing from the darkness, the words leaked out of him. "I want to live."

"Then fight for it," Kara said, and almost immediately Marc felt the ground move beneath him. Looking down in alarm, Marc was just in time to see a dark hand burst from the soil, fingers curling around the cloth by his shoulder and yanking him down. Throwing out his arms to the side purely by instinct, Marc was able to push hard and keep himself above the ground, but something came up to meet him. Another, bony hand burst out of the grave and grabbed his throat, and Marc was forced to see a decaying head emerge with a roar.

In horror, Marc realized that it had his face.

"You wanted to live, right? So don't let anybody take it from you!" Kara shouted, but it was much easier said than done. Before she even started talking, the corpse had lunged for Marc's throat, and it continued to pull him down even as Marc tried to avoid its teeth. After a frantic few seconds of avoiding the decomposing copy, Marc pulled back and pushed hard with his legs, trying to break free from its grip.

He only succeeded in pulling the zombified clone out of the ground and falling back with the corpse on top of him.

"Don't let anybody take it from you, Marcus! Fight it! Reclaim your life; reclaim your world!" Kara shouted, but Marc could only focus on the saliva dripping from the zombie's mouths and the snapping of its jaws. One of its teeth even came loose during one bite, bouncing off Marc's cheek before falling to the soil. It was too real, too dangerous, and this other version seemed so much stronger. Before long it had pinned Marc's arm to the ground— his other hand occupied by pushing against the monster's neck— and it seemed like the end. The zombie's face was getting closer and closer, Marc's arm was becoming weaker and weaker, and it seemed like fate that Marc would become food for his own corpse.

Then Marc realized there was no corpse to feed. Everything here—everything trying to kill him—was entirely a product of his own imagination. Kara wasn't egging him on, his grave wasn't five feet away; this was all the result of the hallucinogen on his tongue. Marc's subconscious had taken over and made him forget, but it was all fake. Reality was hidden by layers of delusion that had gotten in the way, but it had not been *replaced*. It was just beyond the corpse trying to eat him, which meant Marc had nothing to fear.

As soon as the fear left him, the corpse disappeared, the cross faded away, and Marc was left lying on his back in the middle of the woods. The moon was still full and bright above him, light scattered through the trees and Marc knew that he was back in the real world. Taking in a deep breath, Marc sat up to find the edge of the park within sight, the lights of streetlamps turning the rock wall into a dark horizon. He had never thought a few lights would make him feel so grateful to be alive.

"Good for you," Kara's voice came again, and Marc turned to see the ghost of his girlfriend sitting on a stump, just as maimed as the last time he had seen her.

"No, I thought I…" he started, but the hallucination scoffed before sticking out her tongue and pointing at her piercing. As soon as she did, the shock of seeing her again wore off and left Marc feeling like an idiot. Sticking out his own tongue, Marc dragged his finger across the surface and collected what was left of the Escape tabs. He could still see some of the infinity symbols, but his saliva had turned it into a soggy mess.

"It's still going to be in your system for a while, Marcus, but it's a good start. You'll be fine, eventually," Kara said, crossing her legs and clasping her hands around her knee. "It's just detox, now."

"So this is the last time I'll see you, then," Marc said, pushing himself to his feet and patting dirt off his clothes. He was a mess after all of that, but it was better than being buried alive or eaten by his own corpse. Looking back at his rotten girlfriend, he realized it was small consolation. "This will be goodbye."

"Maybe," she replied, sighing heavily and looking away. When she looked back, Marc realized he was not speaking to Kara. "*Hopefully*. I have a feeling it won't be so neat and tidy."

"And you're me…" Marc said, drawing a nod from the hallucination.

"You've caught on," Kara said, dropping her hands and pushing herself off the stump. Marc was about to reply—say something snarky—but then all the muscles of his torso went rigid, cramping and forcing him to bend over in pain.

"What's... what's..."

"Left over, I'm guessing," Kara said, walking over so she could rub his back. It should have come as a comfort, but the touch of her hand only made Marc feel worse. It meant that part of him still thought she was there. "It probably won't be long before you get sucked into something else. This is all psychosomatic, unfortunately."

"What do I... what do I do?" he turned his head, looking for answers, but Kara only pointed at the rock wall at the edge of the park.

"*Live*, Marcus. It's all you *can* do. And hopefully, you'll make it mean something." Kara smiled at him with her ruined face, and then she faded from the world.

Once he was alone, Marc felt an odd mix of emotions. As relieved as he was that the hallucination was gone, being alone was more than he could take in his current state. He needed to be around someone—he needed to feel something *real*—and whimpering in the middle of the forest would not help him. Cradling his stomach, Marc pushed through the trees and shrubs between him and the rock wall, ignoring the manmade path on the other side of the shrub, and it was only a few minutes before he was looking up at the layered stones.

Jumping as high as he could, Marc's fingers wrapped around the top of the wall, and he felt a sense of victory before realizing he was about to slip. After a split-second of panic, however, Marc was able to find footholds and breathed out in relief. Once the pain set back in, Marc climbed the wall until he was able to pull himself over, his arms so weak they shook from the effort. Rolling onto his back in full view of the street, Marc closed his eyes and breathed in cool air for a few minutes, grateful that he still could.

"Marcus? Marcus!" Marc opened his eyes and sat up, watching as Lewis sprinted a hundred yards down the sidewalk, coat flying out behind him. As Lewis got closer, Marc could see the panic and relief in his eyes, and he wondered what he could possibly say to him after what had happened in his apartment. Marc stood up, hoping to find the words in time, but then another series of cramps bent him over again.

"Marcus! What's wrong?" Lewis asked in a hurry, skidding to a halt a few feet away from him, which Marc only understood once he remembered how his intervention had ended.

"No… knife," Marc said, putting out his hands to show that he was unarmed, but his body betrayed him further, driving him to his knees and forcing him to wrap his arms around his torso. Psychedelic hallucinations assaulted him, fractals appeared in the air around them, but Lewis kneeled down in front of him and anchored him. With him right there, Marc was able to keep hold of reality.

"You're dosing?" Lewis asked, and Marc nodded quickly. "How much?"

"Too much," Marc said, throwing out his hands and gripping Lewis' shoulders tight. "Fifteen. Was trying… was trying to kill myself."

"God, Marcus…" Lewis said. "I—you…"

"It's okay," Marc interrupted, struggling to keep his eyes open so he could make eye contact. "I want to live. I'll—I'm not going to…"

"Marcus, just… I didn't know I would push you over the edge," Lewis said, but Marc shook his head.

"Not you. It's not your fault. I fucked up, man," Marc said, closing his eyes and letting out warm tears. "I'm sorry, Lewis. I'm so sorry…"

"No, man, *no*," Lewis said, his voice refusing to cooperate and cracking between the words. "I'm sorry, Marcus. I pushed you too far. I fucked up."

"I'll… I'll have to come back to work Friday. I'll… I'll need a day, I think," Marc said, trying to laugh, but his mind was swarming with visions of medieval torture, his clones a victim in every one and their pain becoming his. If he had not been holding onto Lewis, Marc would have screamed.

"Fuck that shit, Marcus! You come back to work when you feel like it. You do whatever you want, just don't do this again. Don't leave me like this, man," Lewis said, wrapping his arms around Marc and holding him close. It was enough to bring him back from the edge, and Marc returned the embrace. "Hell, dude, I'll even call you Marc if it'll keep you here."

"Hah… like you would," Marc said as he pushed back and sat back on his knees, so drained he was not even surprised when he saw Kara standing behind Lewis. When she nodded in approval, Marc realized that he was ready, that it was time to let go. Smiling at his friend, Marc shrugged as if it was any other day.

"Besides, Marcus sounds better anyway."

CHAPTER 13

SWEET SURRENDER

The pain would not leave him, no matter how many doses Jeremy put into his system. There were five tabs on his tongue—adding to the four doses he had taken throughout the day—but the pain would *not* go away. Entire worlds rose and fell, galaxies exploded around him, men and women fell in love, explosions rocked the surface, electricity surged through the air and rock stars destroyed their instruments; infinity stretched out before him, but Jeremy still felt it all. No matter what he imagined, Jeremy could not forget what Shriver had done to him, what the world had done to him.

Compared to *that* pain, his battered body was secondary.

"Don't feel stupid," Allison said as the dream girl appeared at his side, her legs dangling over the edge of the pool. Jeremy did not bother to look at her; he just kept looking down at his hands as they turned from one genre convention to another. No matter how scaled or furry they became, even if he lost a finger or grew suckers, they were still his hands. In reality, they were still weak, pale, tiny little hands that belonged to a teenager, and he could not forget.

"I am stupid, though," Jeremy said, looking up from his hands and seeing the trees surrounding his backyard. They transformed without rhyme or reason, becoming mountains, a cityscape—even notes on a sheet of music—but Jeremy knew they were just trees. If he walked forward long enough, he would feel their rough bark or smell pine needles beneath him. Reality would always conquer his fantasies.

"I'm stupid. I never should have thought I was worth anything."

"You *are* worth something, Jeremy." Allison shook his

shoulder and tried to make him turn, but Jeremy kept looking ahead. "You're worth something to *me*."

"Oh, yay, I'm worth something to a figment of my imagination," Jeremy replied, throwing a rock into the pool and hearing it clatter and echo, coming to a stop near the drain on the far end. It turned into an insect for a moment, then a fairy, but Jeremy was bored soon enough. He looked back at his dream girl and shrugged. "Sorry, but you don't really matter."

"That's not true, otherwise you wouldn't be talking to me," Allison argued, but it had the opposite effect than intended. Jeremy scoffed as he swung his legs over the edge, knocking the heels of his sneakers against the wall and setting off a volcano to his left, which sent out plumes of ash and fire.

"I'm not talking to you because you *matter*," Jeremy said, abandoning the volcano and letting it become a tower of rotating gears and pulleys, banishing the entire hallucination once he realized he didn't know what to do with it. "I'm talking to you because you're the only one who *will* talk to me."

"You have nine doses in your system, Jeremy, you can imagine anyone to talk to you," Allison said, Jeremy scoffing at the suggestion.

"*Who?* Just who would I imagine to talk to?" he asked, pulling his legs out of the pool and facing her, sitting cross-legged. "Apparently my ability to think up real people is *questionable*."

"There are thousands of people out there—"

"And I don't like a *single one!*" Jeremy interrupted, slamming his chest with his fist and feeling his ribs complain. Taking in ragged breaths, he collected himself before looking back at Allison. "I know lots of people, Allison, but I don't like *any* of them. The only person I can spend three minutes with without wanting to shoot them is *you*, and *you're* completely made up!"

"Jeremy—"

"No!" Jeremy screamed, jumping to his feet and pointing down at his dream girl. "You don't *get* to talk! You aren't real!

I made you up because I felt like a piece of shit—because I *am* a piece of shit—and I found out today what happens when you ignore reality. The real Allison Hayes is a prissy, little idiot who knows how to smile and be nice to people. It's fine—it's great for her—but she isn't you. When I created a person I'd want to spend my time with, I took her body and put you in it. Who are you, Allison?"

"Je—"

"Trick *fucking* question, bitch, I already know! You're me," Jeremy stated, jabbing his thumb into his chest. "Because I didn't fit in, I made up another version of me that I could put into a fucking shell! I don't fucking *know* people, goddamnit! I couldn't make up someone real; someone who could actually feel or make *me* feel like I wasn't an outcast. You're… you're…"

"Jeremy, don't do this…" Allison said, but Jeremy looked at her and shrugged.

"You're a fantasy, Allison. Just like all the rest of it. You're part of the life I always wanted but I'll never have. I can create a tornado that takes me to Oz, I can imagine myself on the deck of a battlestar, I can meet aliens and I can ride dragons, but it's not *real*. I can never have a real life," he confessed, sitting back down beside Allison. "You're the realest thing I made up, but it doesn't *make* you real. It just shows how much I don't belong here."

"You don't want to do this," Allison replied, pausing for a long moment as Jeremy conjured up a hundred people who looked at them from the other side of the pool. "There's more, Jeremy. If you just stick with it, if you keep going, you'll see that there's more."

"Of course, there's more—I didn't say there wasn't—I just don't *want* more. I want *nothing*," Jeremy said, nodding at the people and pointing at them. "Do you know who those are?"

"…no," Allison answered softly, Jeremy smiling at the attempt.

"Don't lie to me, okay? Not when it comes down to this. I know you know," Jeremy said, slowly dragging his finger along the group. "But screw it, why bother with the game? These are the real people in my life, Allison. These are the people I know, that I speak to or think about on a regular basis. Look at them all."

"What's your point, Jeremy?" she surrendered, which felt less satisfying than Jeremy thought it would. Sighing, Jeremy dropped his arm and gripped the edge of the pool, feeling the rough texture on his palm.

"You're in there, just like all the others. You talked to me, or at least the real one did. And you know what? Most of you aren't terrible people, minus a few exceptions. Even Shriver isn't all that bad, he's just figuring his shit out. I *understand* why he picked on me," Jeremy said, his eye throbbing through the haze of Escape in his system. "I was an easy mark. Didn't make any noise, didn't stand up for myself. And I did it to myself. Locked myself away. But you want to know the deep, dark truth of it all, Allison?"

"No, Jeremy, I don't want to," she said, but Jeremy clapped his hands and three people were left on the other side of the pool. Dr. Ruby and his mother were there, but so was a man whose back was turned to them.

"Too bad, Allison, because I might be talking to myself, but I'm still talking," Jeremy said, pointing at each person, starting with the women. "You want to know what these people have in common? They *knew* me. They talked to me a decent amount, and you know what else they have in common?"

"Just say it," Allison said, the words slightly garbled, and Jeremy turned to see her crying. "Tell me that they hate you. Tell me all the reasons why it matters that they hate you. Because why not, right? These three people matter the most in your world, no matter how terrible they are. Your therapist hears all your bullshit and thinks you'll shoot up a school, and your mom gave up on you because you're a lost cause. Your dad hasn't spoken to you in months because he never really wanted you."

"That's enough to kill yourself, isn't it?" Allison asked, wiping snot from her nose and glaring at Jeremy through tears. "Is that what you wanted to say? Was that going to be your big victory, Jeremy? Good job! You won at convincing your fake dream girl that you don't deserve to live."

"I..." Jeremy paused, looking away from her to see the three people standing on the other side of the pool. His therapist disappeared soon after that—she didn't need to be there—and his father followed. His mother stood there on the other side, a phone pressed to her ear, and Jeremy realized how much of it came down to her. "It's not that."

"Oh, then where did it come from, Jeremy? If I'm just you, then that means everything I just said might as well have come from your mouth," Allison argued, but he continued to watch his mother.

"It probably could have," he admitted, a tear falling down his black eye. "But it's not that. It's not that I don't deserve to live. It's that I shouldn't have this life. I don't belong in my own life, and I don't belong in hers. If I did... if I did, things would be different."

"So you're going to blame your mother, then?"

"I can't blame her," Jeremy said, his throat aching as his mother shifted into a lighter, more vibrant woman, the years slipping off of her. "It's not her *fault*. She fits into this world just fine. Tonight, she's heading up a benefit so kids won't get hooked on drugs. The same fucking drugs on my tongue right now," he said, laughing at the situation before turning back to Allison. "It's kinda funny, isn't it? She couldn't notice her own kid getting hooked. She's chasing her own tail..."

"Stop it..."

"It's okay! Really," Jeremy said as he stood up and walked over to the towel he had laid out before sitting by the pool. "It was my fault that she didn't notice. I hid away and locked myself in my room. I locked myself in my head, because it was the only place that really felt like home. All of that out there... it's not for me."

"So you're really going to go through with it, then?" Allison asked, still sitting by the pool and looking away from him. As he knelt down on the towel, Jeremy wished she would look at him, but he also knew that it was a trick, some sort of survival instinct kicking in. His subconscious was trying to make him feel guilty, and he would not give in.

"I... don't have any reasons not to," Jeremy said, grabbing the steak knife from the grass where it had fallen. "It doesn't matter what I want or where I belong, because I can't ignore reality anymore. I locked myself in my head, but it wasn't a *home*. It was a *prison*. And I just want to be free, Allison."

Rolling the handle of the knife in his hand, Jeremy waited for Allison to argue, to scream at him—to do anything to stop what was about to happen—but his dream girl did nothing. When he turned back to look at her, she was already gone. Jeremy waited briefly for her to pop up behind him, but then he realized why she was gone and why she stopped arguing.

"I guess I won," Jeremy muttered to himself, trying to prepare for this grand moment, but it felt hollow. He was not achieving some victory—most people would say that he was running away—and Jeremy's Allison had pleaded with him to stop until the end. Still, Jeremy had made his choice, and no part of his brain still fought against him. Closing his eyes, Jeremy breathed in deep the warm air of spring, the world shifting around him one last time.

When he opened his eyes, Jeremy was in the middle of an orchard, cherry blossoms flowing along air currents and filling his nose with their scent. He breathed in again and wondered how it would feel or if he could avoid the pain. The kitchen knife had transformed in his hand, becoming a katana gleaming in the afternoon sun. If Jeremy had wanted to be traditional, he would have used the shorter tanto, but this was his fantasy and he could do whatever he wanted.

Stretching his arms out in front of him—his left hand curled over his right—Jeremy set the tip of his sword against his gut. In reality, the point of the kitchen knife was barely any closer than his hands and his gut was almost sticking out of his shirt, but in his fantasy, Jeremy was thin, majestic and his katana was held with the blade pointing to the left. It was an important detail—one he made sure to imitate with the kitchen knife—because there was no way to try again if he messed up.

Breathing in and out, Jeremy prepared himself. He had his doubts—part of him still thought he should rule the world—but it was just not going to happen. There was no way Jeremy would ever fit in, no one would ever accept him, and the worst part was that the world would always fail his expectations. Reality only held the promise of disappointment and pain, and Jeremy knew he would rather die than suffer through another day.

Plunging the katana through his body in one thrust—cherry blossoms falling all around him—Jeremy almost felt at peace. As the blade was halfway through his body, Jeremy felt there were worse ways to go, worse ways to fade from the world, but then reality caught up with him. Pain exploded in his midsection, his body trembled and something cold devoured his insides. Feeling the warmth flow out of him, Jeremy looked down and saw the hilt of the katana pressed against his stomach, but the pain destroyed his fantasy and Jeremy was left looking at a wooden knife handle and an inch of blood-covered metal.

Breathing in shock, Jeremy felt his muscles seize and cause even worse pain—the blade in his belly cutting more tissue as he moved—and Jeremy fell onto his side while gripping the handle, screaming in agony. He laid there for a few seconds gasping for air that only caused more pain, but eventually Jeremy remembered that he had meant to do this. It was just pain, and he had to keep going.

Pushing hard against the ground with his hand and finding his body heavier than he remembered, Jeremy's head was swimming as he knelt upright, taking short breaths so he wouldn't spasm and lose his nerve. Gripping the knife again and hoping to get this over with one hard yank to his left, Jeremy prepared to finish his ritualistic suicide. At least by committing seppuku, Jeremy could have an interesting death.

However, when he pulled to the left, Jeremy's strength left him at the first notion of pain. Moaning, Jeremy accidentally pulled out the knife as he fell to his side, losing his hold on it once he hit the ground. Pain tore at him—made it hard to think— and Jeremy pressed his face against the dead grass in frustration. Tears came even though he didn't want them, snot flooded his nose and made it even harder to breathe, but Jeremy had his mission. He had to do *this* right; he couldn't lose this fight, too.

But when he sat back up, Jeremy realized he had lost the knife.

"No…" he whined, trying to crawl around before the pain became too much. "No, no, no, no… No!" he squeaked, collapsing once he realized he would die before he could find it again. It was all over, Jeremy had run out of time, and he had failed.

"Why…" he muttered as he rolled onto his side, warmth running out of his belly and the rest of his body going numb. If it had been intentional, it may have been nice, but Jeremy knew it was just shock. This was how it felt to die, to lose everything.

In that moment Jeremy realized that he did not want to die, but it was too late.

"Jeremy," a strange voice said, and he almost didn't recognize it. Lifting his head, Jeremy saw a blond woman approaching him in an elegant, white dress. He had seen it earlier that week—his mother had brought it in from the car—but he had not seen the woman in a long time. Then he remembered that he had seen her just minutes ago, seen the years and all the resentment melt away.

"Mommy," Jeremy leaked out, barely strong enough to say the word. Propping himself up on his elbows and ignoring the pain and the life flowing out of him, Jeremy watched as his young mother knelt on the ground in front of him, just beyond the towel.

"Come here, little boy. Mommy's here," she said while patting her lap, and Jeremy the teenager vanished. All Jeremy wanted was to curl up next to his mother and feel her hand on his back; feel her fingers scratching his head. He wanted comfort; anything to run away from the pain. Crawling forward even as his limbs became weaker as shock set in, Jeremy was not going to let anything stop him.

"Mommy," he said as he collapsed on her lap, his arms slowly wrapping around her back as his face pressed against her stomach. "It hurts, Mommy."

"Shh, I know, baby, I know. Mommy will make it better," she said, her hand rubbing Jeremy's back, the fingers of her other hand gently scratching his head. "Mommy will make the pain go away."

"Thank you... it feels... better..." Jeremy said, drifting off to sleep in his mother's arms. Or, at least, that was what he thought; that was the mercy given to Jeremy Stafford. In those few precious seconds, he was loved, and loved back.

In his last moments, Jeremy got to feel like he belonged.

CHAPTER 14

SURREALITY

ynn swallowed down her anxiety and tried to keep it together, but nothing was going to calm her down at this point. There was a microphone on the table in front of her— there was a placard with her name in front of that—there were a thousand things of no consequence in this room, but Lynn was trembling in fear. That was because there were twelve other representatives sitting on the raised platforms with her, most of them familiar faces. Most of them were her colleagues—part of the committee she had created—but no amount of friendly faces would help her in this congressional hearing.

Especially since she had een dosed with so much Escape that her colleagues had turned into brightly-colored, felt puppets.

It wouldn't have been an issue if she could hang back like the others and wait until the hearing was over, but each one of those puppets was looking at her like she was a circus attraction. In reality, they were probably looking at her from their periphery— the bold ones like Janice actually turning to look at her—but she was on the spot either way. Lynn was supposed to be asking questions and leading their investigation, but she could shuffle her papers only so many times before someone would notice.

Lynn had exceeded *so many times* a few minutes ago.

"Ms. Stafford," Senator Price said over his microphone, shocking Lynn enough that the puppets transformed back into their real-world counterparts. Seeing that she was back in the real world for the moment, Lynn cleared her throat and shuffled her papers one last time. It was all a stalling tactic—she had forgotten where they had left off—but one look at Vincent Cartelli was all she needed.

As the Deputy Director of State, Local and Tribal Affairs for the Office of National Drug Control Policy, Cartelli had been called to testify, poised to be ripped apart by Lynn's subcommittee. He was skinny, had tanned skin and black hair and reminded Lynn of a rodent, but more importantly, Cartelli was responsible for the programs designed to keep kids away from drugs and drugs away from kids. This was the man Lynn needed to shame, expose and accuse of incompetence, just to further her career.

It made no difference if he was competent or not.

"Mr. Cartelli," Lynn said, her voice stern and confident as she looked down at the man. "I understand that your branch of the Office of National Drug Control Policy is responsible for a number of programs, the High Intensity Drug Trafficking Areas, Drug Free Communities and the National Youth-Anti-Drug Media campaign. That is correct, yes?" she asked, causing him to look around the room skeptically before leaning toward the microphone.

"Yes, that is correct, Ms. Stafford," he said, leaning back as Lynn nodded.

"Now, these are all good programs—and we'll be speaking to the other Deputy Directors after your testimony—but I wanted to speak more about those last two campaigns with regards to the new wave of designer drugs, specifically Escape," Lynn explained as she picked up her pen and prepared to write notes. "What measures has the ONDCP taken to ensure that drugs like Escape are not falling into the hands of young people?"

"I'm sorry, Ms. Stafford," Cartelli said as he leaned forward, "but as far as our policies are concerned, designer drugs do not fall under any specific programs nor warrant aggressive measures. The popularity of these substances rise and fall quickly—far too quickly for a reasonable response—and new substances take their place. To issue new policy for every specific mixture of hallucinogens, narcotics or other substances would be a waste of funds that could be used elsewhere."

"So what you're saying, Mr. Cartelli, is that you have no

programs in place to combat the spread of Escape?" Lynn asked, writing down nonsense on her page in order to intimidate the Deputy Director. He seemed to be sweating profusely, fear in his eyes, but Lynn had forgotten that her perception was flawed.

"No, there is no specific program in place," Cartelli said, stammering at first, but a sudden flicker across the room revealed the confident Deputy Director that Lynn had *actually* questioned. "There is no need for one, as most of the components of Escape are already considered Schedule I controlled substances. If arrested for possession of even small amounts of Escape, drug offenders face years in prison and severe fines. Any specific legislation or policy concerning Escape would be redundant."

"Is that so…" Lynn said, her confidence abandoning her even if there were no outward signs. Setting her pen down, Lynn laid her arms across her notes and stared at Cartelli in an attempt to salvage some part of her argument. This was supposed to be easy—Price had sent her the questions that morning like he had promised—but the Deputy Director was more than capable.

"That is correct. Despite your media campaign, Ms. Stafford, Escape is a very new strain with limited appeal. Outside of the Northeast there is very little evidence of its popularity, and what little has been seized through law enforcement is nothing compared to other more prolific and harmful substances," Cartelli explained as he sat back and looked pleased with himself, and Lynn had a difficult time finding any weakness.

Although that difficulty may have had less to do with his argument and more with how the Deputy Director was turning into a rat before her eyes.

"Mr. Cartelli…" she said, trying to find some way to speak to a giant rodent in a suit, but her stalling only made things worse. Squeaks and hisses seemed to resonate throughout the room— Lynn's subconscious had given Cartelli support—but Lynn closed her eyes and urged her mind to change him back. For a long moment, she pleaded with her brain and told it that she did not want to see the Deputy Director as a rat, and she almost thought she was making progress until Senator Price got her attention.

"Lynn, what are you doing?" he whispered, and Lynn turned to right, expecting to see the senator holding a hand over his microphone.

Instead, Price had become a walrus wearing a top hat, a massive flipper draped over the microphone.

In fact, all of her subcommittee had been turned into various animals and they were waiting for Lynn to continue her assault. Sherman had turned into a bloated hippopotamus, his dress shirt about to burst its buttons; Gainsborough had become a seahorse shooting bubbles in an arc over the room. There was a tortoise and a flamingo—there was one unfortunate woman who turned into a horse—but Janice's transformation into a baboon was enough to force a giggle out of Lynn.

Immediately she was horrified—she knew what they must all be thinking in the real world—and Lynn hastily tried to figure out a reason why she had giggled in the middle of a restricted substances hearing. It was almost too much—she was already wording her resignation in her head—but then she saw something miraculous in the back of the room. A man in robes entered the room and closed the door behind him, but it was the halo on his head that caught Lynn's attention. She thought it may have been Jesus himself, but then Lynn recognized his face.

In her entire life, she could never have imagined seeing Noel Silverman dressed up like a messiah and smiling at her from across the room, but his appearance did save her, oddly enough. With the knowledge that it was absurd and it was all in her mind, Lynn was able to focus and all of the hallucinations fell away, revealing the congressional hearing she had left behind. Not bothering to look at her colleagues, Lynn readjusted her microphone and cleared her throat.

"I'm sorry, Mr. Cartelli, I had a tickle in my throat and I was just making sense of your claims in my head, trying to put myself in your shoes," Lynn said, picking up her pen once more and staring straight into the man's dark eyes. "I understand it must be difficult for you to allocate your funding to the right places, weighing the costs and benefits of each program and campaign. I want to thank you for your ability to see past the fad trends and focus on what really matters."

"Thank you, Ms. Stafford."

"*However*," she spoke over him, bringing out a document and skimming the highlighted portion. "You mentioned that you prefer to focus on the more prolific and harmful substances, am I right in saying so?"

"That is… correct," Cartelli answered, his eyes narrowing, and Lynn had to hold back her smile.

"And your department is also responsible for programs that target children and youth culture, trying to deter them from starting drugs in the first place?" Lynn could hear her colleagues whispering to each other, unable to understand where she was going with her questions.

"As I've stated before, Ms. Stafford, that is my responsibility as the Deputy Director," Cartelli said, annoyance seeping through his voice.

"Then tell me, Mr. Cartelli, why has there been such a culture of acceptance in youth demographics when it comes to marijuana?" Lynn asked, looking back at her reports. "I'm reading here that there has been a massive surge in popularity for marijuana over the last twenty years—starting with the younger generation—which has now led to certain states legalizing it completely. Why did your anti-drug campaigns not work in the case of marijuana?"

"That's… a different situation, Ms. Stafford," Cartelli said, flustered by the question. "Marijuana has been prevalent for half a century, especially popular with young people, and does not have the same harmful effects. The comparison between marijuana and designer drugs like Escape falls flat."

"So you believe that the surge of popularity in marijuana is because it has been around longer, because it's easy to spread among young people, and due to the fact that it is not a harmful substance?" Lynn asked, imagining Cartelli rolling his eyes as he answered and the Escape giving life to the thought.

"That would be what I *said*, Ms. Stafford."

"Well, then I guess Escape is already well on its way, Mr. Cartelli, because you mentioned that you did not consider Escape to be a threat. Not when you could focus on *more prolific and harmful drugs*," Lynn said, dragging her pen across her page for emphasis. "Your words, Mr. Cartelli."

"The context is…"

"Now, Mr. Cartelli, I have another report here talking about the failures of the Youth-Anti-Drug Campaigns of the last decade," Lynn said as she rearranged papers in front of her. "For the millions of dollars that were spent in the period between 2001 and 2003 to curb marijuana consumption, we have some rather surprising results. A five-year study from an independent contractor showed that not only were children who saw those commercials just as likely to experiment with marijuana, but others were actually *more* likely to start smoking."

"I'm aware of that study, Ms. Stafford, and I will remind you that I had nothing to do with those campaigns," Cartelli replied, actually sweating, and he became more nervous once Lynn smiled at him.

"Bear with me, Mr. Cartelli," Lynn said while settling the report in front of her, but maintaining eye contact with the Deputy Director. "Now, instead of being scuttled for being a defective program, the Youth-Anti-Drug campaigns have been given *increased* funding over the years, with little to no results. In fact, it seems like the American people are growing and more accepting of a drug culture."

"What does this have to do—" Cartelli started, but Lynn tapped her microphone and shook her head.

"I was not done *speaking*, Mr. Cartelli," she stated firmly, stopping the man midsentence. After reclaiming her smile, Lynn continued. "Now, there are likely too many reasons to count for this shift, but I feel like it's a logical leap to say that the reason that so many states are decriminalizing marijuana is because a great deal of the voting public *grew up* exposed to these substances. Why would they punish anyone for smoking marijuana when they did it themselves?"

"I—" Cartelli tried to speak, but one look from Lynn was enough for him to lean back in his chair.

"The reason I bring up the example of marijuana is that I believe almost *any* drug can become the next marijuana with the advent of social media," she said, hearing the murmurs going through the crowd in front of her. "Not because it's easy to use, or it's hard to get, or even because it's cheap. The way the internet has changed our world and prepared the next generation, it will only take the smallest nudge to turn an unknown substance into the next big drug."

"This is absurd," Cartelli said while crossing his arms, and Lynn even heard Price whispering at her.

"Get back to the script, Lynn," he said, forcing Lynn to look at him out of the corner of her eye. Although it amused her that he had turned into the Monopoly mascot, Lynn put up her finger to silence the senator.

"It would be an absurd theory if I just made it up, but the trends on social media, the general distrust of authority and government—the many, *many* avenues that people now have to acquire contraband—every one of these contributes to a growing issue when it comes to young people and substance abuse," Lynn continued, holding up another sheet of statistics. "I have here a report concerning aggregate data on popular websites for youth groups. You mention that Escape is not popular, that it is restricted to the Northeast, correct, Mr. Cartelli?"

"That is my understanding," Cartelli answered, wary, and

Lynn had to think of something awful just to keep herself from smiling.

"Then your understanding is *wrong*. The sad truth of it is that Escape has exploded in popularity. It is trending on a number of platforms and reaching millions of users. Escape-related tweets have become commonplace, as are internet memes depicting the experience. There are even browser-supported games that either reference or try to emulate the feelings one might feel under the effect of Escape. I will spare you the rest of the lingo—I barely knew what half of these were before I educated myself—but it is *clear* that there is overwhelming support for this drug and there is a nationwide network spreading its roots as we speak here today."

"Then, according to you and this dubious report, it is already too late to stop the spread of this substance. Just *what* are you proposing? Is this some sort of attempt to lay blame at my feet?" Mr. Cartelli asked, too irritated for it to be real, but Lynn humored the Deputy Director.

"Calm down, Mr. Cartelli, we're on the same side," Lynn said with a smile on her face. "I was merely explaining to you my perspective on this issue, and how we must act quickly. Right now, Escape is enjoying a surge of popularity—no matter how much I expose its dangers—and I believe our most efficient course of action would be to counter with a social media campaign of our own."

"You want to sink to their level?" Cartelli asked, raising an eyebrow, and Lynn knew for sure that she was imagining it. Almost everything around her was shifting and becoming less rational, but she could not break now. Ignoring the transformation of Noel Silverman from messiah to professional at the back of the room, Lynn gave a congressional shrug.

"Don't think of it as sinking to their level," she said, covering her bases by repeating the phrase. "To effectively communicate with youth culture, we have to appropriate the same tools. Escape has gone *viral*, and the best way to combat that kind of popularity is to *go viral* ourselves."

"Reorganize your media campaigns into something more comprehensive, focus *more* on pursuing the digital crowd, make our children feel like we understand them—that we *care* about them. At this point, our main concern should be to raise awareness for the harmful effects of the drug and the consequences that come with it," she concluded to scattered applause, but it died down when Cartelli leaned forward to reply.

"And how should we do that, Ms. Stafford? How do you propose that we cater to a generation with collective Attention Deficit Disorder?" he asked, his familiarity finally striking a nerve.

"You are the Deputy Director of one of those most influential offices in the United States government, Mr. Cartelli, and you have almost unlimited access to a handful of intelligence organizations, any one of which would be able to teach your employees how to manipulate social media. If *they're* not enough, you can always just hire a firm to do it *for* you, and I'm pretty sure it will still be cheaper than your current tactics," Lynn explained before leaning back, her last statement dripping with condescension.

Lynn had made it to the end; there were no more questions for her to ask. She would have smiled, cheered, and possibly jumped out of her chair, but it would have been highly inappropriate at a congressional hearing. Remembering the chemicals affecting her brain, Lynn realized that she could *try* to enjoy it, and so she imagined that everyone in the room was giving her a standing ovation. Even Janice stood for her, and Lynn smiled as she saw the hatred in her eyes. It was too good to be true—she could not imagine a scenario where the woman would fold like that—but it was nice to imagine.

Turning away from her colleagues, Lynn realized that Noel Silverman was staring at her from the far side of the room. She gave him a smile out of habit, but Lynn was surprised when he smiled back and walked down the aisle as the hearing continued. Not only was it inappropriate for a congressional hearing, but they were supposed to be enemies in public. To show affection, to even smile, would be a surefire way for them to get caught.

Yet Silverman continued on his way, stepping past stunned onlookers, and Lynn's jaw dropped when he started to undress. Once he was standing by Cartelli's table, Silverman tossed his sport coat to the side before pulling out his tie. Lynn was horrified by the act, but she could not speak as he unbuttoned his shirt with one hand and removed his belt with the other. Soon enough, Silverman was standing in a white undershirt and his slacks, but Lynn could see him reaching for the last button.

"Mr. Silverman," she whispered, covering her microphone with her hand, but no one seemed to hear her. Silverman continued to smile at her as the button came free, as his hand pulled down the zipper. Before a congressional hearing about restricted substances, a known spokesperson for personal freedom pulled down his slacks, removed them, and then draped them over the head of a Deputy Director of the Office of the National Drug Control Policy.

And instead of watching the world explode from the absurdity, Lynn's jaw dropped as a hundred cheers went up around the room.

Looking around, her eyes wide, Lynn watched as politicians and prominent figures yelled and screamed and applauded for Noel Silverman as he danced in the middle of the room. Once he jumped onto the table in front of Cartelli, it was not long before Silverman tore off his undershirt and started to flex his stomach, showing off his perfect abs. Lynn was so stunned by the act that it took her a few seconds of staring, but then she realized that Noel Silverman did not look like that in real life.

As soon as she made that connection, almost every aspect of the congressional hearing fell apart. People started to expand and stretch, others switched genders entirely, Cartelli even jumped up

and started grinding up against Silverman's crotch. As carnival music filled the room, Lynn knew that she had lost her grip on reality. There was no way any of this was happening; there was no way she had not lost her mind on national television.

There was no way that she wanted this.

"I don't *want* this!" she shouted, standing up and slamming her fists on the surface in front of her. "Escape is supposed to be what you want, and I sure as hell don't want this!"

"Sure, you do," Silverman replied as he continued to grind his hips against the Deputy Director. "You didn't want to take it, so what your mind *really* wanted was to know what's real. It started out slow, but we eventually had to start getting more creative."

"What are you saying?" Lynn asked, her voice shaking, and Silverman laughed hard as he pushed Cartelli off his table. "What's real?"

"Just you, Lynn. You're still in bed."

"What?" Lynn asked, but Silverman had disappeared before she had even said the word. *All of it* had disappeared, and Lynn looked around to find that she was in her bedroom. She didn't quite know how she got there—her body hurt all over for some reason—but she was grateful. With the circus that congressional hearing had become, there would have been no recovery if it had been real.

Lynn realized she should have suspected earlier—before she launched into her tirade against social media—but it made no difference. She was home, safe, her mind essentially her own. Even though she felt a little strange, Lynn assumed it was just the endorphins rushing through her. Now that the nightmare was over, she almost felt like it was a good practice run.

Looking at the clock on her nightstand, Lynn realized that it would be an hour before Jeremy would need to get on his bus. Almost every morning had turned into chaos for them, just barely making it out the door in time, but Lynn had more than enough time to surprise her son with a nice, warm breakfast.

Getting ready for work could wait this time, especially since the hearing wasn't for another five hours.

As Lynn made her way down the stairs, she realized she did not really have five hours. Just getting to D.C. was more than an hour commute, but she thought it was worth it to keep this house. It was much larger than they needed, but it was private, away from the press and the busy atmosphere of the capitol. Jeremy didn't need to grow up around that—he would have hated it even more—so it was a sacrifice Lynn was willing to make.

Once she got to the kitchen, Lynn had to open up three of her cabinets before she found the pancake mix, cursing herself for forgetting where it was. It almost seemed like the kitchen belonged to someone else, which was Lynn's fault. She used to cook almost every night—especially when she was still married—but her career had stolen all of her time and energy. It was obvious that Jeremy resented losing home-cooked meals and sharing dinner, but Lynn had no choice. Life had changed on them, and they had to change with it.

However, Jeremy was going to get a nice, tasty breakfast surprise this morning. After setting the pancake mix on the kitchen island, Lynn turned around and opened her refrigerator, noticing the awful smell coming from inside. Pinching her nostrils shut, Lynn inspected her groceries and found that almost all of it was past the expiration date. Scowling for a moment, Lynn eventually surrendered and brought out the trash can from the pantry before breathing in deep. One after the other, Lynn inspected each item of food, looked closer at the questionable ones, and threw away almost all of it.

By the time she was finished clearing out her refrigerator, Lynn saw bare shelves and empty cubbies on the door. It should have been depressing, but Lynn almost felt relieved after cleaning it all out and, fortunately, there was a carton of eggs and a half-gallon of milk for Jeremy's pancakes. The milk *smelled* alright, at least.

After retrieving her ingredients, Lynn went to work mixing

up the pancakes, humming as she paced around her kitchen. It was just a nice melody at first, but eventually she recognized it as one of Jeremy's favorite cello pieces; a Bach prelude she had played for him when he was being fussy as a child. No matter what tantrum he was throwing, that song calmed him down and made him sway to the music.

That was why Lynn had given him a cello when he got into middle school. He complained about it, of course—the cello wasn't cool—but Lynn remembered hearing that prelude echoing through the house when Jeremy thought he was alone. There were so many times that Jeremy would practice and send dark, warm notes through their house, and Lynn would just sit on the couch and listen. If nothing else, the acoustics were not an issue.

Sighing, Lynn set down the mix and retrieved a skillet from one of the lower cabinets, turning the dial on her stove until it started clicking. Blue flames flared out from the bottom of the skillet before Lynn turned the dial back down, and she poured a fair amount of oil onto the surface.

Once she stepped back and watched the flames dancing underneath the skillet, Lynn realized how much she had failed Jeremy. She had given him a nice place to live, comfort and safety, but she had sinned as a mother. Since she was so busy with work—and all of the drama and chaos that go along with it—she had made Jeremy think that she did not care about him. She had thought taking him to a therapist would help, but after what happened at Jeremy's session a few days ago, Lynn realized that she may have been pushing him even further away, further still once she took on the crusade against Escape. For Jeremy to hear all the rhetoric and spin, Lynn could not blame him for being resentful.

Sighing, Lynn brought the mixing bowl over the skillet, pouring enough batter to create a pancake as big as a plate. As soon as she thought of the comparison, Lynn reached up and grabbed a plate for Jeremy and a plate for the extras, but then she realized she would need a tray to bring up the pancakes, a glass of milk and the syrup. After grabbing the milk and the syrup from the refrigerator, Lynn tried to remember where she kept the trays.

As she bent down to look in the island's cabinet, Lynn promised to herself that she would try harder with Jeremy and let him know how much he meant to her. Even a tough kid like him shouldn't have to go through adolescence thinking his mother didn't care about him.

"Hopefully this will be a nice start," Lynn muttered to herself as she pulled out a tray covered in cartoon characters, smiling at the worn plastic. After setting it down, Lynn flipped the first pancake and then proceeded to pour out a series of smaller ones. It was something Jeremy had loved when he was a kid—a tower of pancakes getting smaller until it was just a silver dollar at the top—and Lynn thought it would be a nice touch. Lynn would come up to his room with a peace offering, and they might actually start talking to each other again. It may have been too much to expect from a teenager, but Lynn would work on him; they had their whole lives to reconnect.

After finishing up the rest of the mix—a mountain of pancakes on another plate destined to be thrown away—Lynn poured milk into a plastic glass and set it on the tray along with Jeremy's tower and the syrup bottle. It had taken her a little longer than she thought it would, so they wouldn't be able to chat, but Jeremy would still be able to eat it before going off to school. All Lynn had to do was bring it to him.

Picking up the tray from the island, Lynn started through the house, careful not to let the milk slosh up and over the sides of the cup. However, a fair amount defied her and ended up spilling all over the tray, which meant Lynn would need to turn around and grab a paper towel.

"Goddamnit. Stupid… milk…" Lynn started in a frustrated tone, but she stopped being able to think straight once she turned and could see out the window. From her vantage point, she had a straight line of sight to her pool, which was nice during the summer. What stunned her and made the breath catch in her throat was the bundle of clothing lying a few yards away from the pool. At first, she tried to trick herself into thinking it was nothing, but when a gust of wind blew through her yard and ruffled a head full of dark hair, Lynn felt a chill go straight through her bones.

With a crash, milk and syrup and assorted pancakes spread across the living room, and Lynn was already out the door before the plate stopped spinning.

"No, please no," Lynn begged, sprinting through her yard. Along the way she stumbled into a piece of furniture and pushed through it, not bothering to regain her balance as she threw herself at the boy lying on the ground. Just as she made it to the edge of the pool, Lynn prayed to whatever god would listen. "Just be asleep."

"Jeremy!" Lynn screamed as she slid into her son's back, shaking his shoulder hard. "Wake up! Oh my god, wake up, Jeremy, please!"

"Jeremy," Lynn said, already crying as she pulled on his shoulder to roll him onto his back, but it only proved what she had already felt. Covering her mouth, Lynn took in the sight of her son's corpse; blood staining his shirt and already dry, his skin white and ashen. If she had been thinking rationally—if her heart wasn't in the process of getting torn apart—she may have realized that he had been dead a long time, but Lynn was not rational.

"*Jeremy! Jeremy!*" she screamed, crawling forward so she could put his head in her lap, so she could run her fingers through his hair. Unable to consider that he was gone, Lynn turned him so she could rub his back like he always loved. "Oh my God, Jeremy, please..."

"The joke's over, right?" Lynn asked, smiling down at her son's face and shaking him gently. "It's all just a joke, Jeremy, right? It's a—it's a good one... You got me good, right, Jeremy?" she asked while rocking back and forth, watching his face and his arms and his legs and *anything* that could tell her that Jeremy was still alive, that her son hadn't died alone and cold in their backyard.

"Jeremy," Lynn whined, admitting the truth as she set her trembling fingers along his cheek. His skin was so cold, devoid of life, and she had seen him just a day ago. This boy—the only thing she had done right in her life—had been taken from her in just a day, and Lynn looked around for some reason, some sign.

Finally, as she clutched Jeremy's head to her chest, Lynn spied a steak knife next to a towel that belonged in their house. Picking it up with her other hand, Lynn saw the dried blood that belonged in Jeremy's body and it took her a few moments to realize what had happened. Turning back to the child in her lap, Lynn realized how badly she had failed as a parent.

"Oh, my, little boy," she said, tears streaming down her face as her voice broke. "Mommy's here." Lynn tried to speak, but pain tore through her throat, made her feel like she was choking, and it was not long before her face was a mess from tears and snot. Lynn shuddered as she leaned over Jeremy and clutched his head to her chest, but there was nothing she could do for him now. She should have listened, she should have paid attention, but Lynn Stafford was trying to save the children.

She just didn't save the one who mattered most.

CHAPTER 15

BODY AND SOUL

Y•ou're going to be late, you know that?"

"Yeah, I know," Marcus said, the second-to-last button of his shirt fighting against him as he stood in front of the mirror. Once it finally slid into place, Marcus looked at his reflection in disbelief. A few months ago, he would have never thought he would wear anything more professional than a t-shirt without a logo, but business casual looked good on him, even if his light green shirt was currently untucked. Spying the sport coat and tie hanging in his closet, Marcus looked at the last button and sighed.

"And what is it now? I can't read your mind."

"Yes, you can, Kara. Are you really going to make me say it?" Marcus said, turning away from the mirror to see the hallucination sitting on the edge of their bed, one leg crossed over the other. It had taken a few weeks to adjust, but Marcus was no longer disturbed by her decayed and ruined appearance. Even the missing eye didn't stop him from looking at her fondly under normal circumstances.

Since these were not normal circumstances, Marcus was looking at her in annoyance.

"C'mon, handsome, I like the conversation," Kara said, playing with her lip piercing as she smiled at him.

"Fine, you win. I have to wear the blazer, but the tie is optional. Should I wear the tie and feel like I'm being choked all night, or can I leave the last button open and try casual?" Marcus asked expectantly, but the hallucination shrugged before laying back on the bed.

"Dude, I don't fucking know, they're *your* parents."

"And it's *their* country club, and they might as well be your parents, too, you stowaway," Marcus said as he turned back to his reflection. "You just act like Kara to get under my skin."

"Oh, you big softie. I do it because that's what you want," she replied as she sat up quickly and rolled off the bed, eventually standing next to Marcus and looking him over. "Go casual. The parental units will understand the trials of a top button."

"Yeah, but I'm trying not to seem like a total fuck-up and the tie might help with that," he said, earning a groan from the dead girl.

"Then fucking *go formal*, for all I fucking care. Jesus!" Kara said as she wandered around the room, tracing bony fingers across each surface. "God, I miss touching things."

"You can't *miss* anything, you're a construct of my mind," Marcus said, lifting the tie and setting it in front of his chest. It was a decent color combination, but it felt too much like growing up for him. "I am *glad* I don't have to wear these things to work."

"Well, not anymore, at least. Ever since you guys got the private lab, it was bye-bye to the formal wear," Kara said, jumping on the bed and out of her boredom. "It *would* look good on you, though."

"Pretentious, snobby, ridiculous... those are the words you *should* use," Marcus said before looking over his shoulder at the hallucination. "And just so you know, Kara would never say that. She'd think I look like a clown."

"Dude, you're going to a country club for dinner. Pretentious and snobby are *definitely* the words. Good thing I showed up when I did," Kara said, stomping on the bed so she could jump even higher, and Marcus could not help but smile.

That part the zombie got right.

"I'm going with the tie," Marcus said as he raised his collar and closed the last button, restricting his throat already. Setting the tie around his neck, Marcus attempted a half-Windsor knot before it turned into a mess of material. After unraveling it, Marcus tried again, but it still looked wrong. "Damnit, it's been so long since I had to wear one of these."

"Here, let me help," Kara suggested, jumping off the bed and stepping in between Marcus and the mirror, but he only looked down at her in dismay.

"Really? How? You can't even touch it," Marcus argued, but the girl scrunched up her face and set her hands on top of his.

"Dumbass, just follow my lead," she said, and Marcus allowed Kara to guide him through the process. He was about to complain and say that it was stupid, but there was a half-Windsor on his neck less than a minute later. Stepping back, Kara gave him a smile that showed teeth through the hole in her cheek. "See? I'm useful."

"You only knew that because *I* did," Marcus said as he lowered his collar, but he could hear the disgusted sigh coming from his left.

"Why the fuck are you so nitpicky today? Yesterday you acted like I was actually Kara. It was fucking nice, dude," she said, and even though she was a figment of his imagination, Marcus felt like he owed her a reason.

"I'm just… trying to remind myself, okay? When it's just— when we're around the others, it doesn't matter if I think of you as Kara. Hell, sometimes I actually forget. But around my parents… I don't know, I just want to keep up a barrier around them. I don't want to give them any reason to think that I'm dosing again," he explained, but the decomposing girl crossed her arms and raised an eyebrow.

"But you're *not*. You've been clean since, well, since a few days after the whole suicide forest thing. I feel like you get a pass for that relapse. You don't have anything to hide," Kara argued, but Marcus turned to her as he tucked in his shirt.

"You and I both know that's not true. I might be clean, but I definitely have something *to hide*. When *you* are responsible for the production of eighty percent of the Escape on the Eastern Seaboard, you might understand," Marcus said, turning back to look at himself in the mirror once the shirt was tucked away. Like this he didn't look sloppy, but the tie still made him feel out of place. Walking over to his closet, Marcus grabbed the sport coat and threw the wire hanger onto the bed.

"The way you're talking, I'm responsible for forty percent, hosscat," Kara said before laying out on the bed and lifting her feet behind her. "What with us being all *Fight Club* and everything."

"We're not… we just share the same brain, yeah? Sometimes, well," he said while throwing his arms through the sleeves and then adjusting the coat as he looked in the mirror. "Sometimes I *do* think you get to keep different parts of my head. Like the tie thing. Used to be able to do it in my sleep."

"Are you complaining about me being here?" Kara asked in mock indignity. "Before you throw stones, remember that *you* were the one who overloaded your nerves with experimental drugs. Just because I'm part of your self-induced schizophrenia doesn't mean I cackle and fucking plot your demise over three-newt stew."

"Three-newt stew?" Marcus asked, feeling confident now that he was wearing the sport coat. Even though it was too warm in his apartment, he almost didn't want to take it off. "Since when did you turn into a witch?"

"Dude, I came back from the dead as a ghost zombie. I have mystical juju just pouring out of every orifice," Kara said, grinning as she pointed at her eye socket. "Even that one."

"*Especially* that one," Marcus said as he sat beside her, returning the smile she gave him. For a moment, he wanted to reach out and touch her, but he knew that his hand would fade right through. His thoughts turning dark, Marcus looked at her until her grin disappeared.

"What?"

"I… it's just been a crazy few months," Marcus said, looking at the mirror and seeing only his reflection. "Almost die, fuck up my brain enough that I see my dead girlfriend, but that's nothing compared to how Escape took off. We fucking hated him at the time, but goddamnit if Ulysses didn't come through for us. Left for two months with all our inventory, but then he came back with double the markup and orders for twenty times as much."

"He's an idiot, but he's *our* idiot. Who knew he'd turn out to be a savant?" Kara said, pushing herself to her knees and looking Marcus over. "Looks like you're ready to go grovel to your parents and eat expensive food that's *really* not that much better than hitting up the deli across the street."

"You say *not that much better* when it's more like *not better*," Marcus said, looking fondly at his constant companion. For the foreseeable future, Kara wouldn't be going anywhere; she would follow him around to the ends of the Earth if he ever left his twelve-block radius.

She was not *the* Kara, but Kara had never really been *his*, either.

"Get the fuck out of here, dude," she said, trying to push his shoulder and breaking against his skin. Still, it made Marcus stand up, so it had the desired effect. "Good luck impressing the folks. May they never figure out you're one of the most powerful men in the black market."

"You say that like it's a bad thing, Kara," Marcus said, adjusting his tie and puffing his chest out. "At least I'm not getting anybody killed; at least I'm just selling a service."

"A service, yeah, alright. Service that gets people to hate their lives and waste away under a hallucinogen," she said, his own guilt coming out of her mouth. Shrugging, Kara bounced off the bed until she was standing just in front of Marcus. "And you're just so kind to anonymously donate to their rehab centers."

"Look—"

"Yeah, fine, you're a fucking good Samaritan, Marcus. I know where the money goes and you drag me along to the soup kitchens and the benefits," Kara said, slapping ephemeral hands against his chest. "You're just a *goodie fucking two shoes drug lord.*"

"No, Kara, I meant *look*," he said, stepping back so Kara could see the full glory of his transformation into an adult. "Looks good, right?"

"Gross, I'll be happy when you're back in t-shirts and shorts. Have fun," Kara said before lying on the bed and burying her head in the crook of her arm.

"What does that mean?"

"It means *have fun*, jackass," Kara explained as she set her face onto the mattress. "I don't feel like going."

"You can just *do* that?" he asked, but Kara yawned before bothering with an answer.

"I don't have to be here all the time; I'm here because part of you wants me around. *Who'd a thunk*, right? Anyway, you don't want me to distract you from your parents, so I won't. I'll show back up at some point and scare the shit out of you, don't worry."

"You're such a bitch," Marcus said, laughing as he left his bedroom and made his way to his door. As he put on his shoes at the entrance, he could hear Kara yelling from the other room.

"Only because you like it that way!" she shouted, and Marcus had to agree. It made things more entertaining, like he had a true companion. If they were just the same person there wouldn't be any benefit to their relationship. For all its side effects, his brain damage was one of the best things that ever happened to him.

Once he opened his door, Marcus paused, nervous about what his parents would think of him, but then he remembered the apparition in his bedroom. With a smile, Marcus left the apartment and let it swing close behind him. It felt like the end of an era—his delusion letting him free like this—and Marcus remembered that night on the roof and what Kara said. It didn't hurt this time, and maybe it was because his Kara was a decent substitute, but Marcus had a feeling that he would see the real one again. So, as he set off into the night, Marcus whispered a few words to the girl beyond his reach.

"Don't wait up, hosscat. I'll find you eventually."

Also From 25 & y Publishing

◈ Anthology ◈

Surviving Tomorrow
A Charity Anthology to Fight COVID-19

Edited by Bryan Thomas Schmidt

◈ Graphic Novel ◈

Behind These Eyes
by Peter J. Wacks

25ANDY.COM

≈ Non-fiction ≈

Common Nonsense?
A Practical Guide to Managing Through Emotional Intelligence

by Susan Fink Childs, FACMPE

≈ Novella ≈

Chasing Your Tale
by Peter J. Wacks